The White Jamaican

Chris Helvey

A Wings ePress, Inc.
Mystery Novel

Wings ePress, Inc.

Edited by: Jeanne Smith
Copy Edited by: Joan C. Powell
Executive Editor: Jeanne Smith
Cover Artist: Trisha FitzGerald-Jung
Image from Pixabay

All rights reserved

Wings ePress Books
www.wingsepress.com

Copyright © 2021 by: Chris Helvey
ISBN 978-1-61309-553-9

Published In the United States Of America

Wings ePress Inc.
3000 N. Rock Road
Newton, KS 67114

DEDICATION

To the memory of Ross Macdonald and Lew Archer

***

One

She stepped out of the stairwell shadows—black heels, black hose, gold chain dangling, skirt cut high, blouse cut low. A big woman, tall and built to match. Then my eyes found her face and a memory moved in the wilderness of my mind. I was tempted to say, "Haven't I seen you somewhere before?" But the line tasted old, like stale cigarette smoke, and I choked it down and fixed a smile on my face.

She came through the half-open door without knocking, walking like she owned the place. Maybe she did. I'd never seen the owner of this dump, only the manager, and that runny-nosed, pimple-faced, wire-haired termite didn't own his own soul, let alone this monstrosity on Hanover.

I got treated to the royal view, a full body profile: chiseled cheekbones, bee-stung lips, breasts that jutted toward daylight, gently swelling buttocks, and slim, well-muscled legs that ran all the way down to there.

I was supposed to be impressed.

I was.

Not that I told her, though. Lots of women have bodies worth dying for, and brains that have been dead for years. I've been around the block too many times to lose my head over any lady, even one who looked as fine as the one silhouetted in my door frame. Besides, I had this lingering tickle in my mind that I'd seen her somewhere before. I didn't say a word. She was the one paying the visit; let her be the one to speak.

I leaned back in my squeaky, second-hand office chair, and put my dusty shoes up on my desk. My desk, I could do what I wanted. I admired the view over my laces and waited.

"You look thinner than you did on television."

Her voice was well-modulated, falling around the equator of the register, but low for a woman, curiously without accent. Broadcasting, maybe, with a national media background. Certainly she'd adapted, or perhaps cultivated, the voice; it wasn't natural, it was a touch too good.

"Really?"

I'd had to think for several seconds before I could remember when I'd ever been on TV. Had to be the McAllister case. Following that bloody gun battle, I'd made all the eleven o'clock news shows and garnered my twenty-four hours as a little hero in a big city.

She was stretching to remember that case, especially as I hadn't lost the beard back then. I caught myself unconsciously running a calloused left hand across the day-old stubble on my jaw.

"You had a beard back then, didn't you?"

"Yeah."

She held the pose for a moment, then turned and strode across the wooden floor, dark with a hundred oilings. She had a good, no nonsense walk. The lady stopped by my hard-backed, poorly cushioned visitor's chair and said, "May I" with her head and hands. I nodded and she sat, revealing a flash of inner thigh as she did. I pretended not to notice as I sipped lukewarm coffee from my *Yankees* cup.

She folded her right hand neatly into her left and crossed her legs enough to make the nylon whisper. "Mr. Quick, I'll get right to the point. My husband has been missing since last Thursday evening, and I need the services of a private investigator."

I thought I detected a hint of emphasis on the word private, or was I reaching?

"I don't know anyone in the business," she continued, "but I remember seeing you on the news last fall and reading all the laudatory reports about your heroic actions."

"Haven't you learned not to believe everything you read or hear?"

"Ages ago. I also checked with some friends of the family, people who are quite high up in the police force. They said you were good, maybe the best, but undoubtedly a royal pain in the ass."

She said the bad word with a naughty smile playing at her mouth corners. Good little girl playing at being bad.

I didn't say anything. What she had said was at least partially true.

For a moment, we sat in silence, studying each other. At least I was studying her. I had to assume she was studying me because I couldn't see through her mirrored sunglasses to get a look at her eyes. I always wonder about people who insist on wearing their sunglasses indoors. Are they really trying to maintain a veneer of privacy, or are they simply trying to create an image?

She broke the silence. "Mr. Quick, let's talk business." Still that firm, professional voice. "My husband is missing and I want him found."

She slid a color photograph across my desk. It showed a darkly handsome man, wearing a tan Armani suit and a thin-lipped smile. He was standing by a new Mercedes convertible.

"He's never been away from home for more than a few hours without telling me his plans. I don't mind letting you know I'm very concerned."

This time I was certain about an added emphasis to the word 'you.'

"Police?"

"My husband and I are both essentially private people, Mr. Quick. We don't care to share the details of our lives with either the venal rank and file of the jackals who pretend to be the police force of this metropolis, or the vultures who form the modern American media."

She made Egyptian eye movements. "I simply don't want to air my linen in public. I have confided in two high ranking police officials whom I trust. They understood both the situation and my family's wishes, and they recommended you. I really need your help, Mr. Quick." Her bottom lip trembled. She noticed the unauthorized movements and bit down on the soft flesh with fine, even, white teeth.

I knew there were dozens of private investigators in this city who were as good, or better, than I was. However, I also know the status of my mind, and that I liked her packaging. Plus, I needed the work. Boredom and loneliness were killing me, slowly, silently, one day at a time. First, however, I wanted a peek at her soul. I like to know who I'm working for.

"Take off the sunglasses."

One slim, perfectly manicured hand moved purposefully to her face.

Blue. The cornflower blue my mother had loved so much. I shivered a little inside myself. My mother was long dead and I needed to live more in the present. Like its cousins—boredom and loneliness— the past was also killing me, one memory at a time.

Back in my church-going days, my wise old Sunday school teacher had told me that the eyes are the windows to the soul. For some reason that statement stuck with me better than ninety-nine percent of the Bible verses we'd recited, and for years I was terrified of anybody looking directly into my eyes. Had it in my childish brain that everyone, not just God, could look into my eyes and see every single wicked thought I was thinking, and register all the sins I'd committed, or planned to commit. I finally figured out that if I couldn't use their eyes as a television screen to their minds, then maybe they couldn't read mine. Still, eyes can give an indication of what lies below.

She looked at me steadily, a hard-to-figure smile turning up only the corners of her mouth. A pulse pounded faintly in her temples.

"Two hundred a day, plus expenses."

"Okay." She reached for her checkbook, at least that's what I figured she was digging for in her gold lamé clutch.

"A week in advance."

Golden head bowed, she simply nodded and started writing. I sat quietly, watching her, trying to recall where I'd seen her face, heard her voice, or crossed her path. Granted, she was of a type, but my memory of her was sharply distinct, as though I'd known her in another time, another place.

She finished writing the check and tore it crisply from the book, then rose smoothly. Standing tall in her heels, she towered over me as she handed me the check. In my gentlemanly days I would have stood. Knighthood was long dead, however, and chivalry was a farce played only in the games of overtly correct men and women.

An emerald set in silver on her right ring finger caught my eye. The stone looked as big and smooth as a robin's egg. If the egg was indicative of her financial status, she could buy me before breakfast. I snuck a peek at the check. The writing was large and rounded, the amount correct, and the name was Allison Grant Dubronski. It has a familiar ring.

"Television?"

"Only a little. You might remember me from an early morning talk show on Channel Five, very early. More likely you saw some of my commercials. I was the Hunt Club Girl. Or you might have caught my fill-in weather gal act."

Laughter tumbled out of her throat like water rushing over polished stones in a Rocky Mountain streambed. "God, I was awful."

I remembered her now, in the commercial—big, blonde, and that hunting jacket up high, riding boots down below, and what looked like acres of gorgeous, glorious female in between. I'd been impressed then. I was impressed now.

I fanned my face with the check. "Thanks."

She nodded. "I'm late for an appointment with my attorney. Can you come by my house tonight?"

"Let's say tomorrow. I need to make some preliminary inquiries first."

Her expression never changed; only the eyes darkened minutely. "Ten o'clock in the morning?"

"Make it five in the afternoon." I always like to set the parameters of a relationship.

She stood motionless while I counted to fourteen. Then she said, "All right."

We shook hands like a pair of business tycoons before she turned and walked across the old floor with quick, reverberating steps.

Two

I hadn't truly wanted the job. I had enough money left over from the McAllister case to last a long time. The amount might not have held the average person for long, but then I've never been average. My needs are few, my wants fewer. These days I had no family, no debts, no obligations, and no dreams. All barriers had flown somewhere over the rainbow. Basically, I didn't give a damn. Being in the unique position of telling the world to screw itself was one I frankly found enjoyable.

After Mona, I'd quit caring and started going through the motions. I only showed up for work when I felt like it, or was too bored to do anything else. If I wanted a job I took it, but it had to interest me. In the past year and a half, I'd taken on only six jobs, and two of them had been on the house. Legal, illegal, or half-and-half, it didn't matter to me; the critical element was that the job had to be interesting.

So why had I taken this one?

Missing husbands were a dime a dozen, even missing husbands with money weren't that rare. It had to be the blonde, although, if I were honest, she wasn't particularly my cup of coffee. The smell had just gotten in my nostrils—that was all. The smell of the case, that ancient musty smell of life. I moaned inwardly at my own stupidity.

Three

The pile of leaves on the corner of Dewhurst and Polk had grown since I'd walked by it in the morning. Old man Talcott, who lived in the basement of my building and kept the furnace running and the air conditioner humming, had said it was going to be an early fall followed by a moderate winter, with one bad period that would produce three good-sized snows. He based his forecast on the bands of color on the wooly-worms and the number of heavy fogs in August. His methods weren't scientific, but the old varmint was right more often than he was wrong. Probably more accurate than that fat weather man with the walrus mustache I occasionally watched on Channel 5.

I kicked absentmindedly at the pile and sent leaves showering in all directions. These were the early dropouts and only a couple of crimson patches blazed among the green and brown.

Between one stride and the next, it struck me that I wanted the company of a woman. I wasn't in the mood to go out and play the amateur hour and I wondered if Debi was working tonight. Not that Debi was what I really wanted in a woman. Chronologically, I'd guess she was twenty, maybe twenty-one years old. However, she'd been out on the streets for well over a year, plying that most ancient of arts.

Debi was short and small-framed and I doubted she would ever become even an average-sized woman. If she didn't get a late growth spurt, she wasn't going to make much more than five feet. Twiggy thin, she looked more like a college student, but the only education she was getting was that taught on the streets.

For months now, she'd been standing on my block. My sense was that she wasn't getting much action. Extremely thin, thick sunglasses, and not exceptionally pretty didn't cut it; the competition was too damn tough. Still, she knew how to keep her mouth shut, did what she was told, and never tried the old five finger discount, which I appreciated.

When I wanted a warm body in bed with me, my place cleaned, or a meal fixed, and all for a modest price, Debi was the best game in town. If the fact that we'd never even kissed bothered her, she hadn't bothered to mention it.

She was there on the corner, high heels and a skirt far too short for her skinny legs and flat ass. She had on enough makeup to be Tammy Faye Baker *déjà vu*. Lipstick was a bright slash of blood red connecting the halves of her face. Rouge reddened her cheeks, and the eyelashes extended long, fake, and black from a purple pool of eye shadow. Hair, bleached and teased to cotton candy, spun away from her head in air-pocked masses. All that excess did was mask her one truly attractive feature: her warm, large, brown eyes. I wondered if Debi was deliberately trying to hide them. After all, we all are hiding something.

The wind was picking up as I came around the corner and approached her from the blind side. She had a blue jean jacket on over a filmy, silvery blouse and the wind was having its way with both. She must have had a ton of hair spray on, however, because, while her hair was standing almost straight out from her head, like a pennant from its flagpole, it wasn't doing much else. No masses of twisted braids or curls intertwined in defeat, just stiffened hair pulled skyward by the wind. Her hair reminded me of meringue on top of pie.

Focusing on the street traffic and facing the wind, she never heard me coming. I put a hand on her right elbow and she jumped like I'd jabbed her with an electric cattle prod. She spun on her heels toward me, a pale right hand raised to slap down the offender.

"Don't you ever put your hands on me like that you...Hey, Frank, sorry. Didn't know it was you. You scared the hell out of me. What you doing sneaking up like that?"

"You'll live."

"Yeah, I know, but baby you scared me out of a year's growth."

"And that you need."

She laughed, a nervous little tinkle of a laugh, trying not to offend the big bad customer. Made me feel like the neighborhood bully, which, in a Byzantine way, I was.

"You need some company tonight?"

I reached up and gently pulled a pair of horrid purple and white-framed, amber-tinted sunglasses from her face. Those nice brown eyes were still there, moist, concerned, anxious to please. I ran a forefinger down her upturned nose and gave her what, for me, passed for a smile. She gave me a much nicer, brighter one in return and slipped a slim arm through the crook of my elbow. Arm in arm we strolled down the sidewalk, just an old married couple headed home.

Four

She scared the hell out of me.

Well, for a moment.

I'm wasn't used to waking up with anyone and when I opened my eyes she was the first thing I saw. If familiarity bred contempt, then I hypothesized the theory that lack of familiarity bred fear.

She was sleeping soundly, clad only in a pair of silky black panties two sizes too big. Some Snoopy jockey shorts would have been more her speed. I glanced at my Casio—almost seven o'clock. I needed to get a move on. I had several pieces of business to tend to; first, though, a shower.

Ten minutes later I'd gotten rid of most of the dirt, but none of the sins. Back in the bedroom, I slipped on brown twill pants and laid out a cream-colored, button-down, long-sleeve shirt. I was venturing uptown today, so I had to look decent. I debated on a tie, but passed. Formality was out these days, not that I really cared. Still, I wanted to talk to some people who had gatekeepers. Sometimes the gatekeepers valued their own opinions quite highly. It wasn't that I was actually concerned about their feelings; I just didn't want any hassle. I grabbed shoes and sat on an oak side chair I'd picked up at auction after old Mrs. Henshaw died. She had no family, nice furniture, and I got an apartment full of furniture at a low price.

"Going somewhere?" Little girl voice, still half befogged with sleep.

I looked at her long and hard. I wasn't much of a conversationalist before I had my coffee. "Yeah."

She knew better than to ask where I was going. She merely pulled the sheet up tighter around her boyish chest, then turned her face to the pillow—which suited me better, anyway. I hate to be reminded of my weaknesses. I finished tying my shoes, put on my shirt, and padded to the kitchen to fix my coffee.

It was still early in the season for the heat to kick on and the morning was chilly. Feeling vaguely guilty, I strolled back into the bedroom, flipped the blanket from around the rail at the foot of the bed and stretched it over her. It struck me that, if I'd started out young enough, she might be my daughter. Hell, I was getting crazier every day. Still, I was glad that sleeping was all we'd done in that big old bed. The fewer apparitions that had any claim on my soul the better.

~ * ~

Steam rose from the coffee mug and drifted upwards through the early morning light that had worked its way through my grime-coated windows. It spilled weakly across the chipped Formica counter and onto the faded kitchen linoleum. Dust motes twirled in the air, hovering like Nureyev.

In the apartment below, old man Dibionfranco cussed loudly at his son Bennie in Pidgin English. Bennie didn't respond. Not anymore. Bennie was what is politely referred to as Missing In Action. Just a sensitive way of saying that he was damn fucking dead.

Bennie, 6'2", 190 pounds, with dark curly hair, jet black eyes, and boyish bravado, had gone off to Vietnam in 1968 and never came home. All the neighbors kept telling Mr. Dibionfranco that there was still a chance his boy might come home, and Mrs. Dibionfranco never went anywhere without her POW/MIA bracelet.

Mr. Dibionfranco and I knew, though. Knew in our hearts that Bennie was dead. Guess it goes without saying, if you're dead, you're dead. Dead is simply dead. There isn't any good kind of dead.

Sure, how you died mattered, mattered one hell of a lot, but in the end it didn't change being dead. Dead was dead, stone cold. That was why Mr. Dibionfranco gave Bennie hell—he was thoroughly pissed at him for dying. Dying was so damn unfixable.

Cool and wet touched the back of my neck and I half jumped, sloshing hot coffee everywhere. Before I turned around I knew what it was. I was full of reproachful glances and vile thoughts ready to spring into words. Debi girl must be going crazy. She knew better than to touch me, let alone kiss me. I was fired up, ready to give her the cussing she deserved, but pyramids of tears welling up in those hound dog eyes at the sight of my anger changed my mind.

I bit my tongue, picked up her blue jean jacket by one ragged end, and flipped it at her. She wasn't so heartbroken or afraid that she didn't grab it to keep from hitting her face. I told myself I was getting soft as Play-Doh. I'd be taking up charity work next.

"Want me to clean for you today?"

Actually, that had been my plan, but I sure as hell wasn't going to give her any satisfaction, not after she'd startled me like that. So I turned away, faced the window, and stared at the garbage truck lumbering down the alley that ran between Polk and Knox.

I heard her softly call my name once. Then I heard the front door open. I kept staring where the garbage truck had been. I counted slowly, silently, to forty-seven before I heard the door close gently behind her.

Five

I took a cab down Desoto and had the cabbie drop me off at the corner of Whitman. It promised to be a nice day and I was running ahead of schedule, so I could afford the pleasure of a stroll through Kennedy Park. I didn't do either the width or breadth, just zigzagged across one corner of the rectangle. Still, it took me a solid fifteen minutes of steady walking. I harbored a secret desire to linger among the falling leaves and squirrels who dashed from tree to tree, then paused to paw among the leaves or dig furiously for a few seconds in earth still damp from the soaking rains of the past weekend. Storing up against the coming winter, an admirable practice I'm sure.

Duty called, however, so I didn't linger. I was now working for Allison Grant Dubronski and didn't figure she would be particularly happy about paying me to spend all morning in the park. Besides, before I got much more involved, I wanted to find out a few facts about my employer. The man who would know was Mick Ethrington. I also needed to see my banker and a lawyer named Fredricks. First, though, Mick.

Mick had been a lot of things in his life: radio announcer, television critic for a couple of papers, playwright for a drama that only made it to Off-Broadway, performer in several amateur theatre productions, and author of celebrity puff pieces for various slick publications. Never a big hit, but always on the periphery of the entertainment world. Mick would know any dirt on Mrs. Dubronski. Plus, for a little cash, he would gladly part with his knowledge.

I wanted to contact Mick before he got involved in his daily duties. These days he was fronting for a number of performers. Their talent agent is how he defined himself. He covered his lack of expertise and dearth of meaningful contacts in a smoke screen of phone calls, letters, memos, faxes, etc. that made it appear he was busier than a one-armed paperhanger. He put out more smoke than a three-alarm fire. Fake it till you make it was his motto.

His dodo of a blonde girlfriend-cum-receptionist was an elevator listener. She listened intently for the opening elevator doors so she could cram her *People* in the middle desk drawer and spit her gum in the trash can. Whenever time permitted, because I've got a mean streak, I always took the stairs and slipped in on her. She fancied herself greatly and put on airs. She would never make the big time, not in a hundred years.

Moving as quietly as I could, I climbed the stairs, skipping the second from the top, which I knew from experience produced an atrocious squeak. Just off the stairs was the side door you couldn't see from the reception area because Mick had lined up a trio of file cabinets to form a mini-wall. I slid the door open soundlessly. It was always unlocked to facilitate Mick's quick escape from ex-wives, ex-girlfriends, and men to whom he owed money.

Sure enough, I caught Blondie in the act. The silly woman actually had her feet flung up on the desk like she was a man. Certainly, she was no lady. Mick's door, off to my right, was closed. I didn't know if he was in with a visitor who had arrived earlier, or if he just hadn't made it in yet.

I tiptoed around the back side of the filing cabinets. Blondie was deep into her magazine. From this angle, I could see the top of her head as she slouched in her well-padded chair. She wasn't even a real blonde.

"Your boss in?"

She dropped her magazine, tried to take her feet off the desk, and turn around to see who or what I was, all at the same time. I don't know if her movements were too violent and swift, or if her foot got hung, but the result was an unceremonious dump onto the floor for her. Her already short skirt rose higher still, exposing panties the color of a blue October sky. I didn't say a word. She gave me a look meant to kill, then began scrambling to get her skirt down and onto her feet at the same time.

Seconds later, I heard the elevator ding and shortly thereafter Mick sauntered through the front door. His eyes swept the room, trying to figure out what had happened. The man had to know something had gone sideways. Blondie was blushing furiously and radiating hatred my way. Leaning against the innermost filing cabinet, I kept my mouth shut.

"Hey, Frank, what's going on? Anything the matter here?"

Blue Panties stood beside her overturned chair, a sullen look on her face. I could sense an explosion of words beginning to bubble up inside her.

"Afraid I frightened your receptionist. Came in the back way. You got a minute?"

"Sure, Frank," he said, glancing at his watch. "As a matter of fact, I've got about five." He and Blondie exchanged glances I assumed were meaningful to them. He jerked his head toward his office. "Come on back."

I followed his blue Oscar de la Renta suit. The door clicked behind me. Nice office: new carpet, cherry desk and credenza, crystal glasses for the afternoon pick-me-up. This year, Mick was definitely uptown.

"Want some coffee? I can get Brittany to make us some. Won't take two minutes."

I shook my head no.

He settled comfortably in an oversized, leather chair, then arranged his hands on the glistening desktop. Who did he think he was fooling? I'd known Mick when he was fetching drinks for One-Eye Didi Gianfrido. I was tempted to remind him that what goes up must come down, often hard.

Mick seemed a touch nervous. I didn't care enough to find out why, but I sat still, letting the tension work for me. A minute tic had started up under his right eye.

"What can I do for you, Frank?"

"Talk to me about Allison Grant."

A who-in-the-hell-is-that look flitted briefly across his face, followed by an oh-yeah-*that*-Allison-Grant look. I noticed a few more lines etched in the skin around Mick's eyes and mouth than had been there six months ago.

I sensed an easing in Mick's tension. My question must not have been what he was expecting. Which made me wonder what secrets he had. I filed the thought away for possible use down the road.

"Allison Grant, the personality? Blonde, built, and acts like butter wouldn't melt between her butt-cheeks? That the one?"

"One and the same." Mick always had a way with words. Give the man credit; he could sure as hell turn a colorful phrase.

"Well, let's see." He pulled open a desk drawer, rooted around briefly, then pulled a manila folder out and thumbed through it, as though refreshing his memory. Knowing Mick, the folder probably had nothing to do with Allison Grant; more likely it contained nude photos of his girlfriend, dirt on the mayor, or last year's top ten goals.

I waited, not patiently, but I waited.

"Like I thought, not much lately. Our Allison Grant was a hot number here in the city, six or seven years ago. Came up fast. Did a brief stint as TV weather girl. With a body like hers she didn't need the American Meteorological Society seal of approval."

He looked to me for a laugh, or at least a knowing chuckle. I gave him half a smile.

The expression on his face said his feelings were hurt. I didn't care about his feelings, just like he didn't care about mine. Most people don't care, you know. They care about their own feelings and nobody else's. Anything other than that is often pretend.

After a few seconds, he shrugged and glanced at the folder. "Okay, let's see. After doing the weather scene for a few months, she graduated to a local talk show. Lots of gossip and chit-chat. Nothing substantial. All the dirt that could be crammed in between commercials. She modeled a bit, for the full-figured look, and did a few political numbers."

"Such as?"

"Oh, appearing with the mayor, doing a voice-over on commercials, that sort of thing. She presents herself real well in public. Has a great voice, and enough sense to know when to quit talking. Rumor had it that she was going to throw her hat in the political ring, some minor office, of course, but it never happened."

"Why?"

"Oh, it wasn't anything she did or didn't do politically. She simply changed direction. Decided to fly out to Hollywood."

"TV?"

"Actually, she tried the silver screen. Got a couple of walk-ons and bit parts in a handful of flicks. With her looks, she should have done more." Mick paused and gave me a wink, followed by a leer.

"Especially when I hear she was willing to do whatever it took to land a contract."

"So?"

"So?"

"What happened? Why didn't she hit it big time? I've never heard of her at all in the movies."

"Like you would." Mick made it sound like I wouldn't know a movie star if one walked up and slapped me. He was probably right; I'm a *High Noon* man—"Do not forsake me, oh my darling..."

"Sorry, Frank, just had to jab at you, you old hermit. Actually, in addition to having a body that won't quit, Allison Grant apparently had some real acting talent. One of my clients, an actor-director himself, saw a couple of her screen tests and it seems the lady could really make a role come to life. And he said it wasn't just one type of character, like a ditzy blonde, for example. She had real range on the screen."

"So why the bailout?"

He shrugged. "What I heard was that just as Ms. Grant was poised to make it big, she up and marries this Dubronski and moves back east."

"Why Dubronski? He's not exactly a household name or a powerbroker I know of."

"Yeah, but maybe he made her an offer she couldn't refuse."

"Such as?"

"Such as tons of money and the promise of more."

"Where did his money come from?"

Mick sighed as he struggled out of his chair. He walked over to the window and stared out at the park for a long time, as though he were waiting for the seasons to change, or hoping I'd take the hint and leave. I never had been good at taking hints. Mick eventually figured that out.

"Quiet money. Real quiet, you understand, but street money nonetheless."

"Dubronski connected? Allison Grant, movie-star-in-the-making, married into the mob?"

"Yeah. So what's going on? Dubronski's a behind-the-scenes kind of guy, but he's nowhere near the bottom rung. So what gives?" The tic was back below Mick's right eye. I wondered what he had to be nervous about. Then I wondered if I should be nervous.

I let him sit and tic for a minute, then got to my feet and headed for the door. I paused with my hand on the knob. I wondered if Blondie had her ear to the door.

"Nothing much, Mick. Just seems Dubronski's just gone missing."

We both heard a sharp intake of breath. Well, well, well, she was nosy as well as inefficient.

Mick pressed his hands together and opened them as though they were a flower unfolding. "Frank, I hope you know I'm sorry. Sorry about Mona. Sorry I wasn't there more for you."

The knot rose in my throat and I nodded while I choked it down. "I know, Mick. But there was nothing you could have done. Nothing I could do." I felt my face rearrange itself. The silence in the room grew loud. "Here I am always helping people, strangers, nice people and bastards and bitches and wierdos and bums. I can help them, but I couldn't help her. I wasn't there. And because I wasn't, I couldn't do a goddamn thing to help."

I flipped him a salute and spun on my heel and jerked the door open. He said something, but I was already gone, moving across the outer office, not hearing anything beyond the voice in my head, the one that told me what a feeble excuse for a human being I was. I tried to ignore it, not terribly successfully. I'd heard it several times a day, every day, for over a year.

Blondie didn't even speak to me on my way out. Not that it mattered. Silence, I was used to.

Six

Late that afternoon I caught a cab out to the Dubronski place. The sun had slid behind the tree canopy and its filtered, dying rays bathed the autumn leaves in crimson. Autumn was my favorite time of the year. Colors always got to me—gold, orange, deep red, and soft, butter yellow turned me into a sentimentalist. Once an October, I wondered why. Over the years the best I could come up with was that every fall I was trying to relive a carefree childhood that had been so fleeting it seemed to have lasted no more than the passage of a single day. But I was probably reaching, trying to find a reason, excuse, for all my lost days and squandered nights.

I should have enjoyed the ride, but my mind was on the upcoming job. I'd gone to Mick because I believe forewarned is forearmed. I'd also made a few phone calls, asked a few questions. I had been hoping for a piece of information or two to give me the inside track on the case. Instead, I ended up knowing a hell of a lot that I wished weren't true.

Dubronski had to be connected. Mick wouldn't be wrong about something as important as ties to the mob. This cast a much different complexion on the case than I'd originally forecast. While it still might be simply another straying husband playing house for a week with his bimbo in Bimini, it just as well could be a whole lot more. If the boys Dubronski was playing with wanted you missing, you stayed missing, and the way I saw things, it might not be a real healthy for anybody to be looking for you. I was tempted to tell the lovely Mrs. Dubronski to find herself another pigeon, but then I'd begun to bore myself. That's the ultimate problem with being as alone as I was. After a few weeks of being my own company, dark thoughts began to gather on the horizons of my mind.

Dubronski's place was in Hampstead. Massive red brick behind black wrought iron gates, with stone lions standing silent sentinel. Curving blacktop driveway lined with tall yew hedge. Beyond the hedges the grass was still green, lush, and cropped close to the ground. An ancient oak stood on the southwest corner of the estate, while a copse of birch trees, broken in half by a stony bank, ran along the eastern edge of the property. The manicured effect put me in mind of the appearance a fine golf course achieves, before too much rough play takes its toll.

Halfway down the drive, I had the cabbie let me off. I told myself I needed to get a better feel for the place, or maybe I simply wasn't quite ready. The cabbie made the loop and headed back toward the lions. I ignored the twinge of temptation to flag him down as he passed.

In two minutes, I found myself on the red brick porch, surrounded by a quartet of massive Ionic columns. The house was huge, even larger than it appeared from the head of the drive. I felt very much a Lilliputian dwarfed into insignificance. I ran the palm of my right hand along the slightly roughened brick exterior, feeling the collected warmth of the sun. The house, masquerading as a castle, faced southwest. I wondered if the inside would live up to the outside promise. One could never be sure about buildings, or people. Only one way to find out. I pressed the bell.

Melodic chimes echoed deep in the bowels of the monster. I waited twenty seconds and was getting ready to press the button again when I heard the clip-clop of high heels moving quickly. Before I put on my game face, there was a click and the door swung open. A young Chicano in a black and white maid's outfit filled the doorway. She had slim legs, dark eyes and a rotten case of acne.

"Can I help you, sir?" The voice carefully neutral, unusual in one so young. Allison Dubronski trained her servants well.

I nodded. "Frank Quick to see Mrs. Dubronski. She's expecting me."

The maid stepped back, taking the door with her, and I stepped into the vestibule. Hardwood floors gleamed. An urn on a marble stand was reflected in a gilt-edged mirror. Oceans of soft, cream colored carpet lapped up to the edge of hardwoods. To my left was a cherry coat rack with mother of pearl inlaid on the ends of each branch. Joe Dubronski might be a behind the scenes kind of guy, but he didn't put all his money in Aunt Olivia's pickle jars.

High heels clomped back. "Mrs. Dubronski asked if you would wait in the parlor." The maid indicated a room to my right with a half wave of her hand. I hadn't heard that phrase in years. I had no hat to leave, so I simply hauled myself to the parlor while the maid click-clacked down the hall.

The carpet was every bit as plush as it looked. Fine cherry furniture, polished till it gleamed, livened up what was basically a neutral room. An exquisitely colored painting of an indigo bunting was clearly the most spectacular piece in the room. A couch, a pair of easy chairs, a couple of coffee tables, and a sideboard I guessed held either silver or whiskey, served to fill the space. A low-hanging chandelier and a single, tall, thin window provided light for the room. In addition to the brilliant bird, a trio of what looked like family portraits hung at the far end of the surprisingly modest room. I wandered down to have a look at them before Mrs. D arrived. Info about your employer never hurt.

The three pictures were arranged like stair steps. The top one was Allison herself. I guessed it was taken in her days as talk show hostess. The setting was some trendy restaurant full of customers. Allison shared a table with a man I recognized as a motion picture star, but whose name I couldn't recall. His right arm coiled comfortingly around her shoulders and they both smiled broadly into the camera.

The middle photo appeared to be Allison at an earlier stage of life, maybe right out of college. It wasn't a terribly flattering portrait, as Allison must have been caught without her makeup. At first glance, she looked pale and lost, and there were dark circles under her eyes. However, there was a certain fierceness in the eyes that was both a promise and a warning, and made you reconsider your first impression.

The third picture was a happy family shot. Allison and a darkly handsome man caught only in profile played with a beautiful golden retriever. The man apparently had just thrown a red Frisbee. The photographer had snapped the shot as the dog leaped into the air and grabbed the Frisbee. The dog's coat glistened in the sun, Allison was clapping, her eyes bright and alive, her mouth open. You could almost hear her laughter.

I felt a moist cool hand on my shoulder. "Memories, Mr. Quick, happy memories." There was a wistful air to her voice. I turned my head and studied her face. She'd aged since the Frisbee photo. Not much, merely a wrinkle starting to crawl away from the eyes. I figured the picture might be a couple of years old.

"Your husband?" I pointed at the man in the Frisbee photo and smiled.

"Yes, but I have a better photo of him in the study, and of course you have a wallet size. Won't you come with me?"

I took a final look at the movie star. Someone like Richard Gere, only it wasn't him. My memory was getting lazy. I turned and followed her out of the parlor and down a long hall.

Both Mrs. Dubronski and the hallway were exquisitely arranged. She wore a pants suit tailored perfectly to her body and a tennis bracelet that retailed well into the thousands. Her rump twitched invitingly with each step. The hallway was paneled in rich dark walnut. Another crystal chandelier, larger and more elaborate, hung midway down the passage. What looked like an original Edward Hopper sketch hung on the wall. Her scent drifted back to me. Over the years I've inhaled a lot of women's perfumes. In fact, I'm a connoisseur of perfumes. This one smelled of lilacs, moonlight nights, and big time money.

~ * ~

He stared at me with dark, rapacious eyes set firmly in a brooding face. Handsome enough, if you like that type. He wasn't my cup of java. His mouth was set too firmly, as if to compensate for a weakness in the chin. Eyes were a touch too close together, but you couldn't deny the animal magnetism, the intelligence, and the power in that face. I got the impression he tried to control his emotions, but if they slipped their leash, watch out. No way of telling from a picture, of course; still, as I held the five by seven in my hands, I was convinced Joe Dubronski was not a man to cross.

I had the funny feeling I'd seen him somewhere before. Or maybe it was that he reminded me of somebody I'd seen recently.

"When was this taken?"

"Actually, earlier this year, February or March, at one of my club functions. Much newer than the one I gave you yesterday. Just a photo for our club's annual membership guide. The club rarely sends in any photos to the newspapers. Joe would certainly have forbidden that in this case. He hated publicity of any kind, for himself anyway. He didn't seem to mind so much if I got noticed every once in a while for some charitable activity. Joe is truly a behind the scenes kind of man. Made me get the negative of this shot and give it to him. He burnt it."

She smiled to herself. "Was mad as hell when he found out I'd had a copy made. At first he wasn't going to let me keep it, but, after I worked on him, he relented." She turned and looked me directly in the eyes. "I can be pretty persuasive when I want to be."

I nodded. Feeling the power of her blue eyes, I could believe it.

"How old is Joe?"

"Let's see...he is a few years older than I am. Thirty-seven, I think. Yes. Thirty-seven."

"Height?"

"Six foot one, two. I'm not positive; I never exactly measured him, you know."

"Weight?"

"That's easy. He weighed himself every morning. In all the time we've been married it never got below one-eighty-two or more than one-eighty-five. He looked thinner, but a lot of his body is muscle. He worked very hard at keeping hard."

She let her eyes travel up and down my frame. "You're about his size and you look pretty hard yourself. If fact, you two favor in general body type, even a bit in your facial features."

I gave her a long hard look, but it didn't appear that her comment was any sort of double entendre.

"Yeah, we're about the same size, but I'm not in what would be termed peak condition."

"Do you work out?"

"Some."

"Do you lift or run or bike or—"

"A little bit of everything, or nothing. Whatever I'm in the mood or have time for. Probably run more than anything else, although I do take it by spurts."

"Well, you look like you're in great shape." Her blue eyes were wide open and appeared guileless. The smile seemed pleasant and unforced. I reminded myself that she listed actress among her previous professions.

"Looks can be deceiving."

She chuckled—a nice laugh, ringing clear and pleasing to the ear. The sun was fading; the brief twilight of autumn had fallen. Outside, something white brushed against the French windows. Through filmy curtains, I caught a hazy glimpse of a figure. My guess was female.

Allison noticed my attention was wandering. Her face turned toward the coming night. Her glance lingered there for a long moment, then she turned back to me. A smile was still on her face, but this one seemed, in some way I couldn't quite define, different.

"Come with me, Mr. Quick. There is someone I want you to meet."

I followed her across the room and waited while she struggled with the catch on the French doors. "Darn these things anyway, the lock is always sticking. I need to get someone out here to work on them. Just keep putting it off."

Eventually, with a suddenness that was almost startling, both doors burst open. Chilly evening air streamed inside, pulled by the newly created draft. I followed her outside.

Darkness was rapidly overtaking the earth. Light streamed from the windows of the house and from dual security lights set high atop twin poles rising from the ground about twenty-five yards from the house and set about the width of the back of the house apart. The overall wattage, from inside and out, surely had to be impressive, but it did little more than cast yellow dents in the darkness.

I glanced at the sky. A sliver of a moon hung low and a handful of stars twinkled faintly. Instead of falling, as it often did with darkness, the breeze had risen. I wondered if a change in the weather was in the offing. I'd neglected to listen to the weatherman today.

I followed Mrs. Dubronski through the gathering dusk. We worked our way down a walk of large, smooth stones set in the even carpet of grass. The security lights crossed arcs here and the stones shone silver in the autumn night. There were about fifteen or sixteen of them, spaced approximately a foot apart. The short walk led to a small garden.

In the near darkness, I fancied I could make out a gazebo and a pair of willow trees set among several smaller plantings, too covered by the blanket of darkness for me to identify. The gurgling and splashing of a fountain sounded loud in the quiet night. The Dubronski's place was so far from the main traffic arteries that the highway noise was barely a dull drone in the back of the ear, the way a horsefly halfway across the barnyard would sound on a hot, humid, summer afternoon.

Pausing, I let my eyes grow accustomed to the darkness, a darkness that felt like an alive element of nature. It seemed as if I could feel it as it brushed against me. In a strangely satisfying way, I welcomed it. Perhaps not as an old friend, but certainly not as a stranger. Old Man Darkness and I were more than mere acquaintances. We knew each other's moods and methods, morals, and the lack thereof. Not that we particularly enjoyed each other's company, but we'd survived some long, rough nights together. We knew how to handle the past, the loneliness, the despair, well, enough to make it on through to morning.

Allison seemed to vanish in the darkness, then reappeared suddenly at my elbow.

"Mr. Quick, I want you to meet someone very special and very dear to me."

Like your mother, I thought to myself. I stepped forward and turned my head in the direction she pointed. There, off to my right and hugging the main path, were a concrete slab bench and two white wicker chairs. A woman sat on the bench. Blonde hair flowed onto her shoulders like a stream of liquid gold. She was dressed totally in white. In the poor light, I couldn't tell whether the outfit was a dress, or a skirt and blouse. Whichever, it hung low, puddling around the ankles.

"This is my sister, Lindsey. Lindsey, this is Mr. Quick, the famous detective, the one you and I heard about on television that time. You remember the McAllister case. I've hired him to help us find Joe."

"Oh, yes. So very nice to meet you." Her voice was sweet and clear, slightly higher pitched than her sister's, a touch more youthful to my ear. "We really need your assistance. Allison and I are very worried about Joe." She shivered. "He's been gone for so long."

The concern in her voice sounded genuine. I wondered if she was an actress like her sister.

"Pleased to meet you." I didn't know her last name and I don't usually get into first names with my clients or their relatives. She extended a hand and I shook it. It was smooth and soft. Quite the lady of leisure was our Ms. Lindsey.

"Lindsey, I'm getting cool out here. Aren't you chilly?" Sisterly concern, or repressed mother image coming out. I hadn't seen any evidence of any children.

"No, I'm fine. In fact, the breeze feels good." As if on cue, the wind gusted. Golden strands of hair billowed out from Lindsey's head. Allison's hair, although essentially the same color, was cropped much closer, so that she wore it like a cap of tarnished gold. It seemed to me to be a touch chilly to be outside in what appeared to be a lightweight dress sitting on a concrete bench after the sun had gone down. I kept my thoughts to myself.

Allison wasn't so circumspect. She sighed audibly and half-turned on her heels. I got the impression that Allison found Lindsey a bit burdensome at times.

"Come on, Mr. Quick, I'll walk you back to the house." Allison took my arm and turned to face the lighted house. Not wanting to be rude, I hesitated.

"So nice to have met you, Mr. Quick. I'm sure we will be seeing more of you."

"Nice to have met you."

I turned and followed Allison down the stones toward the lighted house. Lindsey's call of "Good luck" came floating to us on the evening breeze.

Allison began apologizing the minute we got back inside, pressing unnecessarily close to me as she began, gently laying one soft hand on my left arm. I could feel the warmth of her flesh through my shirt sleeve. The performance made me feel as if we were co-conspirators in an unsanctioned covert operation.

"I'm sorry about that little scene, Mr. Quick."

"No need to apologize."

She did anyway.

"Lindsey is younger than I am, and, since we lost both our parents at an early age, I've had to be more than a sister to her. You know, sort of a father-and-mother-knows-best all rolled into one. I realize she is a big girl and I need to give her some space, but I suppose I'm actually a bit of an old mother hen."

Allison Grant Dubronski did not fit my idea of an old mother hen. Her physique, style, mannerisms brought other images to mind. I nodded, looked away at an innocuous black, baby grand piano gleaming under a crystal chandelier, and mumbled something incoherent, more of a soothing sound than words.

Silence sat between us for a long moment. I wondered if I should break the quiet. I wondered if Allison or Lindsey, or maybe even Joe, played the piano. Perhaps they all did. A family affair. Piano *a' trois*, if you will. I even wondered a little about the case. After all, that was what I was getting paid for.

"Would you like a drink, Mr. Quick?" Her hand on my shoulder, her voice in my ear.

"No, thanks. I'd better be going. Got a rather important case that needs my attention, you know."

She made a pleasantly agreeable sound in the back of her throat—deep and comforting, as though she understood the process and agreed.

"When you last saw your husband, did he say anything about being gone for a few days?"

A furrowing of her brow, as though she were thinking my question over. Her breasts rose and fell gently, like twin ships at anchor in a sheltered bay.

"No. I saw him at breakfast for a few moments on Thursday. As I remember, I had a glass of orange juice, he had coffee and a bagel. Said something about some business downtown and that he should be back around five. Afraid I wasn't paying much attention."

She squinched her eyes and peered up at me like a child expecting a scolding. "I had a volunteer day at the hospital scheduled, which, to tell the truth, was what I really had on my mind."

A serious look swam in her blue eyes. "I was back home by three, and Joe did phone about four-thirty and said he'd be late."

"Did he sound worried, concerned?"

"No, just business taking longer than usual. You know business deals, Mr. Quick...they always take longer than anyone expects. No, I can't say he sounded the least bit out of the ordinary. In fact, he suggested we go out for Chinese after he got back. The Royal Peking, one of our favorites."

"And he didn't show?"

"No, I've never heard from him after that call."

"You haven't heard from anyone else about it? A friend or an acquaintance, someone who said, 'Hey, I saw your husband at such and such place at such and such time?'"

"No, no." Her voice was tinged with impatience. Sorry lady, I thought to myself, you're paying me to ask questions.

"Has he ever gone missing like this before?"

"No." She smiled, shrugged. "Oh, he's gone on trips, business trips that have lasted a day or two longer than he expected, but he's always called, or had a friend call to let me know he was okay. Nothing like this." Her voice cracked and she turned her head, dabbing at her eyes with a tissue quickly pulled from a pants' pocket.

I counted to thirty to give her a chance to pull herself together. "How long have you and Joe been husband and wife?"

"Two years this past June."

"Any children?"

"No."

"Boyfriends, girlfriends?"

"None, Mr. Quick, and I resent you asking that question. I hired you to find my husband, not to ask questions about our personal lives." She had drawn herself up to her full height and turned to face me. With her heels, we were nearly eye to eye, and I'm six-two. Allison Grant Dubronski was nobody's little girl.

"I've got to ask all the questions. The one I leave out because it might hurt your feelings could be the crucial one. Don't take offense. I'd ask the president's wife the same ones if he were missing."

I gave her the benefit of my smile, so she'd know I wasn't offended. Down the hall a phone rang once. I could hear the murmur of a voice, faint and distorted, as though it had come from somewhere far away, say Sheboygan, or Neptune.

"Now, don't get huffy, but how did you two get along at home? Was it good or bad for you? Him? I'm looking to see if he had reason to stray."

For a minute I thought that she was going to slap me. A tremor quivered its way through the length of that beautiful body. She gave me a hard look, then sighed. The sound sounded sad, as if she were disappointed in me.

"Not that it is any of your business, but our home life, including our love life, was fine. Joe and I have a good marriage, at least by our standards. I don't know about yours, Mr. Quick. Apparently they lie somewhere beneath the gutter."

"That's the side of life I see the most. Anyway, Mrs. Dubronski, you hired me just like you hire a painter, or an electrician, or an auto mechanic. You probably don't tell them how to do their jobs, so..." I let the sentence fall unfinished.

Her blue eyes tried to burn a hole right through me. I wasn't concerned. A lot of people, bigger, uglier, and meaner than Mrs. D had done one hell of a lot more than stare at me.

"Anyway, if you don't like it, you hired me, so you can fire me."

She whirled around and stepped quickly across the room. She paused before a highly polished, walnut credenza. At least one person in the Dubronski household, or their decorator, had exquisite tastes. She ran one long slender finger absentmindedly across its obviously well-dusted top.

"Sorry, Mr. Quick. I do realize you have to ask these questions. Guess I'm just upset and worried about Joe. I try not to be, but each day that goes by makes it that much worse."

"I still think you should try the police. They've got hundreds of times the resources I do."

"Yes, and nine times out of ten they are as corrupt as hell. Some of them would sell their own mother if the price were right."

"We all have our price, Mrs. Dubronski."

She turned and stared at me, peering straight into my eyes as though she were trying to look through into my soul. Good luck to her trying to find that.

Eventually, she found what she wanted, or gave up. I voted for gave up. "Maybe so, Mr. Quick. What's your price?"

"Don't know. No one has ever tried hard enough to find out."

The truth was I didn't know what my price was. I figured I had one, and was scared to know what it was.

Time slow-danced with itself while we stood like two strangers who have met and conversed in an art gallery, and in the process come dangerously close to revealing something significant about themselves.

This silence felt awkward, heavy as it pressed against me. Time to ask another question.

"Enemies?"

"Enemies?" The puzzled look on her face seemed genuine.

I strolled over and leaned against the piano. As it turned to night, the day was getting long in the tooth. It was starting to grind me down.

"Yes, enemies. Could your husband have created any enemies, Mrs. Dubronski? Personal? Or maybe some of the people he did business with were upset with him? Disgruntled employees, ex-wives, that sort of thing."

Long legs crossed, she propped her body on the edge of the credenza. It seemed a natural move, and she was probably tired just like I was, but all that lovely female flesh arranged just so seemed somehow calculated to provide me with a brief, albeit enticing, moment of viewing pleasure. Very pleasant. A touch distracting. Then again, perhaps I was merely too damn old and cynical.

The tip of her tongue gently rubbed the right corner of her mouth. She sighed softly. "My husband is a businessman. Naturally, people he gets the better of in a deal are going to be unhappy. Not that he was running any kind of a scam, it's just that in the day-to-day world of business, one party generally gets the best of any deal. My husband is a good businessman."

"What kind of business?"

Her blue eyes crinkled in a gesture which blended boredom with frustration. She was tired of all the questions. She was through with me for the night. She wanted me to go home, or get to work; whatever, just get out of her life for right now. However, she didn't say it. Instead, she answered my question.

"He buys and sells, and loans people money for business opportunities."

"What sort of things does he buy and sell?"

Anger flared in her eyes, but she quickly banked it. "I really don't know all the details, but, for example, he deals some in real estate. You know, buy a building here, fix it up, then sell it for a profit. Then repeat the process. He also plays the market quite well."

"Stock market?"

"Yes. Stocks, and I have heard him mention bonds. T-bills, too, if that term means anything to you." She pushed herself off the credenza and gave me her brightest model's smile. Her teeth were even, straight, and whiter than they had any right to be.

I had several more questions I wanted to ask, but I'd already pushed my luck. "Good night, Mrs. Dubronski, and thank you for your patience. If you show me to a telephone, I'll call a cab."

"I'll have Rico drive you." She walked across the room and pushed a small round ivory button. Then she turned to face the door. I looked at a small abstract on an adjacent wall. Blues and greens swirled together, with flecks of silver splashed haphazardly about. I'm not much of a modern art fan, but this one at least gave off a sense of power and motion. It reminded me of the ocean at breakpoint, waves dying a powerful, foaming death. We stood in silence, waiting for the maid to come show me the way out.

Seven

Even the city slows down at night. You can't say this town ever truly sleeps—it never does. Still, after dark the overall pace slows. Picks up, of course, in the night spots, with their bright splashes of light, flashing neon, pulsating rhythms. However, the offices and stores close and the ranks of cars, cabs, and trucks thin. The pace of life decelerates. Sidewalks and streets clear dramatically as darkness falls. Sometimes, just for the hell of it, I run in the night.

I run to see what's around the next corner.

I run to kill time.

I run to lose myself.

I run to run.

Waves of dark pavement passed beneath my feet. Blurs of street lights came and went. Sweat glistened at the end of damp tendrils of hair and slid silently down my spine. In the distance a horn blared, muffled by brick and mortar. A dog howled from inside a gas station closed for the night. Shadows without definition stood guard on the right and left.

I ran down the withering blocks that formed the dying west end of Washington Avenue. Abandoned warehouses and offices long emptied of the daytime human flotsam formed a corridor of silent spectators. A single yellow cab cruised by, its light on. The legs of a derelict extended from a darkened stoop. Pungent odors of cheap wine and stale urine hung in the air.

Voices, mumbled and muffled, grazed my ears as I cut the corner at DeWitt and headed east. A large, charcoal-gray Cadillac, its windows tinted against God and humanity, idled against the curb. A scrawny cat and I crossed against the light. A hunk of fur hung by a slim strand from the cat's hindquarters. In the flash from green to yellow, I caught the vulgar display of raw flesh.

Memories flooded my mind. Long Saturday afternoons at the library, reading the books about famous Americans, determined to be one. The smell of fresh doughnuts. My mother's silent tears. Daryl Lamonica deep to Billy Cannon when it was third and only a short yard. Memories as haphazard harbingers of a past that both delights and destroys. They come unbidden, on their own schedule, without guile or warning. They speed by in their own uncharted orbits, their return unscheduled. Always uncertainty reigns. The unknown always awaits.

So I run.

I run to see what's around the next corner.

I run to kill time.

I run to lose myself.

I run to run.

Eight

Faded to gray, dirty gray. White paint over dull red brick too many years ago, Dubronski's office stood on the corner of Whitlow and Twenty-third. Across the street, a bakery emitted aromas of fresh-baked bread and brewing coffee. Next door was a men's clothing store I'd never heard of. They seemed to specialize in tuxedo rentals, probably why I didn't recognize the name. My senior prom was ancient history. Not a slum block, but not upscale either, slipping into pawn shops, holding out against porno palaces.

I eschewed the ancient elevator and took the wooden steps with their peeling gunmetal gray paint. They creaked and groaned with every stride. Suddenly the stairwell began to vibrate. A low hum seemed to fill every inch of air. With mournful moans and protesting gears, the elevator began to ascend. No way to sneak up on anyone here.

The main office, according to my client, was on the third floor. *Equity International, Inc.,* was hand-painted in white on a green, pebbled-glass door. Without knocking, I tried the door. It opened—I was halfway surprised. The thought had been playing around in the back of my mind that if Mr. D. was missing, maybe the place had closed.

Not so. Doubly not so. Two women sat at matching metal desks facing each other across the square, high-ceiling room. The one on my left was heavyset, middle-aged, with no-nonsense glasses and mud brown hair, chopped short. She had a ledger book spread out before her; her hands flew over the number pad of an ancient calculator. She didn't bother to lift her eyes from her work.

The other occupant was young, late teens or early twenties. Red hair out of a bottle and fashion model thin. A can of diet cola and a clean yellow legal pad rubbed edges on her desk. Her smile, flashed over the top of the telephone she cradled on her left shoulder, invited me to come on in. I did. Glass rattled in the door as it closed behind me.

I stood and waited until the redhead finished her conversation. I didn't pay particular attention, but it sounded like she was canceling an appointment. I wondered if it was for the missing Mr. Dubronski. I listened with half an ear and tried to peer through more green pebbled glass on a door marked *Private*. The door looked like a relic from the 1950s. I wouldn't have been surprised if it were.

"Yes, sir, can I help you?" She went for the low throaty pitch, trying for sexy. She almost made it.

I gave her the once over. Promising, but at her age she could go either way. "Yeah. My name is Quick and I have been hired by Mrs. Dubronski to see if I can locate Mr. Dubronski."

A happy light came on in her sea green eyes. I could hear the "Oh, I'm so glad" starting to bubble up in her throat. I waited. It didn't happen. Instead, the numbers lady stepped in. "Well, it's certainly about time." Authoritative, never-wrong tone. No nonsense voice, just like her glasses.

I half-turned to face her steady gaze. "Been worried about him?"

"Yes. It is just not like Mr. Dubronski to not let someone know where he is." She paused, looking me over as if she were preparing to pass judgment. A minute passed, and apparently so did I. "Especially with a couple of big deals only half finished."

"When did you last see him?"

"On Thursday."

"Did he seem himself?" I stepped back so I could look at either of the women without doing more than tilting my head.

"Yes. Don't you agree, Monica?"

"Yeah. He was real busy that day. I remember he was still here when I left at five-thirty. You left at four that day, Jo Ann. I remember you had to leave early for a dentist appointment."

"That's right. An old filling had fallen out the day before and Dr. Bernstein worked me in." She made a face like a kid does after swallowing a big spoonful of rotten-smelling cough syrup.

"I've been thinking about that day, you know, since he hasn't been, well…er…ah…back since then." Monica's green eyes misted over and her long carmine-tipped finger fluttered like broken-winged butterflies across the polished desktop.

"And?" I prompted her, as she looked as though she were wandering down a dead-end trail. I'd begun to wonder about her brain power.

"And it seemed like he was feeling real good, not acting nutty or anything, you know. He never does. Yet, he seemed excited."

"Excited about what? Do you know if he had a big deal in the works?"

Monica looked like the question was a high, hard one, by her before she was ready. She looked across the room to Jo Ann for help. The unflappable bookkeeper considered the query. I pictured the computer inside her brain searching through the files.

"Not really. He had just closed the Decatur-Ward apartment complex sale and, of course, that would make anybody feel good, but that was finalized on Tuesday, no, Monday. So that wouldn't really account for the way he was on Thursday. Monica is right. Mr. Dubonski was different. More upbeat than usual. As though he had something exciting to do after work, instead of being happy about something he'd already done."

"Was he scheduled to meet someone that night? You know, for dinner maybe, or could he have had a late night appointment?"

Two heads moved side to side in unison. The older lady served as spokesperson. "However, he wouldn't necessarily have told us about dinner plans. In fact, most times he wouldn't. Oh, he might have once in a while, or on occasion he'd have us make reservations, especially if it was some place unusual, like Thai or Indian. Otherwise, he made most arrangements himself. Not that he ever said much, but judging by the odd comments I'd overhear and putting two and two together, I always figured he did a lot of business over drinks and dinner."

"Does he have a business partner?"

"Not a regular one. It was this way. He'd do a deal with a couple of guys, then partner with some others the next time, or go solo."

"Did he have you pull any files for him on Thursday, or even Wednesday, that he didn't use? You know, data on a project he might have been boning up on for Thursday night."

Jo Ann looked at Monica. Big green eyes that were wide and empty; prominent cheekbones that poked at her skin. Her red hair swung slowly from side to side.

Nine

Armed with the names of his usual haunts, plus his current and most frequent business partners, I'd gone looking; looking for Joseph Molina Dubronski.

From trendy upscale restaurants serving Nuevo-American cuisine to a half-dozen dark, solid working-man neighborhood bars, Joe Dubronski surely covered a lot of territory. Maybe the spectrum of his haunts was due to his clientele, or maybe Joe Dubronski was a more complex man than I'd figured.

In most of the places, one or more of the staff knew him by name or recognized his picture. None, however, remembered seeing him in the past few days and nobody particularly remembered last Thursday.

No one seemed alarmed or upset because they hadn't seen him in a while. Just as Jo Ann had said, he had a couple of regular places where he often met his business associates, but regular to him was once every couple of weeks. He might stop off for drinks at a bar near his office a couple of times one week, then maybe not make it again for a couple of weeks. He was remembered as a good tipper with nice manners who liked to order steak, and drank bourbon in a highball glass. The kind of customer you like to see come in, but don't have a book full of war stories to tell about.

His business partners I located were quiet and circumspect. Sure, they knew Mr. Dubronski, a couple of them referred to him as a business associate, but nobody had seen him last Thursday, or since. No one told me much, and I endeavored to tell them less. If they got the impression that I was some kind of insurance adjuster or IRS agent on an audit trail, I couldn't be held totally at fault. I never actually claimed to be either, just dropped the telling word or jargon laden phrase here and there and let their imagination do the rest.

Mick was seldom wrong, at least I never caught him missing often. This time was not the exception either. It took me two long, hard days of digging before I made the connection, but I finally did it. The business was called Arlington Associates, a multi-faceted corporation dealing in real estate, antiques, and travel agencies. A mild enough sounding operation until you ran across a certain officer of the corporation, an executive vice president named Anthony D'Angelo.

Mick had said the word he heard was that Joe Dubronski was connected, as in connected to the mob, organized crime, the Mafia—whatever you chose to call them. I'd begun to wonder about the reliability of Mick's information, until Fat Tony popped up. Fat Tony, aka Anthony Joseph D'Angelo, II. Fat Tony, consanguineous to Gotti, Conella, Giardello, and Bennetti. Accused of dozens of bloody, senseless crimes, or at least of ordering them done. A few nights in jail early on for carrying a concealed deadly weapon. Later, a couple of overnight stays until his high-priced lawyer managed to spring him on bail. Fat Tony had danced nimbly through the years, waltzing just along the water's edge, never getting more than a hairy toe wet.

Tony had been on page two of the list of clients and partners of Joe Dubronski that Jo Ann and Monica had worked up for me. Right there between Michael A. Davidson and Charles Edington, Jr., two guys I'd never heard of. I wondered if they knew Joe dealt with Fat Tony D'Angelo. If they did, it might cast a different light on their relationship. I know it made me look at the case a little differently.

Fat Tony wasn't your average Mafia lieutenant. Rolls of fat covered one of the hardest hearts and quickest minds going. He had all of the cruelty and love of violence that any traditional mobster might have, but without any noticeable sense of honor or love of family that those boys traditionally held in high esteem. Then again, maybe that was all phony for them, and Tony was simply being honest.

I tracked him down about one o'clock at the Marble Swan, an upscale Italian dining establishment on the east side. I'd heard of it, even sauntered by once to glance at a menu. At the time, my budget had been too modest to go the prices.

Even in mid-afternoon, there was a chill in the air, but as I stepped into the vestibule, a comforting warmth accompanied by a plethora of wonderful aromas engulfed me. If the food tasted as good as it smelled, it might just be worth the prices.

Slick black tiles on the floor, tiny strands of white running through them; sepia-tinted glass in the vast mirror that ran the length of the antechamber on both sides. Dim, fluorescent lighting encased behind curving brass. A tall, black-jacketed maître d', who still looked incredibly handsome, even though he had to be pushing fifty. Call him a Mediterranean Rock Hudson. The Marble Swan was quite a place, indeed. I walked in like I owned the joint. I wondered if Fat Tony had a piece of this action. It would be legit to the hilt.

"Yes, sir?" Mr. Handsome put it in the form of a question. I wasn't sure if it was a nice way of asking "Do you have a reservation?" or "What is a scruffy sort like you doing here?"

"Mr. D'Angelo, please."

Nostrils quivered for a split second. Black eyes narrowed fractionally. "Just a moment, please. May I have your name?"

"Quick. Frank Quick, and I'm here representing Mrs. Joseph Dubronski."

Our glancing gazes met, held. I couldn't read his face that time was just begun to line. I hoped I was similarly inscrutable. He broke eye contact and turned on his heel, leaving me to stare at a pair of alabaster swans sitting in the pool of a small fountain that gurgled soothingly in the corner.

I cooled my heels and let my brain free fall. A memory of visiting my grandfather Withers' farm as a boy came floating to my mind. Especially vivid were the memories of the old chicken house, full of Wyandottes cackling softly to one another, their nesting boxes lined with straw and set in rows along the east wall. As a small boy I'd been afraid of the old hens who would sometimes furiously peck your hand when you tried to gather the eggs. Later, after life had toughened me, I just pushed them firmly aside.

Footsteps on the tile pulled me back. "Mr. D'Angelo will see you now." I still couldn't read the maître d's expression.

I followed his angular form through a large room of well-dressed patrons. For a restaurant, the noise level was low. The guests spoke in hushed voices while the waiters and busboys moved with quiet efficiency. Even the sound of the dishes clattering together as they were removed from the tables seemed muted.

We passed from the main room through a smaller chamber that held a half dozen booths, all curtained off for privacy. I ran my right hand along the deep blue curtain material as we slipped by the last booth. It felt like velvet. I wanted to look inside.

My guide didn't slow his pace, however, so I quick-stepped after him. Just when it seemed as though the room would end against a plastered wall or a back door, a small corridor appeared, tunneling us left. Seven steps and we halted in front of a heavy oaken door. A slim hand rose and rapped, twice, short. The massive door swung open without a whisper. A thin man with gumdrop eyes held the door open. Tony D was wedged into a booth.

Rolls of fat hung from his neck. Thick, red, blubbery lips. Little black eyes set like twin marbles in a Pillsbury Doughboy face. Fat Tony D'Angelo was a work of art. He was also younger than I'd expected. Because I'd heard of him for years, I'd pegged him for mid-fifties. Truth was, he looked like he was in his early forties. He was dressed in a suit that cost roughly three times what my best one did. Latest cut, fine silk, Fat Tony was ready for the cover of *Gentleman's Quarterly, X-Large.*

His luncheon companion looked like she belonged on the cover of *Hustler*. Blonde, big blue eyes, bee-stung lips, scud missiles for breasts—ready to explode through the shiny material of her dress, a creation more suited to a summer party at the beach house than a mid-autumn luncheon in one of the city's nicest Italian restaurants. To go with the body to die for, she had that certain curve of face that turns men on at eighteen, photographs enchantingly at twenty-one, and begins to turn hard by thirty-five. The first of the concrete had yet to set. Fat Tony liked them young. Maybe she was his niece. Maybe I was Lew Archer.

Tall, dark, and handsome made eye contact with Fat Tony, and some signal I couldn't catch passed between them. My guide withdrew, leaving me alone with the charming couple. I waited for the big man to go first. It might have been my show, but it was clearly his turf.

Tony resumed chewing—spaghetti, salad, or bread. Those were the only things on the table. He must have had a mouthful when we came in, because I hadn't seen him take a bite. Jaws moved slowly, rhythmically, as he studied me carefully out of sunken marble eyes. I couldn't see them well enough to take a reading. He swallowed. A tiny fleck of red clung to the right corner of his mouth. A fat pink tongue slipped out of his mouth and cleaned it up. Eyes still focused on me, he slid his right hand out from under the table and grasped his companion's left breast, or as much of it as he could wrap his pudgy fingers around. He gave it a firm squeeze. Disgust mixed with pain swept across her face and distorted the fine features for an instant. Then the come-on smile popped back out. She shot him a furtive glance, but if he noticed the aberrant expression he didn't let on. She put her head on a fleshy shoulder and snuggled closer. I got the message.

"So you're Quick?"

"Yeah."

"Word is you're looking for Dubronski."

"That's right."

"Is he missing?" A half smile on that fat face.

"His wife certainly seems to think so." Stimulating conversation so far.

"Oh, you mean the glamour girl, the one who never cares what you think?"

I let that one slide. Fat Tony leaned back on the dark maroon leather of the private booth and pulled young, adorable, and hot to trot—provided the price was right—closer to his meaty body. I didn't know the girl, and didn't care anything about her. Nonetheless, it made me uncomfortable to see her attractive face and body mashed against his blubber. I kept my thoughts to myself. Fat Tony wouldn't like them.

He leaned over and nibbled on her neck while he waited for me to respond. I hoped he enjoyed himself. She must have tasted good, because in only a few seconds he French kissed her ear. A fat hand strayed back to her left breast. The blonde kept a cover girl smile stuck on her face. Her teeth were uniformly white and even, and had cost somebody a small fortune. I wondered if it was Fat Tony, or a predecessor.

The free show went on for a minute or so, then he got tired, or bored, or hacked off. I didn't know and didn't care. The ball was in his court.

"Why have you come to see me? Joe's a big boy. I don't have to hold his hand. As you can see, peeper, I've got better things to do. Much better." He gave his companion a gluttonous leer.

"I heard you two did business together?"

"So? I do business with lots of people. I do business all the time. I'm a very busy guy. That doesn't mean I know where every damn one of my business associates is every fucking minute." There was a harsher edge to his voice now. I could understand why the average citizen would be reluctant to cross him.

Our glances locked and we stared into each other's eyes for a tense moment. Then Fat Tony tired of the contest, or got hungry. Anyway, he resumed eating. A heaping forkful of spaghetti disappeared into his greedy mouth. The blonde nibbled daintily on what looked like grilled salmon. I wondered if the verbal jousting had affected her appetite, or if she were simply dieting. I still suspected her of having secret aspirations to be a model. Not that she was interested, but my advice was to take her best shot before Fat Tony used her up. If he devoured her like he did his food, it wouldn't take him six months.

"I hope you understand, Mr. D'Angelo, that it's nothing personal. Just that I have been hired to locate Mr. Dubronski, so you understand, naturally I've got to check out all the possibilities."

Fat Tony grunted. His eyes never left his plate. He was working with all due diligence on his spaghetti mountain. Already, he'd reduced it to a foothill.

"Thought maybe you might have seen him around the last couple of days. Or, maybe you guys had some business going that you wanted kept private."

He raised his head, chewed eight times—I counted—and swallowed. "If we did, Quick, I sure as hell wouldn't tell you." His snorted and then his eyes flickered back down to his plate.

"Did he ever talk to you about some secret place he wanted to slip away to? You know, over drinks or lunch? Because everybody has their South Sea island or Australian outback where they'd like to get to, somewhere far away from the rat race. Do you know what Dubronski's idea of paradise is?"

"Look, Quick, it ain't really none of your fucking business, but, no, we never talked about any romantic cruises or hideaways or any of that shit. Dubronski ain't blood. We did a little business together, that's all, if you get my drift."

He paused and pushed his fat lips together and out in a way a child puckers up. He rolled his eyes to the heavens. "Once, twice, nah, make it three times, total. Nothing big, you understand, just a little business, and for your information I like this here rat race just fine."

He gave Blondie's left boob another twitch. "In fact, the only thing I want to get away from is you, you nosy son-of-a-bitch."

Another forkful, sauce dripping, spaghetti dangling over the sides of the tines, disappeared into his mouth. The rhythmic chewing began again. Footsteps shuffled behind me and a hand firmly gripped my elbow. Mr. D'Angelo was through with this conversation. It was time to leave while we were still exchanging pleasantries. Still, I hated to leave without getting the chance to turn down dessert.

Ten

Light sparkled and tap danced off crystal wine goblets. Fine gold rimmed the Noritake china, and heavy flat silver bearing an intricate design lay around the dozen or so plates. White coated waiters carted silver trays of hors d'oeuvres and martinis. Quite a soiree was being thrown this night by Mrs. Allison Grant Dubronski. Certainly more than a little dinner party that needed one more man to make it all come out even on the boy-to-girl ratio. I wondered why I was there.

The guests had broken off into three small groups, each of which had found its way into a corner of the huge dining room. Actually, when I looked closer, I could see there was a small rail built into the floor about two-thirds of the way toward the far wall. The rail ran the entire width of the room. Looking now with a purpose at the wall on either side of the track, I could see where the panel slid into the recess, allowing the room to be converted from a good-sized dining room and a modest den to a huge open room with a massive polished walnut table at one end and some comfortable furniture at the other. Such a conversion made it perfect for before dinner drinks and after dinner conversation.

The smallest of the three groups consisted of three men in expensive suits who had captured a corner near the dining room table. Two of the men had their backs to me. Both were smoking; one kept putting his cigarette in his mouth, only to almost immediately take it out again. I figured he liked to talk more than he liked to smoke. The other smoker was into cigars. He had a fat one dangling out of the corner of his mouth. I could catch a glimpse of it whenever he turned his head to clear the blue-green smoke cloud that threatened to surround him.

The third man was about my age, tall and handsome, with a face I'd seen before. It took me a minute before I came up with where. Television. I'd seen man number three on television. He was a local politician, and, if I had my commercials straight, he was trying to move one step up the political ladder. His commercials aired often these days as the November elections approached. I tried, without success, to remember his name or something that he stood for, or against. To be fair, that was probably more my fault than his. I pay little attention to television in general, even less to commercials, especially political ads.

Arranged in a circle in front of the living room window, the second group consisted solely of large, fleshy, middle-aged women. They were a rather formidable bunch, looking much like a retired quartet of female linebackers. One horse-faced lady looked particularly rough. She was almost as tall as I was and probably weighed more, and I go six two, one eighty-five in my birthday suit.

The third group was a mixed bag of ages, sexes, and racial origins, including one androgynous creature who could have fallen into several categories of sub-species. Most of this group were seated in easy chairs in front of a fireplace that contained a real fire.

Allison was part of this group, sitting next to a fat, middle-aged man who sported a salt and pepper beard. A tall, sharply thin young man with longish brown hair and round tortoise shell glasses appeared to be telling a joke. At least there were grins on the faces of those who didn't have their backs to me. He delivered the punch line dead pan and the entire group exploded into laughter.

Allison noticed me, disengaged herself, and came bustling over my way. She was in silver heels and a blue dress that almost came together at the breast line. Her hair had been brushed up and pushed to the left side. A silver cross hung low between her breasts. She looked absolutely stunning. I had to wonder about Joe Dubronski's safety, or his sanity.

"Please forgive me, Mr. Quick. I was listening to Peter...he is so clever with his jokes, and didn't see you come in. I am afraid you must give me poor marks as a hostess."

I smiled as I listened. I wasn't upset, but I surely was more than slightly disarmed.

Long slim fingers and a cool palm encircled my right wrist. Her fingernails were long, manicured, and coated in silver, flecked with blue. I bet myself the color scheme extended all the way to her panties. I figured that for a safe bet—no way I'd ever know.

"Come with me, Mr. Quick. I want you to meet some people. Now, this is just a little dinner party I've thrown for my friend, Mark Stephenson. He's running for Congress. You must have seen one of his ads. They are on television all the time. I especially like the one of him with his family at the ball game. So American—the family united, sports. I think he has a real shot at winning."

She followed my gaze to the group of three men. "Yes, that's him. He's talking business now. I'll introduce you in a few minutes. First, I want you to meet some of the other folks." She began to maneuver me toward her group.

Halfway across the room, she paused and bent her golden head toward me. Her whisper echoed in my ear. Soft strands of hair caressed my face. It had to be my imagination, but I could almost swear I felt a soft, moist tongue graze my earlobe.

"I've brought you here under false pretenses."

I rolled my eyes to the right and caught the devilish glint in her eyes. Hard blue, like marbles. They seemed to reflect my look back to me. I wondered if she wore contact lenses.

"I'll tell you later, or I'm sure you'll figure it out for yourself. For now, you are just a friend over for dinner." As we resumed walking, she hurriedly added, "Joe is just out of town on business. Okay?"

I nodded, and then we were on the fringe of the group. A plump little number in a see-through blouse of pale peach was telling an involved story about a sailing accident. As I had missed the start of her story and, as she tended to ramble, I never caught the real drift of her tale. The fact that her round little breasts with their prominent nipples pointed right at me didn't distract me in the least.

Allison Grant Dubronski and I waited patiently. She clung to my arm as though I were a pole on the merry-go-round. Her body pressed against my side. She was one tall girl and her head rode easily above my shoulder. The sweet scent of her perfume filled my nostrils. Heady stuff—it made for easy waiting.

The story ended to a chorus of "oh no's" and "my, my's." Her interviewer's voice cutting through the residual hubbub, Mrs. Dubronski made a number of introductions that few would remember in six hours, let alone six weeks. I met all in the covey and, despite my good intentions, promptly forgot most of their names.

The plump girl who had given up bras was named Melanie, and I gathered she was into sales for some aspect of the broadcasting industry. The tall, thin, bespectacled man was Peter von Something-or-Other, and he wrote horror stories for juveniles and made a mint doing so, at least that was his story. The man with a beard was Don Cartwright, a name, and the only one, I recognized.

Cartwright was a television producer in Los Angeles. I figured he and Allison had worked together in the past. There was also a stock broker, a lawyer, an artist, and a lady who claimed to be in real estate but who looked suspiciously like a brunette who used to perform tabletop dances about five years ago at a dive called Crazy Charlie's. The rest got lost in the blur of introductions. I wasn't disappointed by this and they didn't act like they were either.

Everyone smiled, or at least nodded. Several murmured, "Pleased to meet you," whether they meant it or not. I hoped they would all go back to whatever topic they had been discussing, but

Peter looked at me studiously out of his little round glasses and asked, "So, Frank, are you in politics, too? Maybe part of the Mark Stephenson entourage?"

"No, politics is not my métier."

"Well, what do you do then?" There was something faintly British about the young writer. I half expected him to add "old chap."

"As little as I can get by with." That brought a few chuckles, although the attorney gave me a fishy eye. "Actually, I'm a friend of the family."

That seemed to satisfy most of the group. Cartwright, however, gave me a longer look I couldn't read. As a long-time friend of Allison's, maybe he was wondering why he'd never heard of me. I looked him in the eye, but without any effect. He held my gaze for a second, then, half-smiling, not at all nonplussed, turned back to the group.

I hung around the fringe, one arm on the back of a comfortably padded high-backed chair, nibbling on salmon pâté ensconced in a dark rye pastry, half listening to the chit-chat. There was some talk of politics, a good bit on the cost of group therapy, but the hot topic of conversation was cruises. Everyone in the group seemed to have been on at least one in the past year. Except for the stock broker, who suffered greatly from *mal de mer*, they all seemed to have had a fabulous time, absolutely fabulous.

I hadn't taken an actual vacation since Mona and I had crisscrossed the Arizona deserts in one glorious, wonderful month, a half dozen years before. Now I worked only when and if I wanted to, so I didn't exactly need a vacation. I sympathized with the stock broker, and harbored no urge to call my travel agent and book a cruise.

I flattered myself that pretty, plump Melanie was ogling me, deliberately bending over at the waist so that her breasts hung exposed like overripe grapefruits begging to be picked. I could feel my neck flushing and was glad when Allison caught the maid's signal and announced that dinner was served.

I meandered across the room at the back of the crowd. Conversation flowed in a desultory fashion. Snatches of "what a lousy bitch," "Georgia in June," and "Did you ever see such an outfit?"

drifted to my ears. My thoughts were few and simple, purely my own, and unlikely to endear me to anyone. I kept them to myself.

From my point of vantage, I could observe the guests as they figured out the seating arrangements. Allison seemed to be assigning them. Her directions were quick and purposeful, and undoubtedly had been the subject of considerable advance planning. I hung back at my observation post, waiting for the pack to sort itself out.

In about a minute Allison had worked her way back to me. A half dozen of us still milled around, waiting for our seating assignment. Melanie and Peter were both still standing. I hoped not to draw either of them as a dinner companion. Foppish young writers and plump, juicy young ladies were not on my agenda tonight. Allison swiped a wayward strand of blonde hair from her face and focused her deep blue eyes on me. Glazed with concentration, they abruptly cleared and she slid through those still standing and rubbed a smooth hand on the arm of my jacket.

"Come on, Mr. Quick," she said sotto voce. "I have a very special assignment for you."

"What's that?"

"Only a favor I'd like for you to do for me." The way she said it left no doubt she expected me to do it. "Just a little one," she mouthed as we walked around the end of the large table and down the other side. I felt like everyone was eyeing me, but then I've long had a vivid imagination.

"Mr. Quick, I want you to sit by someone very special to me. This is my younger sister, Lindsey Grant. Lindsey, this is the wonderful gentleman I have been talking to you about all day, Mr. Frank Quick."

It was the same girl I'd met briefly the night before. I mumbled "hello," and began to pull my chair out. I'd been uncomfortable coming in the first place and now longed to be anywhere but here. Fancy little parties and entertaining my client's little sister were not high on my goal chart this season.

Peach polish on beautifully manicured nails, long slim fingers, a fine hand extended to me. A mellow, throaty, "Hello" accompanied them.

I shook the hand—soft skin, firm grip—and gave the younger Ms. Grant a look. Lovely oval face, fine cheekbones, alabaster skin that instantly made you want to touch it. For a second I thought I was seeing double—she looked that much like Allison. If she was younger as Allison had said, it couldn't be by more than a year or two. I wondered if Lindsey had Allison's blue eyes and if they were a family trademark. I couldn't tell as she sported darkened glasses. Maybe she was in pictures. I hit my internal recall button, but nothing popped up.

I slid my chair back and my body on in. The maid I'd seen earlier along with a jacketed manservant were serving. Crystal goblets stood in rows like a brigade of tabletop soldiers. Silver gleamed dully under dimmed lights. Laughter bubbled up from the head of the table. I could clearly see Allison flanked by Stephenson, the politician, on her right and her old Hollywood chum Cartwright on her left. Over the top of my water glass, I slipped a glance at Lindsey.

Soft lighting flatters most of us, but she looked exquisite, refined, and a touch delicate. Ethereal beauty personified. I covertly watched her sip her water. The lines in her throat were good. The glass caught the light and glittered wickedly. I looked away.

My neighbor on my right was a nondescript fellow in a dark gray suit. I judged him to be about forty-five, trying to look thirty-five. His hair was combed straight back from his head and hung moderately long on his collar. In the weak light, it looked faintly damp. A large amber stone was set in a class ring on his right hand. His wristwatch hinted at pseudo-Rolex. I figured him for black magic mind games. He gave me a cheerless smile and half a nod. We both decided to be bad boys and not introduce ourselves. I felt positive he would tell somebody on me.

Except for a stale pretzel and the hors d'oeuvres, I hadn't eaten since breakfast, having found several unproductive ways to fritter away my time. I wondered what the main course would be. I guessed chicken, probably free range, certainly not fried.

"So you're the Frank Quick my sister has been telling me about?"

"Suppose so." I watched as she chewed small bites of her salad with startlingly white teeth. The woman had to be in pictures. She wore a layered dress, teal and silver, which left a good deal of her figure to the imagination. Her hands were pale, good-sized, with long, strong looking fingers. I fancied her for a piano player. Heavy silver hung around her throat and an oval garnet adorned the first finger of her right hand. Understated, but expensive. I liked her taste in clothes and accessories.

"Allison's been talking a great deal about you. She has a lot of faith in your abilities. Apparently she received several high quality recommendations on your work. We both trust they are well-founded."

"One way or another, I tend to get the job done."

My tone must have been harsher than I'd intended. I saw her wince, crow's feet forming just outside the range of the glasses. She laughed, a clear tinkle at the back of her throat.

"Well, the rest of the reports on you were accurate. Universal opinion among your former clients, those we talked to anyway, is that you are a prickly sort. One even compared you to a cactus."

"At times I can be a bit, as you said, prickly."

"Most times?"

"Probably."

The tinkle again. A strange little laugh, like a series of bells setting each other off one by one in the back of her throat. "You really are a bit of a character, Mr. Quick."

Aren't we all, in our own way, I thought to myself, but I didn't say anything. I gave her one side of a grin to show I wasn't offended. After all, she was my client's sister. I glanced toward the head of the table.

Lots of fun and games at that end. Allison was in deep conversation with her guest of honor. Heads bowed toward one another, leaning so that their shoulders touched. If Cartwright felt left out, he didn't show it. He appeared to be spinning some yarn to a buxom redhead seated to his left. She appeared to find the story delightful, leaning over so that a good deal of the front forty was offered up for Cartwright's viewing pleasure. From the not overly subtle glances he kept sneaking, he appeared to enjoy the view every bit as much as she did his story.

The main course came around conveyed by the same pair that had been on duty all evening. They worked smoothly and efficiently, virtually no wasted motion, moving quickly, but not obviously hustling or hurrying anyone. They were worth every penny Mrs. Dubronski was paying them.

"Who are the couple serving? Do they work full time for the Dubronskis, or does she hire them for special events?"

"Rico and Diane work for the Dubronskis full time. In addition to serving at parties, Rico serves as gardener and chauffeur, while Diane does a bit of cleaning and a lot of running for Allison. She's almost exactly the same size as Allison, so she can go try on clothes and bring home only the ones that fit. That way Allison can decide what she wants without devoting a lot of time to her wardrobe. My sister has an awfully full schedule, what with all her charity work, and then she and Joe entertain a good bit."

"You look about the same size as your sister and closer to her age. In fact, you two could pass for twins. I'm surprised she doesn't get you to try on outfits for her. Then again, you may be pretty busy yourself. What do you do to pass the time?"

I was making conversation while looking for information on the side. Lindsey's face wore a funny look as she turned her head toward me. "I don't have a regular job, Mr. Quick. I help Allison occasionally by making a few phone calls, and I've done a few public service announcements for local public radio." There was an uncomfortable strain in her voice. "I used to teach public speaking at Saint Stephens, but gave that up after Allison and Joe married." She lowered her head, then came back up with her lips freshly arranged in an intriguing smile.

Saint Stephens I had never heard of, so I nodded my head in what I hoped was a sage-like manner and let Rico serve me. I was right, dinner was breast of chicken in an Alfredo sauce surrounded by a slender serving of colorful vegetables that appeared woefully undercooked. A roll roughly the size and density of a baseball, accompanied the bird. I was glad I'd eaten a pretzel before I left my place, and wished I'd eaten more hors d'oeuvres.

The bird cut easily and passed the palate test. The vegetables I wasn't sure about. The man on my right crunched on undercooked carrots. They seemed less appetizing all the time.

"Mr. Quick?"

"Yeah?"

A quiet sigh. I wondered what she was up to. Seconds of silence grew up and became a minute. Before they could become two, I broke the silence.

"Yes, Ms. Grant?"

"Lindsey."

"All right, Lindsey. What can I do for you?"

Something almost discernable hung in the air. I could sense it was there, but couldn't grasp the meaning, much like a delicate seasoning teases the palate, hiding among the more flavorful spices. Not knowing what else to do, I chewed my chicken.

That little sigh again—it spoke of lamentations and regret. I found it oppressing.

"What's at ten o'clock?"

"What?"

Another moment of silence for the dearly departed, those about to depart, or those we wished would depart. I was ready to admit I was a lost ball in high weeds.

"What's at ten o'clock?"

"What? Please forgive me, Ms. Grant, er, Lindsey, but I don't have the faintest idea what you are talking about. All this talk of time doesn't have any point to it, as far as I'm concerned."

"Didn't Allison tell you?"

"Didn't Allison tell me what?"

That special little throaty tinkle of a laugh.

"Obviously she didn't. Mr. Quick. However, for a private detective of some renown, you seem to be, shall we say, somewhat unobservant."

"What do you mean?" I could feel myself getting a touch hacked off and not a little tired of this idle prattle, aimless word play, or whatever dear sweet little Lindsey was playing.

Long, slim fingers spread themselves imploringly on the white linen. The peach-colored polish was perfect. I studied a blue vein on the back of one hand. It wound its way just below the translucent skin like a subterranean river seeking a jidden sea. A nerve ending flickered and a finger twitched.

"I'm sorry, Mr. Quick. I thought my sister would have told you by now. I know she intended to. I didn't mean to criticize your abilities. You only really met me a couple of minutes ago and there is no real reason for you to have uncovered my little, shall we say, ummm, secret." The words were clear and distinct, the regret genuine, only the meaning was still shielded, hidden by murky misunderstanding.

"No, no. I'm sorry, Ms. Grant. It's just that I truly don't have any idea what you are talking about."

"I know, and, it's Lindsey."

"Lindsey."

She smiled, a sweet sunrise of a smile—one that covered palms and pelicans, sand and surf, countless miles of emerald green movement cresting, before breaking and then moving forward again to the timeless rhythm of the ages.

"That's okay. You couldn't have known. I try hard not to be, but there are times I know I'm over-sensitive." Five little enamel pearls bit her bottom lip. She pulled them back. Indentations remained. A half sigh. Of regret? Discomfort? Acceptance?

"You see, Mr. Quick, I'm blind."

I felt the hot rush of blood and knew my neck and cheeks were colored with blush. I felt foolish, awkward. What do you say in a situation like this? "I'm sorry" seemed fickle, limp, and pathetic. I wanted to slide down my chair legs to the floor and out the door. Anywhere but at this party, this embarrassing moment, is where I wanted to be.

However, I've been in this old world long enough to know one gets very little of what they want and virtually nothing of the rewards they're convinced they deserve. Both these outcomes are probably in our best interest. My tongue felt thick and my lips seemed stuck together by a white, gummy substance. I swallowed a mouthful of emotion.

"There's some really delicious chicken in Alfredo sauce at two o'clock and a mound of vegetables that don't appear to be overcooked at nine. Oh, and there's a hard, round roll on a separate small plate at eleven thirty. Your wine glass is at high noon."

Her hand slid across the table. I surmised it was seeking for mine. I covered her smooth, soft, fragile hand with my own old, rough, calloused one.

That transporting smile blessed me again.

"Thank you, Mr. Quick."

Words fail me at times. Their inadequacy is overwhelming. So I simply squeezed her hand gently, once.

Eleven

Shadows moved with me in the night. Flickering, changing forms that danced with grotesque abandon on bricks and walls the color of faded blood. Neon flashes pulsated, automobile horns called to each other across the thin evening air, revelers poured out their passions like new wine from old wine skins. I was looking for a man who always seemed to have existed only in the misty murkiness of a dim past, never yesterday, nor even the week before.

Joe Dubronski seemed to have stepped through a portal and vanished, taking with him not only his flesh and bones, but his spirit and memories as well. People remembered him, but couldn't say precisely where or when they'd crossed his path. Gone only a week, he was an enigma fading from a charcoal sketch of life. His trail seemed as cold as an iceberg drifting through the Arctic Ocean in January.

Midnight had grown old and crawled off into the deeper shadows and I was tired, and discouraged. I felt as old as Methuselah. Aching feet protested every step. Determination alone drove me on, fueled by a desire to find a tangible trace of the man, something I could hang my hat on. I hated to go home without a sliver of hope to take with me, balm for my empty soul and aching feet.

I'd hit a baker's dozen of places. Trendy, upscale, yuppie havens like the Pacific Rim. Middle class, working man bars like Grogan's. Down and out, dollar a shot, high-heeled hooker hell holes like the Black Moon. I'd surely met an array of interesting folks, from greasy bikers with wind-blown hair, to pot-bellied factory workers stopping by for a beer after bowling with the guys, to hotshot young lawyers— handsome in their Gucci loafers and Giorgio Armani suits. Joe Dubronski's picture had passed through dozens of hands. Nobody had seen him in the last week, and nobody offered to buy me a drink.

Outside the door to Le Metro, I paused, Dubronksi's smudged photo in my hand. In the last half hour, the wind had picked up. It had also developed a bite. The hawk was flying tonight. It felt good to be protected from the full brunt of its force; only wind whispers swept around the corner of the arch. My body was cold, my brain befogged and I wanted to go home. Yet, I hated to quit. As old Coach Mathis had been fond of saying, 'Losers quit, winners do it.' If I never showed Joe Dubronski's picture to another person it wouldn't be too soon for me. I pulled the door open anyway and stepped inside.

Talk about your den of iniquity. If it wasn't one, it sure as hell felt like it. Strobe lights pierced the smoky darkness in dual beams that made wide orbits, as though the room were an airport landing strip instead of a bar. An infectious reggae tune vibrated from a jukebox cranked to maximum density.

"Who's that singing?" I asked a tall man with a face like a horse's. He was lounging against the bar just inside the door.

Old horse-face looked at me like a preacher viewing a lost soul. "That's Bob Marley, man. The late, great, undisputed King of Reggae."

I nodded like a bobble-head doll and tried to look wise. A crew of three faced me from behind the bar. I sized them up as possible sources of information.

There was a tall, black kid with a six-inch flat top and eyes half-closed as though he were ready to go to bed. Next to him was a slender girl with dishwater blonde hair. She was nearly slobbering over a good-looking young man on the other side of the polished wood who looked to be of Jamaican or West Indian descent. The third staff member I figured as ex-service. Ramrod straight back, slim, yet well-built. Muscles worked in his forearms like a small army of stubborn soldiers on the march. His gunmetal gray hair was streaked with silver, worn in short spikes like you see on the tops of certain fences in New Orleans. Flat, green eyes surveyed the room constantly, while his head was cocked to one side as though he were listening for something special. I wondered if he was hearing something I wasn't.

I elbowed my way through a rowdy crowd. It was a mixed bag, mostly white teens, with generous splashes of dark-skinned islanders, adrift in a sweating sea of humanity, far from their Caribbean home. I took a shove from a steroid stud in balloon pants and a muscle shirt and stumbled the last few steps to the bar in a poor parody of a dance routine.

"Hey, mon, you like the music, yeah?" A long arm from the lady's man at the bar steadied me.

"Yeah."

"You like Bob Marley? You into reggae? You like Jamaican?"

"Yeah, I like it. So much they call me the White Jamaican." I told it like the truth—one of the marks of a good liar.

"The White Jamaican? That must mean you good, Mon. That your good name? Your inland name?"

I nodded. "Sure."

G.I. Joe with green eyes came to parade rest just behind the polished oak. "What can I get for you, sir?"

"I'm looking for a Bud, and some information."

"The beer I got for sure, however, the information ain't always easy to come by."

I slid the smudged picture out onto the counter. He pushed a bottle in my direction and picked up the snapshot carefully by one corner, as if he were afraid he might tear it. His hands looked strong, with clean, carefully trimmed nails.

"You a cop?"

"Private."

He waved the picture back and forth like a funeral parlor fan. "This guy did something wrong?"

"Gone missing."

His green eyes made contact with my mud brown ones. Flat and opaque, I couldn't read them at all. His face was stiff and expressionless. I was glad I wasn't playing high stakes poker with him. "Who wants him found?"

"His wife."

White teeth pulled strongly on his upper lip. His nostrils flared. "Yeah, I've seen him around. Name's Joe, ain't it?"

"That's right. Happen to remember who he used to come in with in particular?"

"Different people."

"Men or women?"

"Mostly men, but a couple of times with a lady, and more than once by himself."

"Remember any of the people he was with?"

"Men or women?"

"Both."

He crossed his arms on the bar, then looked at the ceiling as if the answers were written there. Somewhere behind me, a woman's shrieks of surprise dissolved into a gale of giggles. She sounded happy, young, and foolishly drunk.

The bartender drummed the fingers of his right hand on the dark wood of the bar. He looked at me and cleared his throat. It took me a second before I realized he wasn't looking to me for inspiration. I dug in my front left pocket, fished out a twenty, and palmed it to the man.

His hands disappeared below the bar. I pushed the bottle of beer in slow circles on top of the bar and waited. Keeping his eyes on the patrons shifting like grains of desert sand before a rising wind, he cleared his throat.

"Comes in here pretty regular, now not every day, not even a certain day of the week, but he's usually in here, oh, say every third or fourth day.

I nodded.

"Well, Joe is sort of regular and sort of not. I mean, sometimes he stays an hour and sometimes ten minutes. Mostly, he's here with someone and I've never seen him get drunk. Might have a beer or a bourbon and water. Likes Maker's Mark."

"What about the people he's with?"

"Well..." The bartender paused, running a flat hand across the top of his spiked hair as if massaging his scalp would help bring memories to the surface. "Most of them I don't remember specifically. I mean, they were in here only once or twice. If I had to guess, I'd say they were like business associates."

"What about the others, the ones you do remember? Were any of those folks in here more than once or twice?"

"Let's see," the man rolled his eyes as he massaged his face. "Couple of them were women. One was tall, blonde, with a body to kill for. I think she was on TV for a while. Believe somebody told me she made a couple of movies. Now, what was her name?" He furrowed his brow, trying hard to remember, or impress me, maybe both. "Allison, that was it, Allison. Last name was Good or Swift or Craft, some short catchy name like that."

Yeah, real catchy, I thought to myself, so catchy you can't even remember it. "He ended up marrying her," I said. "What about the others?"

He rubbed the top of his head again, as though he were both Aladdin and the bottle with the genie inside. Then he pursed his pink lips—not a pretty sight.

I was sorely tempted to chug the beer and go home. Like I said, it had been a long night. Allison's party, or rather its food, sat heavily on my stomach, and my body and mind longed for sleep. Still, I'd come this far...what was another ten minutes?

"The others?" I prompted him.

"Well, there was this short, stocky redhead with boobs like missiles. You know, like out to here." He made extravagant gestures with his hands. I found his demonstration fascinating to consider, but hard to believe. He caught my eye. "I swear."

"Okay. That particular lady shouldn't be hard to find. Any others come to mind?"

He squinted. "There is Sam Bonner. To hear them talk, they do some business."

A tall woman in velveteen trousers and a sweater with a teddy bear on the chest came up to the bar and ordered a Bloody Mary. Her eyes were pale and opened wide and her bones were prominent beneath taut skin. I waited until she took her drink and headed back to her table. It looked like the main event.. Half a dozen housewives out on the town. Trouble any way you cut that layer cake.

"So we got Bonner and a redhead with a pair of heat-seeking missiles. Any other regular companions?"

"Two. One a tall, super thin guy with one of those old mustaches, like what's-his-name used to wear."

"Who?"

"Ah, you know him. Movie star from a long time ago. Big ears. What was that movie? Oh, shit." He paused and wrinkled his forehead with thought. The bartender's thinking process was painful for both of us. Something clicked and he gave me a half grin, displaying stained teeth with more than a few fillings. "*Gone With the Wind*. That's the movie. Now what's the guy's name?"

"Clark Gable."

"Yeah, that's right. This tall, thin guy has got a mustache like that."

"Does he have a name?"

"Not that I ever heard."

"What about number two?"

"That would be Al."

"Al who?"

"Don't know his last name, but he comes in all the time. Local guy, lives around here. I heard him say where once. Now, let's see, where was it? I've got a real good memory for street names. Oh, yeah, he lives over on Monticello, next to the gas station."

The man put both elbows on the bar and leaned across like he wanted to tell me a secret. I inclined my head closer. I could smell the garlic on his breath as he whispered in a hoarse voice, "Al works for Tony D."

"Fat Tony?"

"Tony D'Angelo, for sure."

Twelve

Armed with knowledge, burdened with responsibility, I made my way home through the vestiges of the dying night. In my benumbed brain, Lindsey Grant and Tony D'Angelo were starting to merge. Past time to shut this night down.

Le Metro had been my last stop, which left me a half dozen blocks or so from home. Flagging down a cab wouldn't be an easy chore at this hour of the night, or morning, depending on how you wanted to look at it. Certainly it wouldn't be worth the effort. I decided to walk. I could certainly use the exercise.

The wind was still strong, drowning out most of the night sounds. I did hear a small animal, probably a rat, scurry out of my path as I came around the corner of Dewhurst. The neighborhood was steadily drifting in the wrong direction. I knew I should get out while the getting was good. I knew I wouldn't.

People of the street had gradually been drifting this direction over the past year. I'd counted them, twenty-four, huddled in doorways, sleeping on benches, wandering aimlessly, since I had crossed Monroe, where the Litkenhous Park and Observatory stood on the right. Litkenhous used to be our Maginot Line. The streeties didn't come south of the park boundaries; a strong alderman and a willing police force had seen to that.

Two years ago, the changing district had elected a liberal lesbian, who, when her girlfriends didn't have her head jammed between their legs, turned out to be a homeless rights advocate. Now the barbarians were on the march, headed for Rome, or at least for my castle.

Maybe I was too hard on them. Maybe a few really couldn't work. But there were some who looked a helluva lot younger and stronger than I felt. I try not to hate, but I do truly despise a sponger.

I cut the corner at Dewhurst and Polk and headed for my place. I lived on the top floor. The other two floors were rented out, too. The bottom one to a middle class black family with two kids. The place was too small for them, but all they could afford on his bus driver's salary. She had been unemployed since April, except for temporary secretarial jobs. The middle floor was occupied by a single white female who taught art classes at Morgenthau Junior College on the east side and fancied herself a painter in her own right. She majored in watercolors, promoting her own pastel version of the world. I'd seen some of her works when I stopped by to drop off a couple of her magazines our mailman had put in my box. I can't say that our views of the world were the same, at least if she believed her pictures reflected reality.

Someone, or something, was piled on the front stoop of my place. I skewed my approach so that I arrived directly out of the shadows. I figured it wasn't one of my tenants, and street people generally weren't anything more than a nuisance. Still, I found it doesn't hurt to err on the side of caution.

In the poor light it looked like a bundle of bones under an old fatigue jacket. I felt my muscles tighten involuntarily and my pulse beat quicker.

I prodded the misshapen form gently with the toe of my right shoe. It emitted a half groan and began to curl itself into a ball.

"Here now, you'll have to move along. This is not a motel."

"Hush, Frank."

It took me a heartbeat to recognize the voice, muffled as it was by the jacket.

"Debi? What in the world are you doing here?"

She began worming her way out from under the jacket, talking at the same time. "I kind of ended up down here toward evening and was too tired to walk back to my place. Figured you wouldn't mind if I came by a while, so here I am." She gave me a sad little puppy smile.

I wasn't crazy about the idea, but I was too tired and it was too late to argue. Sometimes it's easier to go along. I stuck a hand out and felt her small one slip into mine. "Come on, let's get off this stoop and inside where it's warm."

She came willingly, scrambling to her feet. A little girl dwarfed by her daddy's old coat. Not likely to be her father's. Hell, she probably didn't even know whose coat it had been. Likely some john's, or else she picked it up at the Salvation Army, or drug it out of a dumpster.

She preceded me up the stairs. I put a hand on her shoulder. "Whatever made you settle on my stoop? Now, don't give me any more bullshit about being too tired. Tell me why in the world didn't you go on back to your place? At least you'd have been out of the cold."

"Couldn't." A catch in her voice spoiled her effort at a defiant tone.

"Why not?" I slid the key into the lock.

She didn't answer till we were inside, and then only after she had plopped herself down on one end of my couch, pulling the oversized coat around her like a blanket. In the lamplight, I could see that it was stained and had one large, unmended tear shaped like Chile. "I got booted out," she finally blurted, as she helped herself to a tissue, then blew her nose.

"How the hell did that happen? Thought you had an agreement with your friend."

I flung my jacket on the back of the couch, eased down on my La-Z-Boy, and began to take off my shoes and socks. I concentrated on the job at hand, giving Debi a moment to get her act together.

Tears pooled up in her eyes as she told me, "She found herself someone else."

"Someone else?" I didn't understand any part of this conversation and wasn't sure I wanted to.

"Denise likes her roommates young and well, er, ah, very attractive." Seeing my puzzled expression, she added, "See, Denise don't give you a room for free. Actually, you share her bed and are expected to buy her little presents from time to time, plus occasionally chip in on expenses. It all works out a lot cheaper than trying to go a place on your own. It's even less than going halves with another girl. The only thing is you have to take care of Denise, whenever and however she wants."

"Didn't know you two had that sort of agreement. Sounds bizarre."

"Oh, it's not too bad. It's just that Denise likes her roommate to be really attractive, and anyway, the new girl, Marsha or something like that, well..." She quit talking and blew her nose again.

"Anyway," she resumed after a brief pause, "this Marsha, or Martha or whatever, she has a whole lot bigger tits than I do, and I guess Denise really likes that. Besides, she's at least two years older than I am," she added defensively.

Even my jaded self was slightly uncomfortable with the direction this conversation was going. I stood and stretched. "Debi, it's getting late, so I'm going to desert you now and go to bed. You want the couch?"

"Yeah, sure."

"Hang on and I'll get you a couple of blankets."

Five minutes later, clothes off and teeth brushed, I slid between the smooth, cool sheets. Tiredness ebbed from my body while tendrils of sleep began to wrap themselves around the corners of my brain. I loosened my mental grip on Joe Dubronski and began to drift toward the galaxy of dreams.

A sound, or a sixth sense, jerked me awake. I wasn't sure how long I had been asleep, but I'd been out. My mind was still foggy with sleep.

Avoiding non-essential movement, I didn't look at my watch, reaching instead for the gun under my pillow. Fingertips touched my bare back and I involuntarily stiffened. My fingers closed on the butt of the gun.

"It's only me, Frank," Debi whispered. "Hope you don't mind, but it was awfully lonely in there on the couch." Soft lips pressed against my back. I let go of the gun.

I gave a long, deep sigh to let her know I wasn't overjoyed with the situation, and to obscure my tap dancing nerves. She already knew too many of my issues.

She slid into bed and, after a minute, I said, "turn over and go to sleep."

Without a word, she rolled over on her side. We lay there, bodies never not quite touching, each staring at a different wall. When I woke again morning was creeping in through the window to join us.

Thirteen

Flat face, black eyes, eyebrows that met to form a single line; hair cut skull-cap tight against the forehead. The bartender's description fit like a glove. The guy I was studying had to be Al. Al, who worked for Tony D'Angelo. I decided I'd better stick with referring to him as Mr. D'Angelo. Fat Tony might want to be called that only by his friends.

I could see Al clearly across the room. It was early evening and smoke had yet to sock in Michael's. The place wasn't the Waldorf Astoria, but it wasn't a dive either—just a nice little neighborhood bar and grill where you could get a beer, a shot, or a steak cooked the way you liked. I sidled up to the counter and pulled myself up on one of the red leather bar stools. The counter was shaped like a horseshoe, and I picked an open stool on one of the upturned ends where I could keep an eye on Al.

He was parked at a round table with three other guys. The table was about the size and shape of a card table, although more sturdily constructed. It could still function as a card table, however, which is what they were using it for. The game looked like draw poker.

A waitress drifted by with a tray full of steaks and fries. Hunger pangs hit me like a middle linebacker. I hadn't eaten all day. On her way back to the kitchen, I caught the waitress' attention and ordered a dressed burger and coffee, medium well and black. A veteran, she didn't need to write my order down. She just kept plodding for the kitchen on thick, well-muscled legs.

Al and his buddies were intent on their poker. While I waited for my food, I watched a few hands. They were betting dimes and quarters, playing quickly, without a lot of talk, as though they were on a schedule and needed to get in a certain number of hands before the hour was up to make their quota.

Al won a couple of hands and so did the man to his left. Then my food arrived. The player on Al's right had light-colored hair mounded like a sand dune atop his head. While I was eating, he won three in a row and threw back his long head in laughter after the third one, cackling at his good luck. Al had his back to the wall and he leaned against it, his chair standing only on its hind legs. The fourth man hadn't pulled in a pot the entire time I'd been there, and I was on my second cup of coffee and nearly through with my burger. Tonight wasn't his night.

From where I sat, it looked like Al's buddies tried to talk him into staying for one more. Al stayed, but his heart wasn't in it. He shifted restlessly in his chair, head slowly turning as he surveyed the room.

The man on Al's left dealt the hand. Bad Luck tossed three of them back and got three more. I figured he was holding a pair. The dealer also took three, Al took four, and the guy who had been so hot ran a hand through his sandy-colored hair and took two.

Al dropped out early. The dealer stayed through one round of bidding, then folded when it got too rich for his blood. After that, the bidding got intense. The man on a run of bad luck started to get loud. I could hear his high, thin voice as he moaned about something. His voice wasn't loud enough for me to distinguish the words, but his unhappiness certainly came through clearly.

A moment later, it was time to shut up and put up. Luck was running true to form. The unhappy player angrily pushed his chair away amid roars of laughter and shouts of "One more, Tommy!" Anger tinged his cheeks and he ignored the baiting as he walked down toward the far end of the bar. Sandy Hair began to rake in the pot and Al and the dealer made leaving motions. I slid off my stool and headed across the cheap navy blue indoor/outdoor carpet that covered the floor.

The dealer was telling Al a story about a race at the Meadowlands. The gist was his sure thing had been beaten by some lousy, lowlife of a broken-winded claimer. He figured the race was fixed. He asked Al what he thought. Al told him he thought all of life was fixed; the strong ended up taking what they wanted. Everybody else fought for the scraps. Before the philosophy got any deeper, they noticed me.

"You want something?" the dealer asked me.

I ignored him and looked at Al. "You the Al who works for Tony D'Angelo?"

"Yeah. Who wants to know?" Voice as flat as the face, and they both went with his flat chest. A cardboard man with a cardboard face.

"Me. The name is Frank Quick and I'm looking into a couple things for Mrs. Joe Dubronski. You got a couple of minutes?"

"Guess so." Al gave the dealer the evil eye and a jerk of his head. Seconds later, the dealer and Sandy Hair drifted off in the direction of the bar. Al eased into his chair, back still against the wall, so that he could watch the whole room. I sat in the dealer's chair. Only two or three tables were out of my view and I could see both the door and the bar. There was a good crowd in tonight and this was essentially unknown territory to me. I was grateful for the comfortable weight of my gun in the shoulder holster under my left arm.

People milled around us, but they weren't close and it was merely background noise. I looked them over casually. Nobody I knew. Nobody I was particularly interested in meeting.

"Well?" Al's flat voice pulled me back into the moment. "You want to talk, talk."

"You know Joe Dubronski?"

"Yeah, what about him?"

"Word on the street is he's done a couple of deals with your boss."

"Mr. D'Angelo conducts business with lots of folks. So what?"

"Tony tells me they have done a couple of projects together." I made projects sounds like the word left a bad taste in my mouth. I wanted to call him Fat Tony, but didn't want to hack off Al before he told me something. That, of course, assumed he knew something worth telling.

Al shrugged his thin shoulders. If the man had a personality, it was under control.

"Like I said, Mr. D. does business with a whole lot of people. It really ain't none of my business who he does his business with. If he said he did some business with Joe Dubronski, he did some business with Joe Dubronski. No crime in that."

A waitress with a touch of Dunlop's disease headed our way. Al shook his head and she veered left. She had great legs, but her butt wobbled as she walked away. I wasn't thirsty anyway.

"Some people say you and Joe have been known to have a drink or two together more than once in this very bar."

"So?" He gave the shoulder shrug again. I waited for him to add something about it being a free country, but he merely pulled a Camel out of the pack he had in his shirt pocket, scanned his eyes across my face, then fired up.

"You remember the last time you saw him?"

He blew smoke through his nostrils and considered my question. I didn't know if he was trying to remember, or if he was conjuring up a story. He tugged the cigarette out of his mouth. "Guess we had a drink last Tuesday night."

Al told it like the truth. I couldn't read his eyes to see if he was telling a lie. They reflected the light like black mirrors. It was like looking at tinted glass. I couldn't get a read on him at all, but if he worked for Fat Tony, he had to have something on the ball. The fat man wouldn't keep losers hanging on.

"What did you talk about?"

"The Chisom fight."

"You have Bobby?"

"Yeah, we both did, dropped a couple of hundred apiece. So we had a beer or two to drown our sorrows and talked about how that Puerto Rican pissant tossed the fight, the prick."

"Does Dubronski bet much?"

"Few bucks here and there. A little on the ponies, a few hands of poker. That's about it, far as I know."

"Can he afford it?"

The black eyes glared out at me from the flat face. I figured he was trying to guess where I was headed. I suddenly found an overly plump blonde two tables over very interesting.

"What business is it of yours?" Smoke from his Camel hung in the stale air between us like a thinly veiled threat.

"What are you so sensitive about? I only want to find out if he was having some money problems, maybe a little gambling fever." A light popped on inside my head. "Maybe our buddy owes you some bucks?" A brighter light went off. "Maybe he owes Tony?"

Al flashed me a black stare that made my heart stumble and sent a chill down my spine. The cold sweat of fear formed Lilliputian puddles under my armpits. If looks could kill, I'd be deader than three o'clock in the morning.

I told myself I'd be better off eating mud than letting Al see my fear. He'd feed on it like a blood-crazed piranha. I stared back at him, long and hard, pretending my eyes were frozen stones buried deep in old snow high up in the Canadian Rockies.

For a moment, he looked like he was working up to do something physical. I felt my muscles tense, and my left leg began its telltale twitch. I watched his hands. Long, slim fingers curled and uncurled.

Somebody punched in Bruce Springsteen on the jukebox. Bruce was born in the USA; maybe I was going to die here, now.

Al slowly pulled the cigarette to his lips and took another puff. Tension drifted away with the smoke.

"Is that why you're looking for him? He shortchange you? Thought you said you were working for his wife."

"I am. No, he doesn't owe me any money. I don't know that he owes anybody anything."

"Then why are you looking for him?"

"Because he is missing."

"What do you mean, missing?"

"I mean he's not where he should be. Hasn't been for the last few days. When he didn't show up at home for a couple of days, his wife hired me to do some looking, especially since she was expecting him."

"Missing, eh?" The question hung in his throat. A sly little crinkle developed around the corner of his eyes.

"Sure you haven't seen him since last week?"

"I'm sure." He took another drag off the Camel, then shifted his flat black eyes so that they reflected my own gaze. "You see him, you let me know?"

"Sure," I told him. I just didn't tell him when I would tell him. What he didn't know wouldn't hurt Joe Dubronski.

Fourteen

Logs crackled and popped as the fire consumed them. Blue-gold flames shot skyward. Stretched out in a La-Z-Boy with legs pointed toward the fire, I stared contentedly into the flames, brain jammed in neutral.

The bottoms of my feet were uncomfortably warm. The farther away the rest of my body extended from the flames, the cooler it became. There must not have been much other heat in the room because the tip of my nose and my earlobes were cool. The fire provided enough light to allow me to watch the shadows dance and leap on the wall like men possessed with a violent vigor. Supper sat comfortably in my stomach, while a final cup of coffee cooled at my elbow. A degree of contentment with life that I seldom achieve slid over me like a Navajo blanket. My eyelids felt thick, heavy.

Two beautiful blonde women sat with me before the fireplace. Allison Grant Dubronski extended her long legs from a Kennedy rocker. She had her shoes off and kept running the toes of her right foot back and forth over the smooth stones of the hearth. Lindsey Grant was on my left, seated on a short, four-legged stool, knees drawn up to her chin, arms wrapped around herself, head cocked toward the fireplace as if the fire were telling an intriguing tale. I wondered what the flames were sharing.

"Any luck, Frank?" Allison's voice, deep register for a woman, brought me out of my half doze.

"Don't know for sure. I've eliminated several possibilities. There are others." A pretty poor way of saying not much.

I studied her in the firelight. She was close enough to touch, less than an arm's length away, and her physical attractiveness was formidable. Her beauty wasn't a classic one…she was too tall and large-boned for that. On television, she'd appeared to be a virtual Amazon, often dwarfing her smaller male guests. Yet there was no denying her physical attractiveness. The big bones were arranged in fine fashion and plenty of lovely female flesh covered them. Allison Grant, with her gorgeous body and face, always made a statement. You noticed her when she was in the room.

However, she didn't overpower you with the sexual angle. Maybe that was due to her training as an actress, or perhaps an innate desire to be known as more than a body. That I could respect.

Lindsey shifted her position on the stool. "Has anybody seen him since he left the office last week?"

"If they have, they won't admit it, or I haven't found them yet."

"What about your idea of the credit card charges?" I had to admit Allison had a good voice. Her words were clear and concise and, even though she pressed you a bit when she asked her question, you didn't feel threatened, just compelled to answer it.

"No luck. Oh, I got the information all right. Just used the info you gave me and pretended I was Joe, checking up on a son who had borrowed my card. Both companies checked their records. There haven't been any charges since you made one on the eighteenth at Lady Killers, whatever that is.

Even in the flickering firelight, I could see Allison's blush. "Lady Killers is a lingerie shop." She laughed deep down in her throat like a man. Her feminine equipment was certainly obvious and undeniable, but there was a toughness, a strength about her that, rightly or wrongly, society more often associates with the male.

Lindsey cocked her head. Shafts of firelight flattered her delicate features. Not that she needed any help; she was a remarkably attractive woman. I found it easy to forget she was blind.

"What about his business associates? His secretary?"

"His secretary tried to help. She simply didn't know a great deal. Apparently, Joe conducted a lot of his business over dinner or drinks and didn't often follow up such meetings with a memo to the file."

"Joe is a great wheeler-dealer," Allison chimed in. "Unlike a lot of men who claim to operate in that fashion, he gets a good deal done."

"So he makes good money?"

"Yes. Why?"

I responded first to the coolness of her tone. "I'm not being nosy, per se. My point is that you guys aren't in any particular money trouble at this point, are you? He isn't in debt to loan sharks, for example?"

"No, we aren't, and yes, I'd know," she went on to answer my unspoken question. "I keep a lot of the books, and while we have our debts like everyone else, the mortgage on this house for instance, we're basically ahead of the game. If there had been financial difficulties I'd have gone back to work. I haven't lost all my marketable skills, Mr. Quick."

No, I didn't think so, I thought to myself. I didn't say anything, however, as I dislike hacking off a client, unless it is absolutely necessary.

For several minutes the three of us sat in silence, each lost in his or her own thoughts, watching the fire burn blue and gold while the shadows danced.

At least Allison and I watched the fire and shadows. I supposed Lindsey saw pictures in her mind. I was tempted to ask her the extent of her blindness. I wasn't sure if it was total, or if she could see light, maybe even make out forms if they were large enough and familiar enough. However, I didn't know her that well. My early impressions of her were that she was refined, delicate, and sensitive. I have a tendency to lean toward the blunt and direct, so I held my own council.

Allison broke the silence. "Where do you intend to go from here?"

I answered her question with a question of my own. "Have you ever heard your husband speak of a Tony D'Angelo?"

"I have heard the name. My impression is that Joe does a little business with him. Why?"

"His name's popped up a couple of times. Like you said, it appears they do a bit of business together from time to time."

"Have you talked with this Mr. D'Angelo?"

"Yeah."

"And?"

"And he says they did business together. One of his people said Joe and Tony did a couple of deals together. So, okay, they did some business. Nothing wrong there, of course. It's just that D'Angelo has a bit of a bad reputation and some of his connections are less than savory."

"Joe would never do anything that was even questionable, Mr. Quick." Allison's tone of voice was as rigid as her suddenly taut body.

I made a conscious effort to keep my voice calm, impersonal. "I didn't say he did, Mrs. Dubronski. It's simply that at least one of his business associates has a bad reputation. The deal, or deals, may have been totally legit and aboveboard, but Tony D'Angelo has the kind of reputation that makes him the sort of fellow you check out if somebody suddenly goes missing."

"You can't possibly be suggesting that one of Joe's business partners has kidnapped Joe, or, er, done away with him?" She couldn't bring herself to say the "killed" word. I didn't blame her.

"No, I'm not. D'Angelo and Joe appear to be on good terms. In fact, one of D'Angelo's people talked to Joe last week. He may have been one of the last, of what I call the outside people, to see Joe. I'm simply curious."

Allison slipped out of her chair, crossed in front of the fireplace, then started across the room. In the half-light cast by the flames, I couldn't read the expression on her face, but I saw her pause to briefly put a hand on her sister's shoulder. Lindsey reached up and squeezed the hand. In my mind, they were a pair of lonely, lovely creatures of the night, unsure about the disturbing promises of the morning.

Allison walked to one of the small, square windows cut high in the outside wall of the square room and turned to face the night.

The only sound was the crackling of the fire. This didn't seem a productive time for questions, and chit-chat is not my forte. Peaceful at first, the silence grew uncomfortable. Lindsey stirred on her stool. A log burst apart at the bottom of the fire and others tumbled down. Sparks flew about like Fourth of July fireworks. I wondered where Joe Dubronski was right now and what he was seeing, if anything.

"Mr. Quick, if expense was no problem and you could get on a plane right now and go anywhere in the world, where would it be?"

"Ummmm, Lindsey, I don't know. Anywhere?"

"Anywhere. Hawaii, Greece, Australia—you name it."

"What time of year?"

"Now, or make it anytime. In this game you can choose where, so why not when."

"England in June, I guess. Although I love the desert outside of Scottsdale, and I have always wanted to go to Australia. England would have to be my choice. On a lovely, early summer day the countryside can be absolutely gorgeous, and I'd like to see Stonehenge once more before I die."

"You've been before?"

"Twice. Once on a job, once on vacation. What about you? Where would you choose if money were no object and you could pick the time?"

"Oh, I know." The eagerness in her voice bubbled through her words. "I have wanted, for as long as I can remember, to go on a long, slow cruise around the islands of the South Pacific. On a sailboat. Lie on the deck and let the soft, warm breezes blow across my face and the sun slowly bake my skin to a delicious shade of brown! Now, don't get me wrong, I definitely do not want to do the sailing myself, neither the steering nor the manning of the sails. I'll leave all that to a crew of wonderfully muscled, hot, sweaty, desirable men."

Laughter gurgled in her throat. Whether she was laughing at herself or contemplating the cruise, I couldn't be sure. Anyway, she had a nice laugh.

"What about you, Alli?"

"What?" She spoke to the window.

"Where would you go if you could go anywhere in the world? Cost not a problem, bags all packed and ready to go. Just get up and walk out the door and there's a taxi waiting to take you to the airport. Now, where are you going? Tell the truth."

Allison turned from the window. Firelight played hide and seek in the shadows of her cheekbones. Her profile, framed by the window and darkness of the night, was something a man might dream about.

"Come on, tell us." Lindsey sounded as excited as a kid a Christmas.

"Prescott."

"Where?"

"Prescott, Arizona."

"Why there?"

"You said I could pick any place, so I picked there."

"I know, but why Arizona? Why Prescott?"

Allison gazed into the fire. Her eyes were opened wide. Her body arranged in an attitude that projected vulnerability. I could see the flames dancing in her eyes, but I couldn't read her. She looked as if she were a thousand miles away.

"That's where I met Joe. I was on location doing a shoot. Cover for a magazine. I'd remember it anyway. I never did many covers. I'm too big for most covers. Magazine editors like their models thin, and thin I never was. This one was for some tourist promotion. They had me all dressed up in jeans so tight I could barely breathe and a checkered flannel shirt, unbuttoned down almost to my navel. God, I was flashing a lot of flesh that day." She paused as though viewing the scene which was projecting across her mind.

"Anyway, Joe was there on vacation. Don't remember the details now, but he'd gotten hooked up with some tour—'The Old

Silver Trail,' or something along those lines. Told me later he was absolutely bored out of his mind.

Joe said he was stuck riding a tour bus with a bunch of senior citizens. Said if he had his own transportation, he would have cut out hours ago. The country was beautiful, but the tour guide was an old fart who kept talking about the Old West and his ancestors. Joe told me he was hunting for some place to get a drink, anything stronger than a Coke, when he saw the crowd where I was doing the shoot. Figured it had to be more interesting than the tour, so he wandered over to have a look."

"Guess he liked what he saw?"

"We both did."

Lindsey smiled. She still had that rapt, attention-paying look on her face, though I figured she'd heard the story before. If Allison noticed her sister's alertness, she ignored it.

"Remember it was damn hot that day, and the magazine had sent out this real young guy to oversee the shoot, and believe me, he was a great deal more of a hindrance than he was a help. Nothing was ever quite right for him: the light changed just as the cameras clicked, I twitched just at the wrong moment, the wind messed up my hair at the last second." She made a strange sound deep in her throat and shook her head.

"Oh, god, it was awful. We just kept reshooting and reshooting and I kept getting hotter and hotter. The makeup girl must have wiped the sweat off me and redone my makeup a dozen times. We had just taken a break and the poor girl was dabbing at me with cotton balls when I glanced over at this shady spot under a juniper tree I'd been coveting for some time, and there he was. Just like in the movies. Tall, dark and handsome, looking so cool lounging against the shaded wall of an old adobe building. Right then and there I wanted him. So I matter-of-factly got up and walked over. First, and only, time I ever did that on location. I'm simply not one of those temperamental, my way or else, performers."

She sighed, without realizing, I think. Loneliness and longing were highlighted on her face as the flames jumped and danced. At that moment I very much wanted to make her happy. I silently vowed to find Joe Dubronski, no matter how long it took.

Allison pulled herself back from Prescott and made a monkey face. "Me and my ancient memories. Hate to see what I'm like when I get old. Bet I turn into one of those little blue-haired ladies who live in the past. Can't you see me in my granny gown, sitting in my rocking chair, telling my grandchildren how wonderful life was forty or fifty years ago?"

Lindsey gave a small snort of disbelief. I smiled to myself and shook my head. I had to go along with Lindsey on this issue. Allison Grant Dubronski in no way reminded me of any grandmother, mine or anyone else's I'd ever known.

"Anyway, to make a long story short, I finished the shoot, finally, and he dropped off the tour to be with me. Neither of us made it out of Prescott that night, or the next. We've been planning to go back, but every year something comes up. Now I don't...I just don't know." She choked back a sob.

I was grateful for the shadows. The night and I were both aging, so I slid out of my chair and made my exit, with what I hoped was grace.

At the door, I paused and looked back. I felt like I ought to again say "Thank you for supper," but the moment wasn't right. Allison's back was to me as she stared into the dying fire and her memories. Lindsey sat quietly, left elbow on left knee, chin in her hand, seeing nothing. I moved on alone into the cool darkness, the White Jamaican on the prowl.

Fifteen

The telephone rang as I was finishing my shower. I twisted the water off and groped for my towel. If I'd been in the middle of, or just starting, my shower I would have let it ring on. The answering machine would catch it. I wasn't that interested in talking to anybody.

However, I was virtually finished anyway and if I didn't answer it, whomever was calling would probably leave a message, which I would only have to return, so I wrapped the towel around me and headed for the phone. I caught it after the third ring.

"Hello."

"Frank Quick?" A cute little voice of the female persuasion.

"Yeah."

"*The* Frank Quick?" Sexier now, hinting at more to come.

"The one and only. Now, what can I do for you?"

"Oh, tons and tons, but I'm calling because this time maybe I can do something for you." A pussy cat purring with an English accent, a Southern drawl, and a throat full of not very subtly hidden sexual innuendos.

I anted up to stay in the game. She'd aroused my curiosity and I definitely wanted to see what her next card would be. "Such as?"

"Such as, maybe you are the Frank Quick who is the private dick looking for the missing Joe Dubronski, and maybe I am the someone who happens to know more than a little about Mr. D. and his current whereabouts."

"So tell me and I'll put in a good word for you next time I say my prayers."

She laughed all the way down the line like she knew when the last time was I had said any prayers.

"No way, baby. What I got is good information. The real thing. But it is going to cost somebody some money. Somebody like that blonde cunt who thinks her shit don't stink. She's got plenty of money, and what I got is worth plenty."

The Southern drawl and British accent had both gotten lost somewhere.

"How much is plenty?"

"Five thousand dollars."

"What do you have? Tell me what it is that you think is worth five thousand and I'll decide."

"It's worth that and more."

"So are you going to tell me, or what?"

"I know where Joe Dubronski is, right now." You needed a Gillette twin-blade to cut the drawl.

~ * ~

I didn't like the deal. I didn't like any part of the deal, but a hungry dog doesn't examine too closely the hand holding the bone.

The voice had said, "Meet me in back of the Watson-Patterson Building," so that's where I was headed, without the money. Watson-Patterson was a block long, four story red brick on the east side used for light assembly and a warehouse site during the Eisenhower era. Watson-Patterson had sold preassembled toilet kits and other assorted bathroom items—towel racks and the like.

If my memory served, the building fronted on Dempsey, but the shipping dock where most of the public work had taken place was accessed via Calhoun. It had been at least five years since I'd had cause to be in that area. At that time, I'd gone there for old man Crenshaw, investigating mysterious disappearances from his warehouse, which had been a block down Calhoun from the Watson-Patterson. About a year ago I'd seen Crenshaw's obituary in the paper. I had no clue if Watson-Patterson was still in business.

This segment of the city appeared to have gone downhill since I'd last visited. It was full of old warehouses, ramshackle storage-for-rent bins, and small factories, remnants from an earlier generation. Less than half of the factories still looked to be operational. There were no restaurants or trendy yuppie bars, no apartment complexes or hotels renting water beds by the hour—nothing more now than a fading outpost of civilization. Traffic was light, a cab or two hauling someone home, a patrol car prowling, a few commuters shortcutting to their home or restaurant of choice, and maybe one or two souls like me, out to earn a buck off someone else's trouble.

Silent ghosts of brick and mortar, the old buildings loomed pale in the white glare of my headlights as I cruised by. Several were already boarded up awaiting sale to a dreamer, or the crash of the wrecker's ball. I felt an empathy for the still serviceable but doomed structures standing their cold, lonely vigils in the nights of their declining years.

I rolled by the Chem-Plex plant on Montclair and began to slow. I had to locate my turn. Calhoun was a one-way and I was running parallel to it. I couldn't recall the name of the crossover street I'd used before and needed to read the signs. I didn't want to cut over too soon and end up below Watson-Patterson.

The drive had taken longer than I'd remembered. In five minutes I was supposed to meet the voice in the night. If she showed, I didn't know how long she would wait. I slid by Henderson, then Young, before Robbins flashed in the beam of my headlights. Memory kicked into gear and I swung the wheel.

Robbins was snowballing down the hill named degeneration. Not that it had ever been Rodeo Drive, but now it looked like the initial phase of hell-on-earth. In the elongated block I traveled, not one building gave signs of being anything except a tomb. Boarded up storefronts, cardboard and plywood atop shattered glass, abandoned automobiles—stripped and rusting, street people in pathetic heaps; all a vulgar commentary on someone's lack of any real, meaningful commitment to their own inner cities. In this country, we had lots better ways of spending money. Like invading middle-eastern nations and sending remote-controlled dune buggies to dead planets. I rolled through with half a stop at the red sign, then grabbed a left on Calhoun.

My memory banks were still in halfway decent working order. I was pleasantly surprised. I traveled only half a block before the Watson-Patterson building came into view on the left. Heinemeirs, where I had bought my first good suit all those years ago, was boarded up, but Allandale's Used Books looked like it was still in business. The little hole-in-the-wall coffee shop across from Watson-Patterson had changed names, but, under a dim overhead bulb, I could see a moderately clean floor, a counter loaded with wire racks of pre-packaged cakes, pies, candy and gum. I would have enjoyed going in and sitting on one of the tall stools covered in red vinyl, with a cup of their foul black coffee in front of me, and watching civilization ebb and flow. However, according to the sign, they'd closed two hours ago. Parking spaces were plentiful and I pulled to the curb.

For a moment I sat in the car, listening to the pop and crackle of the cooling engine, riding herd on my nerves. The bulk of the gun under my left arm was a satisfying weight. It was too quiet in this rundown sector. The wee-oh, wee-oh of an ambulance running toward St. Joseph's pinged through the chilly night air. The logical side of my brain told me to start the engine, turn around, and go home. I didn't listen. Instead, I popped the door and got moving. Time to rock and roll.

Vandals had somehow missed the security light that jutted out about halfway toward the back of the building. I was traveling a narrow alleyway strewn with refuse and was grateful for the light. I didn't know the building on my left, but the fire escape had rusted and pulled loose from the crumbling brick and lay in the passageway like the bones of a long dead dinosaur. Rats scurried along the framework and I stepped with extra care.

The pool of light faded behind me as I reached the end of the building and rounded the corner onto the backside. I could see very little in the near blackness, but was able to make out the loading dock. I picked my way through a covey of old barrels, apparently abandoned when the plant closed. I hadn't read the obituary. Once I stepped on an unseen bottle and stumbled forward, banging into one of the barrels, scraping a hand and setting nerves on edge. In my ears, the collision sounded like a cannon going off. I paused to unzip my coat and slide my right hand in and across my body to the butt of the pistol. Strange what brings a man comfort in the dark of the night.

The loading dock was slab concrete. I ran my hand along the edge and chips of dying paint clung to my hand. Wooden pallets lay scattered haphazardly about, soldiers fallen on a long-forgotten battlefield. The security light was inoperative, whether broken or burnt out I couldn't tell, and the only light came from street lamps on surrounding corners which filtered through the dust and grime and maneuvered its way over and between buildings. A white drainpipe, about halfway down the back of the building, had twisted in two, and it moved with the wind to measured time of its own. I listened as it scraped across the roughened bricks, then fell back.

I stood silently listening to the rasp of the drainpipe, letting my eyes grow accustomed to the near darkness. A car rolled down Calhoun with the radio blasting. Some adenoidal group hip-hopped all the way to my ears.

Never saw it coming. Think maybe I heard an aberrant sound just before it happened. Perhaps sensed is a better word. Instincts, long covered by the veneer of civilization, sprang suddenly to life and I half-turned to him before the blow was delivered, cursing myself for being a dumbass.

Stars exploded before my eyes and an ocean roared in my ears. I had a vague sense of falling and I heard a man moan. Just before I hit the asphalt, I wondered if I was the moaning man.

Sixteen

I was only inches from the sun. Fierce light assaulted my eyes, burning a hole straight through to my brain. I opened my mouth to scream, but a hoarse "ahhh" was all that I could produce. My throat was sand-laden desert, and sticky, tacky, silly-putty lined my lips like salt around the rim of a margarita glass.

I prayed for the forgiveness of my sins, but if God was still out there He knew I was lying. I only wanted my suffering relieved. As soon as I felt better, I'd sin again. Dead, smarter than I am, or just too disgusted to give a damn, He didn't answer. After a time I didn't much care…death could have me.

~ * ~

Pulse pounded in my brain like a nuclear sledge hammer. Wham, wham, wham, wham, wham…I tried to put my hands up to the side of my head to reinforce my skull. It seemed a legitimate threat to crack. My arms didn't want to work properly. They felt like the old, heavy, wooden Indian clubs men used in gymnasiums seventy-five years ago.

There was no sensation in my fingertips and my sense of direction had gone missing somewhere in the ionosphere.

"Nice to have you with us, Mr. Quick."

I didn't recognize the voice, but I wasn't so far gone I couldn't recognize sarcasm. I tried lifting the corner of my right eyelid to see if the face was familiar. Brilliant light poured into the tiny crack like fire blazing through a pool of gasoline. I shut the eye, very tightly.

"Painful, isn't it." More a statement than a question. I decided silence was golden and lay as still as I could.

"Sorry if we were a bit rough, but you do have a bit of reputation in certain circles, you know."

"What kind of circles" is what I tried to say. My lips felt like they had been pumped full of helium. It came out more like "dat dined d dirdles."

"Try again, Mr. Quick. Surely you can do better than that."

I ran my tongue over my lips to moisten them. It felt like sandpaper rubbing across an exposed nerve. I gave the tingling a minute to die down and tried it again. "What kind of circles?"

"Humph." As if he had to puzzle out the answer. "Unfortunate, I guess. Yes, Mr. Quick, unfortunate circles. Circles of the unfortunate society. Clans of the underground people of a lost civilization: the homeless, the drug pushers, missing young girls, and dirty old men. The lost of the lost, if you will. I've heard quite a lot about you from them."

"Such as?" Stalling for time as I tried to gather my wits. I really didn't give a rat's ass what those people, this man, or anyone else thought about me. Piss on all of them.

"Violent, Mr. Quick. You have a reputation of being a violent man in an increasingly violent society. Naturally, we didn't want to take a chance on you giving us any trouble. Furthermore, we were not particularly desirous of you knowing exactly what route you took to arrive at your current location. Ergo, smash and grab."

With his phony British accent and manner, the man talked like some jerk trying to impress some other jerk. Strength was beginning to seep back into my arms and legs. The jackhammer inside my skull paused between beats. I decided to take another shot at seeing who little Lord Pain-In-The-Ass was.

I cracked my right eye open and let light stream in. It wasn't as bright this time. A single bulb hung naked from a wire about a foot and a half below an acoustical tile ceiling. I gauged it at a hundred watts.

Two or three of the ceiling tiles were cracked, and one had a large triangular slice missing. Cheap maroon indoor/outdoor carpet covered what felt like a poured concrete floor. My guess was a basement someone had finished for a rec room. I decided to try and sit up and come to grips with what was going on.

To the elbows first, then to a sitting position. The room whirled like a tilt-a-whirl, and I closed my eyes and fought down a wave of nausea. Seconds later I opened them again, with better results. Everything was a touch blurry, like looking through binoculars one twist out of focus. Still, the room had stopped spinning. I looked around for the man with a phony accent.

He swam into focus from four feet away and slightly left of center. He was half-sitting on a stool of the type that you see pulled up alongside kitchen counters in *Good Housekeeping* advertisements. One foot was on the metal ring that encircled the legs of the stool. The other shoe was firmly on the floor. He was round-faced, with a mass of tight curls of snow white hair covering the top of his head. From the lines on his face and his wattle, I judged him to be in his mid-fifties. A long, black trench coat obscured my view of his body. About all I could tell was that he wasn't particularly heavy. I'd never seen him before.

"You're too old for the permanent." My voice sounded hoarse and raspy, even to me.

He chuckled and smiled, but only with his lips. His blue eyes remained as cold as frozen stones. "So good to have you fully with us, Mr. Quick. I was starting to become disappointed with you. You don't seem nearly as tough as your reputation."

"Fuck you."

"Ah, tough talk. Unfortunately, the vocabulary seems rather limited. You really should work to expand your repertoire of insults.

The commercial is correct, you know—people do judge you by the words you use."

"You didn't bring me here to critique my vocabulary. What do you want?"

"Observant and astute, also direct and to the point. I like that in a man." The British accent was still thick as real cream, but there was a faint lisp sliding in now and then between the words. Curly also had an effeminate air about him. Nothing overt, just something in the way he moved his hands. I liked him less all the time.

"Yeah, so what do you want?"

He turned and gave me his profile. From the stillness of the pose, it appeared he thought it was a fine one. "I want to know why your sudden, intense interest in Joe Dubronski."

All of those inquiries must have made some impact. I was glad my efforts hadn't been a total waste. "So why didn't you just call me on the telephone and ask?"

"Would you have told me?" It wasn't really a question. He already knew the answer.

"No."

"Exactly. So you see, I needed an opportunity to have a few minutes alone with you, where we could discuss the entire situation in an open and frank manner. Face to face, you might say. I felt sure that, after you understood the situation, you would be glad to share your findings with me."

God, the man could ramble on, and someone was still doing some major pounding inside my skull. It was down to an old-fashioned sledge hammer on an anvil, but it still took all the joy out of listening.

I wanted to get up and out of this rec room from hell and stumble back to my place. However, my arms were still weak and my legs trembled slightly. Strength was slow in returning to my body, flowing like tired water into my extremities. I simply needed more time. I put my head in my hands.

"Yes, sorry about the head. However, as I said before, you do have a certain reputation, and I did want to try and make a particular point with you. I am a serious fellow, Mr. Quick, and I have some serious business I very much need to transact with Mr. Dubronski. So you see, it would, er, ah, be better for all of us, shall we say, if you were to tell me what you know about Mr. Dubronski. You can start with where he is right now."

If my head had not hurt so very much, I'd have laughed in his face. That would have probably resulted in him slapping my face or, if he were in an extra nasty mood, giving me a sharp kick to my kidneys. Still, I would have laughed anyway. This pompous cretin hadn't done his homework at all. He wanted me to tell him what I didn't know myself. I wanted to just get up and walk out. Unless this curly headed phony had a gun, I didn't figure him to be able to stop me, even in my current condition. However, he might have a gun, and, more importantly, there was definitely somebody else in the room. I'd heard the scrape of their shoe across the thin carpet, and once caught the faint sound of their breathing. They had either allergies or a cold. I needed to buy time and maneuver to where I could see them.

"Sorry. I'd like to help you, but I can't. Please notice I said can't, not won't. I'll make a long story very short and simple for you. Thanks to your thugs, my head hurts like hell, so I'll give you the *Reader's Digest* condensed version."

I gave the old boy a glance to see if he was paying attention. He was eyeing me like a hungry dog checking out fresh hamburger. "No one knows where Joe Dubronski is right now except Joe himself, and he ain't telling."

Anger colored his cheeks so they stood out in sharp relief against the skullcap of cottony curls. He opened his mouth to say something, but I cut him off. "Sorry, but that's the way it is. He's missing and I've been hired to find him, but I haven't found him yet. That's it, short and sweet."

"Don't mess with me, Mr. Quick. You are not that tough."

I didn't say anything. Smarter to keep your mouth shut every once in a while.

Sir Curl's patience had run thin. "I'm going to give you one last chance. Tell me all you know about the whereabouts of Joe Dubronski. Tell me, or you are going to regret it."

The promise of anger ran like an underground river beneath his actual words. I heard more shuffling behind me. Whoever was back there half-cleared his throat. I wondered if he had a gun.

"I'm not holding out on you. Joe is missing and no one seems to have seen him in almost a week now. He's not in the morgue and he's also not a John Doe at any hospital within thirty miles. Unless he's using an alias, he's not in jail. He hasn't used a credit card in eleven days, and he hasn't booked a flight since last June when he and the missus flew down to Freeport. He's just flat out missing and I've been hired to find him. So far I've asked a whole lot of questions, but not received many answers. Sorry to disappoint you, but those are the facts."

"Who hired you?"

"None of your damned business."

A blue vein did jumping jacks in his forehead. His white face was painted with a pinkish tint of anger. I had an urge to tell him the coloring suited him, that it nicely set off his snow white curls. I didn't. Figured I had better not push my luck too far.

He made a real effort to get himself under control and partially succeeded. "You don't understand the situation, Mr. Quick."

"So tell me." I pushed myself up on one knee. The movement wasn't easy or elegant, but I made it. He watched me like a scientist observing a white rat during an experiment. I wondered if I should tell him my new nickname was the White Jamaican. I decided he wouldn't be interested.

A pink tongue came out of his mouth and wet his pasty pink lips. Women might find him attractive. I had a strong desire to pound his pink face into hamburger. Something about those curls just brought the violent side of my nature to the surface.

"I need to find Mr. Dubronski. He and I have been doing some business together and it is now time for another financial transaction.

He needs to make a payment before we can proceed on to the next level of our operation. Time is of the essence. You do see why I need to find him?"

"I do see. However, I'm afraid I can't help you. Like I just told you, the man is missing. I've been looking for him for a couple of days already. Without any luck. Plus, I'm already working for someone else, so sorry, but I can't help you."

I punctuated the sentence by struggling to my feet. I was quite careful not to get any closer to the man with the questions. I was betting on the man behind me having a gun and didn't want to give him any reason to use it.

"I can pay you well."

"I'm already being paid well." Moving in slow motion, I began to ease around to his left. I needed to open the room up and see who else was there before I made my next move. I was still a touch woozy, but the room was coming into sharper focus. A faint, damp, moldy scent hung in the air.

"Mr. Quick, you are a singularly uncooperative fellow." He was growing tired of our unfruitful conversation. Things were not going as he planned and he was growing restless. I couldn't imagine just walking out of this cool, damp room on my own. I needed to stall until I got a better handle on exactly what I was facing.

"Listen, I tell you what. Let me go on out of here tonight, no harm, no foul. Give me a way to contact you, and if I find out something, I'll let you know."

I eased another baby step to my right. Still couldn't see anybody else. Wouldn't it be a sad joke on me if I was the only other one in the room?

"Sure, and my fairy godmother will keep an eye on you and remind you." Sarcasm thick enough to need a knife to cut it, adorned with a British accent. A unique combination in my experience. I took another step, watching his eyes as I made it. My instincts were screaming at me that my time was very short.

"Look, what have you got to lose? I simply and truly don't know anything right now. Give me a little time to dig up something. Hell, I haven't been on the case a week yet."

Another step.

He came off the stool and took a half-step back. His eyes never blinked, but his head bobbed an inch. I tried to spin around but my reflexes were stuck in slow motion. My mind screamed hurry, but my body was sluggish, as though I were standing chest deep in water. My right hand was coming up from the waist, aiming for a face I could only glimpse. It never arrived. Something very hard and very heavy crashed against my skull. Stars exploded by the hundreds in the little room and a great roaring swept over my ears.

~ * ~

Someone kept tooting his horn, driving me crazy. I decided to get up from my bed and tell him to stop. I couldn't make it. A great iron helmet covered my head. The damn thing had to weigh a hundred pounds, maybe more. I strained against the weight. The room went spinning into black.

~ * ~

Cold had seeped into my bones by the next time I awoke. I reached to pull up more cover, but there wasn't any. My pillow felt damp. I stretched out my hand and discovered I wasn't in my bed. Not in anybody else's either.

I was facedown on cold wet ground. As I raised my head, a great bell began to toll inside my skull. I very carefully eased back to the earth.

I rested a while and tried again. Not great, or even good, but better. Struggling, I got myself up on one elbow and looked around. Shrubs, low lying bushes, and thick-trunked trees dominated the landscape. A long, motionless expanse of grass sloped away from me to the west. A hazy mid-morning sun hung in the eastern sky. Sounds of the street came from behind the tall hedge that rose up against my back and obscured my view. In the depths of my cranium, a hive of bees buzzed angrily. I sat up, then stood, moving slowly, stepping with care.

Brushing the damp earth that clung to my rumpled clothes, I began to work my way through the grove of trees, mostly oak, with an occasional hickory and pine growing haphazardly. Gradually, they became less thick and then gave way to a patch of open ground. Under normal conditions, it would have been an enjoyable stroll. With my head pounding and legs moving more as they felt like than as I desired, it was an adventure, and not a pleasant one.

Still, the grove wasn't large and after six or seven minutes I was out of the trees and onto the long field of grass. Bees still buzzed at the base of my brain, but in muted tones.

The grass was a brilliant green, one of the new fescues that holds its color after the onset of cool weather. It was closely trimmed and I figured I was either in one of the city parks or on the backside of an estate. Taking the route across the green veldt veered me slightly away from the road, but it was pleasant walking. The sun's rays fell through the smudge of clouds and warmed my bones. My brain throbbed and it was much easier to keep walking than to stop and think. I knew who I was and where I wasn't and there was tingle of excitement to see what lay at the end of the long, green sea of grass.

I hadn't thought to look at my watch when I started my trek, so I couldn't be sure how long I'd been walking. I figured that, counting the struggle through the trees, it might have been fifteen minutes. Even with the cool morning, a stream of sweat had formed under my shirt and jacket and was running down the middle of my back. Gradually, the grassland turned uphill and as I crested the second of twin knolls, I could see where I was.

Thirty-five miles out of town, the state maintains a modest park and animal research facility. I'd been out there a couple times to view the fall colors and try to capture a white tail on camera. I recognized the shiny dome on the visitors' center about a half mile to my right. That certain animal scent filled my nostrils. I felt in my left back pocket. My billfold was still there. I pulled it out and checked the contents: thirty-seven dollars, auto insurance card, two credit cards, and a ticket to pick up my dry cleaning. The ticket was dated over a month ago. I should be able to finagle some way to get a ride home. If not, I had a marathon of a walk. I slid the wallet back in my hip pocket and started down the hill toward the visitors' center. The "Colonel Bogey March" from *The Bridge on the River Kwai* swam to the surface of my battered brain and I began to force an off-key version through my teeth. The tune blended nicely with the faint buzzing of the bees. No reggae for the White Jamaican today.

Seventeen

Every square inch of my body ached. From the bottom of my feet to the top of my head, pain oozed from every pore. My scrambled brain hurt the worst, and the telephone sitting on Granny Hitchcock's scarred maple bedside table refused to quit ringing, absolutely refused.

Overriding protesting joints and muscles, I rolled over and stretched out my left arm. Dirt under the fingernails. I needed a shower. "Hello."

"Frank?"

"Yeah," I growled.

"You sound a little rough around the edges." Flat voice over the phone line. I could picture the flat face in my mind.

"I am." Never tell a lie, at least not when the truth won't hurt you.

"A little too much of the night before?" the voice snickered.

"Yeah." Way too much, I thought to myself.

We sat in silence as though each had exhausted his conversation quota. The pillow under my head was soft and yielding and I felt myself slipping back into sleep. I didn't fight the urge; I hadn't placed the call.

"You there?" The flat voice, harsh and accusatory, pulled me back to daylight.

"I'm here." I recognized the flavor of bitter acceptance in my voice.

"Thought maybe you'd left me." I didn't respond, and in a few seconds the flat voice continued. "Heard you been making some phone calls about Joe?" Al made it sound more a question than a statement.

"A few."

"Who all you been talking to?"

"Just some people I know, and a few I've met recently.

"What are they telling you?"

"About Joe Dubronski?"

"Of course. Who else, numbnuts?"

"Al, why are you so interested in my conversations?"

"Mr. D'Angelo is interested in Mr. Dubronski, remember? They sometimes do a little business together. Not that it is any of your business. Now, what have you found out?"

"Not much. There's not much to tell. I don't know much. Nobody seems to know much. However, lots of folks are all of a sudden very concerned about Joe Dubronski. But nobody seems to have any idea where he is. Don't you find that strange, Al?"

"Don't worry about what I think, Quick. Just remember, if you hear anything, and I mean anything, about the current location of Mr. Joe Dubronski, Mr. D'Angelo is very interested. A little telephone call to me would be much appreciated. Call me at Michael's. If I ain't there, just leave your name. I'll get back to you. Understand?"

"Say hi to Fat Tony for me, Al." I dropped the receiver back onto its cradle. Then, before it could ring again, I pulled it back off and tossed it on the floor. That swarm of bees was back inside my skull.

Eighteen

"Oh, he was so good! I can't believe that he sounds that good after all these years."

The excitement in Lindsey's voice was almost palatable. I hadn't realized Tony Bronson could still inspire such enthusiasm. I sank back in the soft upholstery of the big Lincoln and watched her bounce up and down like a child. It was a relief not to have to drive in the swarm of cars that had spilled out into the streets immediately after the concert. Apparently, very few folks had hung around to chat with, or try to meet, the performer. The result was a monster traffic jam in the narrow streets outside the auditorium. I grimaced and reached for a brake pedal that wasn't there as a blue Chevy van tried to force its way in front of us.

I shot a quick glance up front to the rearview mirror. The Grants' driver, Rico, seemed undisturbed. His brown face was void of expression. I judged his age to fall in the mid-fifties range. In his nearly thirty years of chauffeuring, he'd undoubtedly encountered and dealt with hundreds of similar situations. He kept the Lincoln easing forward smoothly, never giving the van a chance to get its nose in front of us. I settled back in the softness and gladly left the driving to Rico.

When I was younger, I had absolutely loved to drive. Many Sunday afternoons had been spent cruising behind the wheel of my Olds. In those long-gone days, it had been nothing for me to hop in the Delta 88 early on Saturday morning and drive a hundred, two, even three hundred miles to catch a ball game I especially wanted to see, or merely to visit a friend.

No more. Too many cars on the highways, rude, careless drivers, society's mad, headlong rush to get somewhere, anywhere, now, had combined to dampen my cruising lust.

"Thanks for filling in for Allison tonight, Mr. Quick."

"Glad I could make it. Enjoyed the show." I gave her my best smile, before remembering she couldn't see it. Lindsey was so vibrant and youthful, so strikingly attractive with her fine features and masses of flowing blonde hair, it was hard to remember that she was blind.

Her confidence and self-assurance amazed me. In the well-known privacy of her own home, such confidence and self-assurance would have been understandable. In an unfamiliar, crowded, public place they had seemed as striking as the sudden appearance of an oasis in a desert. Pleasant and welcome, but quite surprising nonetheless.

Tonight had to have been tough for her: strange building, hundreds of noisy people pushing their way through the throng to get to their seats, a long, curving staircase full of short, slick, marble steps. Yet she'd taken my arm with poise and self-assurance and we'd gone bounding up the stairs like a couple of teenagers hurrying to get to our seats before the first number.

"It was good, wasn't it?" She stretched a hand across the seat and felt for something. Turned out to be my hand. Her long fingers felt smooth against the back of my rough hand. "Oh, that was such a nice concert." There was a happy lilt to her voice. If you listened closely, you could catch the smile interwoven among the words.

"It was real nice." Tony Bronson was not in my top ten, but he had put on a good show, flung a lot of heart into his performance. The theatre had been designed to be appealing to the eye, as well as to the ear. Acoustics had been good, seats wide and well padded, the audience reserved and well behaved. Little Richard live and in his prime it wasn't, but I had enjoyed myself.

"Do you go to a lot of concerts, Mr. Quick?"

"Not many. You can call me Frank. Mr. Quick is a bit formal for my tastes. How about you? You go to many?"

"Not so many anymore. Allison and I used to go a lot a few years ago. Before Joe and she hit it big. She still tries to get us out together some, but, with her schedule, a lot of times she has to cancel."

"What happens when she does? Do you go by yourself, or get someone to go with you?"

"Usually someone goes with me. Joe's been a couple of times. We went to see The Eagles last year. Rico has filled in a couple of times, although he once passed on Vanilla Ice. Absolutely refused, didn't you, Rico?" She punctuated her question with a laugh.

Rico smiled into the rearview mirror like it was a camera. "Sure did, and damn glad of it." Lindsey laughed again.

We caught the light at Connecticut and Dupree. As the car idled, I watched the neon flashing atop a bar on Dupree reflect in her face. The light changed in the same instant as her expression.

She turned to face me. I knew she couldn't see me, but I had the distinct impression that she could sense exactly what I was feeling. Silly, I know, a touch spooky, but...

"Frank?"

"Yes."

"Where do you really think Joe is?"

"I don't honestly know."

"I know, but where do you think he is? Do you think he's alive?"

"Well, Lindsey, there are several ways of looking at it." Blood ran hot up my face as I realized what verb I'd used. I was grateful for the dark. "Sorry."

"What? Oh, don't be." She squeezed my hand. "Please go on."

I stared out the window, pissed at my insensitivity. I wondered if Rico was laughing at me. We swept down the road, which was now carrying a significantly lighter load. We passed Hoffmann's where I had once, in a previous life, purchased the only suit I'd ever gotten married in. I thought of Mona, and the memories of her and the knowledge that she was gone forever from this world writhed deep inside me; my throat began to swell, so that for a moment I could not speak.

She came to me like that sometimes, unbidden and unexpected, her arrival triggered by a face from our past, a place we'd gone to together, a silly song she'd liked to sing.

For a moment I savored the memories; memories so real I could almost taste the sweet scent of her soft skin. Then I told myself to be a man, grow up and face the music. What is gone is gone, and all the hoping and wishing and praying in this world won't bring it back. I bit my lower lip and watched the blur of lights from my window as we rolled through the night.

I felt the pressure of her fingers on my wrist and turned from the window. Concern furrowed Lindsey's brow. I patted the top of her hand with the palm of my free hand to let her know I was back with the living.

"Please, go on. Really, it's all right. I know it is simply an expression. People use it all the time. In fact, I use it myself, and I've been blind for the longest time. Just say things the way you want to say them and don't worry about my sensitivities. They aren't here, at least not where my sight is concerned."

She gave me a smile, her silhouette illuminated by the big round globes the city used for street lamps in this section of town. Those monsters had to be relics from the past. With today's budget crunch, they wouldn't be affordable. We were in a pretty decent segment of town; two out of every three lights were still intact. In some sections of this city, if one in ten burned we'd be lucky. I swallowed the lump in my throat and smiled a smile she couldn't see.

"Three ways things could be. One, Joe is dead and gone and it may take months to find his corpse." I recognized the words were blunt, but I sensed Lindsey wanted to deal with reality.

"The fact that Allison hasn't heard from him tends to support this. She says there have been no calls, no letters, no possible sightings by friends or acquaintances. Number two, kidnapping. But I'm doubtful there. If it were a kidnapping, the kidnappers surely would have called by now.

Three, if he had simply decided to leave for a while, for whatever reason, odds are somebody would have spotted him by now. That is, if he were anywhere close."

"But he could have amnesia, walking around lost in some strange town. You hear of such cases."

Mostly fiction, I thought to myself. Out loud I said, "Guess that's another possibility. Joe could be somewhere far from home because he has amnesia, like you said, or on purpose. The fact that he hasn't turned up in a hospital, police station, or the morgue gives us some reason for hope. Depending on how you look at it, every day he stays missing could lend credence either to the idea that he is somewhere far away, say Argentina, or the possibility that he is dead."

Impossible to see her face in the Lincoln's dimly lit interior, but there was no mistaking the sob she failed to choke back. I looked for somewhere else to be and caught a glimpse of Rico's stony stare in the rearview mirror.

Okay, he didn't like seeing Lindsey unhappy. Hell, I was sorry to have to spoil her evening, but I really hadn't told her anything she hadn't already suspected. I stared out my window. In the lighter traffic, Rico had the big sled rolling and the lights of the stores flashed by like we were on the world's fastest merry-go-round.

Left onto Baxter and within three blocks the neighborhood began to change. Shopping centers and drive-in restaurants gave way to old, but well-maintained brownstones. Brownstones soon gave way to uniformly ugly apartment buildings built for the growing, lower-middle class. Unfortunately, of late this class of people was achieving much of its growth by having its members slide back a rung or two on society's evolutionary ladder. In today's America not many were climbing out from poverty.

Three blocks of monstrosities designed for the masses, then we crossed the C&O tracks. My territory now. A certified melting pot of architectural styles, in various stages of disrepair.

Many inhabitants of Regis Park proper tried hard. Most of the residences were lived in, only a few were boarded up, with the occasional empty lot where fire had burned someone out and they hadn't had the money, or courage, to rebuild.

Maybe the roofs were patched, the sidewalks cracked, and painting two years overdue, but for the most part the yards were neat and trimmed and the abandoned automobiles were few and far between. In Regis Park, people still tried to keep the old clunker running, glass in all the windows of their homes, and a few brave flowers standing guard in long, wooden boxes. Not a prosperous neighborhood, but a peculiarly proud one.

He'd come here earlier in the evening to pick me up. Whether he had been here before I didn't know, but Rico drove like he knew what he was doing. He made the zig onto Colfax and then zagged onto Dewhurst. I'd read of people who have a photographic memory for what they read…maybe he had a photographic memory for streets he drove.

As we entered my block, the Lincoln began slowing. I saw Debi shivering bravely on her corner, her short, skinny legs exposed to mid-thigh. I didn't wave.

Sometimes my hypocrisy disgusts me. Not many cars out tonight, and I saw her bright, eager head follow the big car to the curb. I breathed an inward sigh of relief when she clung to her post.

Rico maneuvered the Lincoln to the curb in front of my place. Tonight, it looked rather shabby to me. Hated to think I'd been dazzled by a night of gilt and glitter. One thing I purely do despise is a pretentious son-of-a-bitch.

I turned in the seat and faced Lindsey. "Thanks again for a great evening. I really enjoyed it."

"You're most welcome, and thanks for going with me. You were good company. Don't imagine Tony Bronson is your cup of tea, yet you managed to stay awake for the entire performance." She laughed, a silly laugh, a little girl's laugh.

As she laughed, she turned her head and the streetlight filtering in through the back window caught, and soft, diffused light caressed her cheekbones and highlighted her lips.

I had a sudden urge to kiss her. It had been a long time since I had experienced that desire. I wasn't sure what she wanted or expected. I didn't want to mess up. I hesitated.

He who hesitates is lost. The moment passed.

She gave my hand a squeeze. "It's getting late. I'd better let you get inside. Thanks again for going with me."

Hand on the door handle, I turned my head back over my shoulder. "Nice ride, Rico, very smooth." He nodded, the hooks of appreciation pulling up the corner of his mouth.

I slipped out into the night and jogged to my door. I lifted my right hand as the Lincoln rolled smoothly from the curb. In seconds the night had swallowed up all but its twin taillights. I watched those disappear.

Nineteen

I smelled him. Smelled the cigarette smoke on his clothes. Smelled the scent of his cologne he'd sprayed too liberally. Smelled the stink of his sins. A man's past never leaves him. He can only cover it with the veneer of a new life. Sometimes, say in the dead of the night when the rest of the world disappears, it filters through all the covering layers and works its way to the surface.

Al sat with his flat face and lean body in my easy chair in my living room. He sat there unbidden and unwelcome. A .38 dangled from his hand, metal gleaming dully in the weak light from the single, shaded, forty-watt bulb glowing in my mother's favorite brass lamp. An aura of death and moral filth pressed upon him, fitting him tighter than his black trousers. I was somewhat familiar with the condition, having experienced it a time or two myself.

Halfway across the room I stopped and slid the key back into my pocket. I longed for my gun, but it was in the drawer of my nightstand. Probably better, on second thought, that I didn't have it. Al wouldn't hesitate. He'd lived too long in a very tough world to let the idea of shooting some run-of-the-mill private investigator bother him. I carefully turned my head to look at the Seth Thomas on my cracked marble mantel—12:17. One more day in the bank.

I gave Al a long, hard look. His flat face conveyed nothing. Only his flat black eyes were alive, moving from side to side, checking the periphery, letting nothing slide by. They didn't give a damn thing away, and they didn't miss anything either.

"Thought you were never going to come home." The voice as flat as a punctured tire.

"Do you always let yourself into other people's houses and make yourself at home?"

"When it suits."

"What if it doesn't suit them?"

"Then let them do something about it."

"Someday, somebody will."

"Maybe."

"Count on it."

The clock on the mantle kept up a measured conversation with itself. I glanced at the watch on my left wrist. One of us was off by two minutes.

"It's late, Al, and I'm tired. Say what you've got to say, then go."

"What's your rush? Blind bitch wear you out?"

"You wear me out. Why the sudden interest in my life?"

"You're important to us, Frank."

"Who is us? And why in hell am I important?"

"Us is Mr. D'Angelo and me. You're important because you're interested in the whereabouts of one Joe Dubronski and so are we."

"Really hope this doesn't hurt your feelings, or Tony's, but I'm not working for you and I really don't care what you think."

"What Mr. D'Angelo thinks matters, a lot." A hint of anger. I was glad to see even a touch of emotion.

"Not to me, it doesn't."

"Could be very beneficial to you to change your way of thinking."

"Good for my bank account?"

"And your health."

"You talk tough, Al, but talk is cheap. So are your threats, come to think of it."

"You don't want to cross Mr. D."

"What about you? Aren't you a tough guy on your own?"

"You cross me, you cross Mr. D." He stood. Slim and cold and standing there in my living room he made me think of a snake on two legs. I shuddered inwardly, but counseled patience for myself. My time would come.

"Goodnight, Al."

He gave me his snake-eyed stare. The clock ticked. Down the block someone leaned on the horn; I wondered if it was for Debi. Al pulled a battered pack of Camels from his shirt pocket, eased one out and fired it up with a brassy square of a lighter. He was as subtle as a porcupine. I was not impressed. Al blew me a smoky goodbye.

Twenty

As I crossed over Colorado, the old legs finally began to loosen up. The first half dozen blocks they'd masqueraded as two blocks of stone. Every stride had been an effort, lightly frosted with pain. Some days they go ahead and work the kinks out, letting the blood flow uninhibited and the muscles move smoothly and powerfully. As I advance in years, however, there are more days when they refuse to cooperate. I figure they are trying to get back at me for the abuse I gave them in my younger days.

Back then I thought I was a marathon man; two or three fifteen- to twenty-mile training runs a week were nothing out of the ordinary for me. Now I pay the price: aching knees, painful hamstrings, quivering calves, tender feet. I won't quit running though, or maybe I can't; the entire experience is a high for me, even with the aches, pains, and assorted miseries.

I turned west on Vissing, then a couple of blocks later, crossed the street and entered Jacobsen Park by one of the service roads. Jacobsen was a small park, no swimming pool, and little used except for dog walkers, bird watchers, and couples in love. I like it, though.

The peace and quiet make it special. To find a triangle of tranquility like Jacobsen in today's urban sprawl is exceptional.

Today's sun was a timid sun. He kept peeking out of large, fluffy clouds that dominated the sky, only to dart back in a moment later as if he were afraid of being seen.

I didn't mind his absence, even though we hadn't seen much of him during the week Joe Dubronski had been gone. Exactly one week ago Joe Dubronski had left his office in a non-spectacular fashion and hadn't been seen since. No one, not even his wife, had any idea where he had gone. Old Joe was on my mind as I plodded around the dirt and wood chip trail that curved for half a mile inside the park. Despite the cool temperature, sweat began to pool under my arms, and I could feel a patch forming in the middle of my back.

Why would Joe Dubronski leave home? He'd left behind a stunning wife, a gorgeous home, and what appeared to be a lucrative business. Why would anyone leave such a setup? Near as I could tell, he didn't have another woman, drug problems, an obsession with southern beaches, or a serious head injury. Why? Stride. Why? Stride. Think. Stride.

Money? No biblical scholar am I, but I recalled from Sunday school days that somewhere the Good Book says that the love of money is the root of all evil. Not that the Bible needs improvement, but I wonder if maybe we shouldn't slip, "or the lack thereof" in there, right after the word money. Maybe, despite appearances to the contrary, Joe had money troubles. I was no corporate whiz; what looked like a lucrative business might be badly overextended. Gambling was the source of financial woes for some men I knew. I made a mental note to look further into Joe's wagering habits.

Two men seem inordinately interested in my missing man. One was Fat Tony D'Angelo. No one who knew anything about the undercurrents of this city had any doubt that Fat Tony was a member of organized crime. The mere fact Joe Dubronski conducted business with a criminal cast substantial doubt on his own moral character.

The second man who was so interested in Joe Dubronski had been responsible for my recent headache. Before our brief encounter,

I'd never seen him. That encounter, magnified by the headache, had left me with a vivid picture of a middle-sized man in his mid-fifties, with an unprepossessing body, a heavy British accent, and a mass of soft, white, kinky-curly, cotton candy hair, who had a vicious partner.

The wind seemed to pick up on my second circuit of the trail, or maybe I was just getting tired and starting to notice it more. I still wasn't fully recovered from the head-smashing earlier in the week. I've begun to notice that the older I get, the slower I recovered from such an experience. I decided to make this circuit my last.

Running time for me is often reflection time. Some of my very best thinking has been accomplished while doing road work. The miles also bring back memories. I try not to think of Mona too often. Even after two years, the pain still rips at my guts.

It doesn't seem possible that she's gone. We were so much in love, so much a part of each other's life there are days when I am thinking deeply about something else and walk into the apartment still expecting to find her there. When the sudden realization that she is gone hits me, it is as though I had been smashed by an eighteen-wheeler going seventy-five. It just crushes my soul.

It's knowing that she is gone forever that really gets to me. If she had just left me, even if we had divorced, I could always have held onto some hope. Death grants no comebacks, however.

Dead long before I got to her. Dead within minutes after the young punk drew his knife across her throat, even though he'd already taken her purse, gold chain, and wedding ring. A totally senseless, brainless, cruel, unwarranted, and worthless death. It made me doubt my sanity, and my God.

The stinging wind brought tears to my eyes as I left the park and pounded the pavement for home.

Twenty-one

Eclectic. That's a good word to describe January's. Actually, the real name of the place is January Jackson's, but as it came to be the in spot for the in crowd, the owners dropped the Jackson part. Too common for folks, I guess. January's had a ring to it and I had to admit it was a cool place.

Greek revival on the outside, fifties Americana Formica as the interior. Real mixed bag of furniture, some modern Danish, a little early American, and a fair smattering of Chippendale replicas. January's was a noisy place. Lots of people talking too fast and too loudly when the liquor flooded against the stress.

However, there were islands partitioned off from the free-flowing mainstream, quiet and darkened alcoves that gave the illusion of privacy.

Allison leaned across the table and whispered, "I had another call today."

"What kind of a call?" It was so dark in our little bay I couldn't read her face. Lindsey's was a faint image a table width away. I could clearly see her bright, shining halo of hair, but couldn't discern her features. For me, merely a taste of what she went through every day.

"A call wanting money."

"You mean someone begging you to donate to their church, or political campaign, or activist front?"

"No, someone wanting money they say Joe owes them."

I could sense Lindsey turning her head. Maybe she was having trouble hearing Allison's whispers, as Allison had inadvertently put a good deal of her body between their faces. Then again, Lindsey might have been picking up on some interesting table conversation going on behind the partition. I could hear indistinct murmurs from time to time. Once I thought I could make out the words "your place," another time I clearly heard "liar."

"How much?" I kept my voice down, wondering why Allison hadn't waited until we were alone, or told me over the telephone.

"He wants one hundred and twenty-five thousand by the day after tomorrow, or he said he wouldn't be responsible."

"Responsible for what?"

"His actions, the consequences, whatever happens next, I don't know." She leaned closer. "Frank, these calls are so upsetting. There's a certain evil in his voice, like he wouldn't hesitate to do something really awful. Sometimes I think maybe he even wants to." I could hear the tremor in her voice. In the sputtering candlelight I thought I saw her chin quiver.

"Did he say what Joe owed him for?" Lindsey's voice was as clear as the ping of a silver spoon against real crystal.

"No," Allison murmured, her voice half muffled by tears. I could see Allison's golden head slowly swing back and forth like a golden ball. Her head seemed heavy on her shoulders, as though it weighed more than it should, or her neck was suddenly weak.

"Allison, was there anything distinctive about his voice? Was it deep? Raspy? Did he have an accent?"

Her chin came up and the quivering quieted. "An accent. He definitely had an accent. It was a British accent, pretty strong."

"Hmm, do believe I've met the fellow."

"You've met him? You actually know the low life?"

"Yeah, pretty sure I've made his acquaintance, and quite recently. Only one time and it wasn't pleasant. He was extremely interested in Joe's whereabouts, and determined to get the answer out of me. He didn't care what he and his friends had to do to get it either. Of course I didn't know anything, and to say that displeased the curly-haired Englishman is to put it mildly. His cohorts gave me a concussion to go with an assortment of abrasions and contusions. We'll want to be careful of him. He's not the sort to take half measures."

"What does he look like? I have imagined the most sinister kind of gangster you ever saw."

I took another sip of my coffee. They brewed it hot and strong at January's. Someone switched the CD to reggae. I felt the island beat lift my spirits.

"His looks belie his actions. He looks like a soft, plump, middle-aged stationery salesman. Masses of snow white hair arranged in tight, kinky curls. He must have it done. Can't imagine anybody's hair growing that curly naturally. The one time I saw him he wore a light gray suit with wide white pinstripes."

Lindsey stirred in her seat and I felt one of her feet brush against one of mine. The errant foot lingered for a moment as if testing the waters of an ocean, then moved on. Allison rested both elbows on the table and put her face in her hands. In the dark the top of her head appeared luminous. Easy to see why men liked her, and women hated her.

We sat there, each of us lost in our own thoughts, until the waiter came with the drinks. Allison didn't move even when he set her gin and tonic at her elbow. I sipped my coffee and leaned back. Even if you are not blessed with patience, and, believe me, I'm not, you acquire at least a modicum of the virtue if you spend much time at the detective game.

The pressure became too much for Lindsey and she broke the silence. "Allison, what's the matter?"

Allison lifted her head. Her eyes had that faraway look, but they were dry and her voice was clear, if a bit brittle. "Nothing, honey. Just thinking about Joe."

"He'll be all right." Brave words from a brave girl.

"I know. It's just that it has been so long and no word at all, and now these damn nasty phone calls. Guess it's all wearing me down." She gave us a smile, albeit a forced one. First a sip of her gin and tonic. Then one beautifully manicured hand reached across the table and sought her sister's. I noticed that a couple of Lindsey's nails were broken off and the polish was cracked and beginning to wear on several more.

I punctured the quiet. "What did the man say for you to do with the money?"

"He just said to get it and he would call and give me instructions."

"Did he give you the usual spiel about small, unmarked bills?"

"Yes. He wants nothing larger than a twenty."

"What did you tell him?"

"Told him I didn't keep that kind of money around the house, but I'd try to get it together."

"What did he say?"

"He laughed and said I'd better."

"He didn't say anything about threatening to harm Joe?"

"No." She paused as if replaying the conversation in her mind. "It was more of an implied threat against Lindsey and me."

"He knows about Lindsey?"

"Yes, the bastard. He mentioned my poor blind sister in that smarmy voice of his. That's why I had to get out of the house. Felt like a gigantic explosion was building up inside of me. One that would tear me into a million pieces, and the ringing of the telephone would be the detonator."

"Now pay attention," I said. "Here's what we'll do. When he calls, listen very carefully and we'll do exactly what he says. Except I will make the delivery and the briefcase will contain index cards instead of green-tinted portraits of dead presidents. I know this asshole doesn't have Joe and doesn't know where he is, so he can't possibly harm him.

If the matter isn't resolved on the spot, I'll come out to your place and bunk with Rico for a while, just to make sure he doesn't try to follow up on his threat. Okay?"

Allison nodded. Our waiter returned with our salads and the conversation ebbed. As I chewed on lettuce and carrots, I became aware of a strange vibration. For a minute I was puzzled; we weren't close to any railroad tracks and I'd seen no heavy machinery in the neighborhood when we arrived. I concentrated on the vibration and suddenly realized its point of origin was much closer than the street. Lindsey was rapidly bouncing her left leg up and down against the bottom of the table. I had a feeling it might be a long night.

Twenty-two

In the final moments before dawn the knock came. I was already awake, lying quietly in the brass bed in the Dubronski's guest bedroom. After some discussion, Allison had asked me if I'd go ahead and move on out to the big estate while she waited on the call from the Englishman. I suspected she had a dual purpose. Probably she was justifiably frightened of that particular caller. Also, I suspected she simply liked having a man around the house.

Nothing to keep me at my place, so I'd packed a bag, holstered my gun, waved goodbye to Debi—standing forlornly at her corner, and come to stay.

The place was even bigger than I'd suspected in my earlier visits. No need to room with Rico. Soft bed, luxurious room, but I hadn't slept well, alternately dozing off and jerking awake. I was lying in the bed, one finger pulling the curtains away from the window, watching for the dawn, when the knock came. Surprised, my other hand went to my gun under the pillow. I became still, silent.

Another knock, actually more a soft scratching. Then the door swung open a crack.

"Mr. Quick?" A hoarse whisper, female, but not Allison. Gentler, in a higher register. "Mr. Quick, are you awake?"

"Lindsey?"

"May I come in?"

"Sure."

Light from the hallway spilled into the room and my eyes followed her progress. She was encased in a white, velour gown that came up high on her neck and fell to the floor. She moved surely and silently across the room, not hesitating when the pool of light fell short of my bed. Hovering over my bed for a moment, she created in my mind the impression of an angel floating in the dark. I let the curtains fall back and rolled over on my side, back against the wall, facing her.

"Hope I'm not disturbing you."

"No, I was awake."

"I know. I've been up quite a bit tonight. I often am. As I walked by your room, I could hear you tossing and turning. Wondered if perhaps you weren't feeling well?"

"No, I'm fine. Just an unfamiliar bed. You know how it is."

"Yes. I don't sleep well most nights. Never have, for some reason, and I think on the first night in a strange bed it's always difficult to get much real rest. May I sit down?"

"Sure." I patted the wedding ring quilt that covered my bed.

Lindsey lowered herself gently and sat half turned away from me on the bed, slender legs dangling over the edge. A velvety sleeve brushed gently against my hand. I hadn't been this close in bed to such a lovely lady in a long time.

"I'm worried, very worried, Mr. Quick."

"About Joe?"

"Oh yes, but even more about Allison. She tries to be so brave and keep up a front. You know, continue on as if nothing has happened. Yesterday, for example, she signed up to shoot a commercial for the Kentucky Derby. I overheard her making arrangements to fly to Louisville. She is simply pretending. Everything is not okay, and I know and she knows it and you know it."

Lindsey sniffed. I wondered if she was trying to hold back tears. There wasn't enough light in the room to view details as fine as tears. All I could make out was a blurry view of her face and her fine golden hair done up in a single long, plaited braid. One white hand lay on the quilt inches from my face. Long, slim fingers stroked the quilt.

"Maybe she's better off keeping busy. Work should help to take Joe off her mind. Better than sitting around the house brooding about it."

"I know, but I'm afraid that if bad news hits, it will be such a terrible shock. It looks like bad news, doesn't it, Mr. Quick?" Her hand, the one that had been restless on the quilt, felt for and found my right one.

"I don't know. I wasn't tap dancing around the issue earlier. Such a complete absence of data could mean several things. You two have to keep hoping, and I have to keep working."

"I try, but it gets harder every day to keep the faith when you don't hear anything. I pray every day and every night that Joe is all right and that he will soon come back to us, but I don't know. It's been over a week now and we haven't heard anything." She sighed. "Do you believe in the power of prayer?"

Her comment about praying every day and night made me think of a child praying that their lost dog or cat would return. Sometimes they did.

To tell the truth, God was beyond the scope of my mind. I only believed in Frank Quick and what he was able to do by himself. Plus what he could coerce, trick, or scare others into doing for, or with, him. Not an appropriate answer in this situation, so I tried for diplomacy. "I've never known prayer to hurt."

She looked away from me. I wondered what she saw in the dark. Darkness, I supposed. Darkness she saw every day, all day. Darkness she would see for the rest of her life. Talk about keeping the faith. I wondered how she kept her spirits so high so much of the time. In my mind, blindness would be pure hell.

Lindsey spoke, so softly I had to strain to hear the words. "Frank, I've prayed a lot over the course of my life. I prayed that Mom and Dad would be all right when their plane was missing, but they found them two days later in sixty feet of water in the Mediterranean off the coast of Portugal. I prayed when I found out about my disease, prayed that I would be spared total blindness, but I haven't even been able to tell day from night for the past three years. I prayed that Allison's movie would be a huge hit and she would make it big in Hollywood, but it bombed and she had to come home. You can't even rent her movie on video. So I don't know about prayer. Some days I don't even know about God."

"Someone, something, one hell of a lot smarter than either one of us made this earth."

"I know, but what if He or She is dead? Maybe earth was just made for fun by some incredibly advanced civilization and now they've abandoned us and things are just winding down like a top, spinning slower and slower until it falters and stops. That's the way I picture the end of the world, not some glorious final explosion, just one revolution after another, each slower than its predecessor, until finally the earth can't maintain the momentum for even one more spin."

"What happens then?"

"I don't know. I've never gotten beyond that point. Guess we are either sucked into the sun and burn up, or drop off into deep space and slowly freeze to death."

"Neither scenario is very pretty."

"No. Well, life isn't pretty sometimes. Look at Allison. She hasn't done one really terrible thing in her entire life, and I would know— I'm her sister. Yet she doesn't have any idea where Joe is right now. Doesn't know if he is dead or alive."

She paused and sighed. One soft hand ran up my forearm and lingered on my biceps. Her touch felt the way I'd imagined an angel's hand would feel, when I was still an innocent boy, all the way back when I lived on Hudson in that rambling three story white job with the concrete front porch.

"Did you have a good childhood?"

I shivered. The woman was psychic. "It wasn't bad."

"Big family?"

"Mom, Dad, older brother, younger sister. Mom was a fifties mom, stayed home, baked cookies, did the laundry, mopped floors, the whole homemaker scene. Dad taught shop and coached basketball at Park City High."

"Sounds nice. Do you still keep in touch?"

"No." I was silent as the memories flooded in.

"Sorry. Didn't mean to pry. It's really none of my business." She stirred as though she were going to get up. I reached up and put a firm hand on her arm.

"Hold on. You weren't prying and I'm not upset. Only, all of a sudden, a lot of memories poured in. Like you had suddenly turned a glass of water upside down, only it was memories instead of water, and they went straight to my head. Overwhelmed me for a minute." I squeezed her arm.

"Anyway, to get back to your question. Mom died of cancer in my senior year, so she never ever got to see me get out of high school. Dad had a heart attack during the district finals seven years later. Died before they could get him to the hospital. Park City won. We beat Brother Sebastian in double overtime: seventy-one to seventy. He would have been so happy. For years he'd had a running feud with old Carl Sternberger, coach of the Brothers. Dad used to call him the motherfucker Brother."

I smiled to myself in the dark. I could still see Dad giving the good brother the finger after we beat them in their own Christmas tournament my senior year. Before that game, both teams had been undefeated. That had been my one really good season. I'd averaged over seventeen a game on a well-balanced squad. The best team in Park City history, even better than Jack's squad, and they'd won the city championship.

"What about your brother and sister?"

"My brother Jack went to Vietnam and came back with only one arm and a boulder on his shoulder. Lives in Philadelphia now, teaches school. We haven't talked in two years. He's still pissed that he had to go and I got to stay. His number came up in the draft, mine didn't. That's how simple it was. So not my fault, but that makes zero difference.

"My sister, Peggy, well she kind of got lost in the shuffle after Mom died. She was only eight. Dad should have sent her to Aunt Pam, but he wanted to do it all, bear all the burdens.

"By the time she hit junior high she was starting to get out of control. Really went wild after Dad died. Aunt Pam was sick herself by then and couldn't handle her. I was single and wasn't around much. Jack was married, stable situation, employed and all, so she went to live with him.

"When she turned sixteen, she took off on her own. About five years ago she called from California to say that she'd gotten married. Then last year, just before Christmas, she showed up unexpectedly on my doorstep. Stayed a week and a half, caged a couple of hundred bucks from me and blew town. Who knows? So, no, I don't talk much to my family. You and Allison seem close."

"We are now. At least we were until Joe turned up missing." She sighed deep in her chest and an image formed in my mind of Lindsey sinking more within herself. In my mind's eye, she was smaller, younger, and suddenly very insecure emotionally. Of course that was only my perception of reality, maybe it was purely imagination.

What wasn't my imagination was Lindsey sinking down onto one elbow on the bed. Her face was turned from me toward the open door and the shaft of hall light that intruded into my bedroom. I wondered why she'd turned that way. I knew she couldn't see the light; maybe she didn't want to be that up close and personal to me. Probably a comfort thing.

I felt a touch strange myself, lying there under the covers in only my jockey shorts, with a very lovely woman just on the other side of the quilt. At the moment, I couldn't get a good handle on my feelings. They were a warm, mellow, comfortable déjà vu, soft and warm, blurry along the edges. I tried not to think about Mona.

"Allison and I are a strange pair of sisters. We always seem to somehow sense what the other is up to, whether we're close at that moment or not. The exact degree of our closeness seems to come and go. We will be very close for a while, as we were in high school. We were only a year apart, both cheerleaders, both on the student council. Then, for some reason, perhaps simply fate—like when Allison went to Hollywood, we slide into a different level of closeness, and may not see each other for months on end. Actually, we have had very few quarrels, we simply seem to drift apart for some time."

"And you've been close of late?"

She shifted position and I felt the smoothness of her dressing gown against my fingers. Her perfume drifted in the early morning.

"Up until the last couple of weeks before Joe disappeared, we were." Lindsey rolled over. Her breath was warm against my cheek.

"Then suddenly she didn't want to talk much. I didn't really notice it at the time because we were so busy: a tea here, a party there, theatre one night, then working at the mission the next. Looking back, it seems as though she was finding a lot of things for us to do, but always with a crowd, never just the two of us. When we're in one of our close phases, we can sit together and talk for hours."

"About what?"

"Anything and everything, the most personal thoughts imaginable, or the latest trivia."

"You think she was trying to avoid talking to you, perhaps about a problem?"

"Maybe. It didn't seem so at the time because we were on the go so much, but I can see now that she cut me out on really personal matters."

"She say anything about having something on her mind?"

"I didn't notice anything in particular, but she could easily have gotten a phone call or a letter that I know nothing about."

"Money?"

"I don't think so. I mean, just look at this house, the car, maid, chauffeur. Allison and Joe are living the good life."

"The good life can be very expensive."

"True, but they seem to have a good income. There are residual checks from Allison's TV shows, and Joe has made some great deals over the years. Plus, he has a number of income-producing investments."

Yeah, I thought to myself. Joe's a wheeler-dealer who, the street says, likes to gamble. Maybe the guy had hit a bad spell on both bets and deals. Allison Grant is an actress and model who hasn't worked in over two years, except for a part-time talk show. The cost of maintaining this castle and retinue had to be enormous. Money talk kept popping up. It made me wonder how well Joe and Allison were really doing. It made me wonder a lot.

Aloud I said, "So Allison has gone back to making commercials?"

"Oh, she says that was just to keep her hand in. Two of the three were basically freebies anyway. Public service announcements she did for the guild minimum, then donated back to the charity." Lindsey shivered and inched closer to me.

"You cold?"

"Maybe a little cool."

"Hang on a sec, I'll fix you right up. Lift your feet."

I half sat up and snaked out an arm to the foot of the bed. There was an extra blanket lying across the foot of the bed, a Navajo weave of soft stripes of brown, red, and gray. Probably more for show than actual use, but what the hell? I grabbed the blanket and shook out the folds as I pulled it up over both of us.

"Better?"

"Yes, but I really shouldn't be here. I was just having a bad night and needed someone to talk to. Hated to bother Allison. She has slept hardly at all since Joe's been gone. I hear her up all hours of the night on the telephone. Last night she was on the phone at two a.m."

"Who was she talking to at that time of night?"

"I don't know. She was talking very softly, just above a whisper, and I couldn't distinguish any of the words."

"Hmmm. Well, anyway, you didn't bother me. I don't sleep a lot anymore. One of the advantages of growing older, your body doesn't require as much sleep as it did when you were younger."

"You're not old, Mr. Quick. I'll bet you're not even forty."

"It's Frank, and I'm way too close to forty for my peace of mind. Besides, I've lived a lot more in this life than most people twice my age. Got a lot of miles on the old body."

"Frank." She let the word roll around on her tongue. "I'll bet you have."

She snuggled closer, sighing as she laid her head on my arm. We lay in the dark without speaking. Then I heard the rhythm of her breathing change as she slid into sleep.

An hour later, she came back to wakefulness with a start. Daylight was streaking the corners of the room. I lay as still as a guard outside Buckingham Palace. Her lips brushed my cheek as lightly as a soft summer breeze on a warm Mississippi night dances through the mimosas and live oaks. Then she was gone. Gone so quickly and quietly she might have been a dream. I put my hand in the hollow of the bed where she had lain and felt the warmth of her body she'd left for me.

Twenty-three

Full daylight greeted me as I rolled out from under the covers. I was tired of fighting a strange bed and a strange room, but I wasn't ready for breakfast, or to face the world, so I slipped on some running shorts, a couple of running shirts, socks, running shoes, and my old blue toboggan, then hit the door.

It was a fresh morning, with temperatures that felt like the mid-forties, accompanied by an incisive breeze. I shivered as the first windy blast hit, then began chugging down the driveway. It was at least an eighth of a mile from the house to the gatepost, and by the time I'd made five circuits I was warmed up and moving easily. Ten laps, and the sweat was starting to form between my shoulder blades. I lost count around lap twenty. By then I was sweating like a race horse and my legs were starting to complain. I refused to listen and did five more as hard as I could. I finished out of breath on trembling legs, but feeling like a new man.

By the time I grabbed a shower, got dressed, and made it to the breakfast table, the ladies were gone. I talked the middle-aged maid, who possessed an even disposition and a faint Latin accent, out of a cup of coffee and a bagel. She moved quickly and efficiently on slender legs, darting here and there like a marsh bird on a mission.

Neither Allison nor Lindsey had shown by the time I finished my bagel, so I lingered over the paper and a second cup of coffee. The coffee was hot, strong, black, and decidedly better than the morning news: one of our intelligence agencies seemed convinced North Korea had stepped up production of nuclear weapons, a taxicab had lost its brakes and crashed doing fifty into a crowd milling around after a pop concert, killing three and injuring a dozen, a top Canadian official was accused of cutting an illegal stock deal with some high-powered clique after getting insider information.

I gave up after reading about the federal judge in one of the Midwestern circuits who was receiving golden showers from his secretary between trials, and went to see if I could find some company.

Wherever the ladies had been, they were back. I heard the car as it made the horseshoe loop in front of the house. I pulled back the filmy, rose and snow shaded curtains in time to see Rico bring the big Lincoln to a professionally smooth stop. He hopped out from under the wheel to open the door for the ladies. These were modern women however, and each already had one leg on the ground by the time he reached them. Rico stood by awkwardly and stiffly, as though his back hurt him and he was ashamed of it. Likely he just didn't know what else to do.

From my window, I was struck by how much they looked alike—same height, hair color, basically the same fine body, at least what I could see under their coats. One had on a hunter green, cloth coat that hung to just below her knees, while the other wore one of a similar cut and material, dyed electric blue. From this distance I'd be guessing as to which was Allison and which Lindsey. Letting the curtain fall, I hustled down the hall to open the front door for them.

"Well, here come the Bobbsey twins," I said as I flung one of the big oak doors open. Lindsey, who had been laughing, only laughed harder. Out of the corner of my left eye I caught a glimpse of Allison's face. I got the impression that, for at least a fleeting moment, she was unhappy with me. Then, as they came into the house, she joined her sister in the laughter. I smiled myself; we were quite the happy trio.

"Did you miss us, Mr. Quick?" Lindsey got out between giggles.

"It's Frank, and yes I did. What have you two been up to? Thought you were concerned about those anonymous phone calls. Tough for me to be of much assistance when you two slip out on me and zap off to the malls."

"Oh, don't be an old silly. It was only the local mall where we've been hundreds of times before. It was broad daylight and Rico was with us all the time."

"Rico went shopping?"

"Well, not exactly shopping. More like he stood around and held packages. Kind of kept an eye on things, you know. Isn't that right, Allie?"

"That's right. Around here, you snooze, you lose. Next time you'd better not stay in bed so late."

I had a snappy rejoinder on the tip of my tongue when the phone rang—obscenely loud in the marbled foyer. I heard Lindsey gasp and saw her go a bit pale. Allison's eyes solidified into two, smooth, polished chunks of lapis lazuli staring straight into mine.

"I'll take it in the library. You grab that extension." She indicated the phone on a brass stand, directly under the Edward Hopper. "Stand about a foot from the wall and you should be able to see when I pick it up." It rang again and she ran on clattering heels across the marble.

I moved into position, cradled the receiver in my hand. Allison and I picked up on the heels of the third ring.

"Hello."

"You and your sis shopping again, huh?" The voice was male and sounded as though at some point in his life the speaker had swallowed a handful of gravel.

"Who are you?" Allison was pure ice.

"Don't worry about who I am. Worry about coming up with the money your chicken-shit husband owes. What's he done, run off and left you holding the bag?"

"Where my husband is now, or at any time, is none of your business."

"It is my business, because I'm making it so. Your no-balls husband owes my boss one hundred and twenty-five thousand large and we want it tomorrow. All of it."

Allison started to say something, but he overrode her. "No delays, no excuses, no bullshit. We'll call you tomorrow with the instructions. Be ready, or else you'll regret it, deeply."

"You'll have to give me a little…" Allison's voice trailed off. No use in talking to a dial tone.

She turned her head slowly and looked at me. There was a lost, trapped without hope, look in her eyes. She opened her mouth as though to say something, but no words came. I could sense Lindsey moving across the hall toward me. Then I could see her hand reaching out. I gave her my right one as I hung up the receiver with the left.

"Different guy?"

"Yes, but he wanted the same thing, the bastard."

"I heard. So, what are you going to do about it?"

"What should I do?"

"That's a tough call. Joe may or may not really owe this English gent the hundred twenty-five thousand. However, at this juncture that isn't really the point. Key thing is the Englishman believes Joe does and he wants his money back. Sounds as if he means business." Lindsey's grip grew decidedly tighter on my hand. I could feel tremors running through her fingers.

"But it's Joe that owes him the money, if anybody does, and Joe is not here."

I understood her implied question. "I know, but I don't think it matters to him whether he gets it from Joe or if he gets it from you. He simply wants his money and he intends to get it. Don't think he cares in the least who gives it to him, how he gets it, or who he has to hurt to get it."

I didn't say the rest of what was on my mind—that with Joe out of the picture Allison moved up to strongest link in the chain and Lindsey joined the chain as the weakest link. Perhaps Allison read my mind, perhaps she was already thinking the same thing, because I saw her looking at Lindsey.

She must have sensed me watching her because she jerked her head in my direction and made eye contact with me. Her look was intense, as though she were trying to stare straight through my eyes into my brain, or my soul. For a moment, I had a glimpse of a new Allison Grant, an Allison Grant I wouldn't want to cross.

I couldn't name the emotion that fueled that look. It wasn't fear and it wasn't greed. Hate didn't quite catch it either, although I did sense a certain negativity. I wanted to squirm under that withering stare, but I wouldn't.

Suddenly, just as suddenly as it started, it was over. She broke eye contact and flipped both hands, palms facing me, up around her head, turned on her heel and left the room with a stride. Her footfalls echoed down the hall.

Lindsey ran the palm of one hand up and down my arm like she was doing one of those tombstones rubbings I'd read about in *Time*. That wasn't far off the mark, as I felt about as ancient as the Mayan civilization discussed in the article. The Bible indicates somewhere, if I remember my childhood Sunday school lessons correctly, that "As ye sow, so shall ye reap." I've often wondered about that passage as it's been my experience that a great number of horrible things happen to a significant number of basically decent people.

"That phone call really upset Allison, didn't it?" Lindsey's face was so close to mine I could feel her breath on my cheek. It was warm and smelled of toothpaste and peppermint.

"Yeah, it did."

"I could tell by her voice. Not the pitch or the tone exactly, but more the timbre. Maybe it is due to her training as an actress, but Allison's voice has very distinctive sounds for different emotions. Today she was upset."

"Scared?"

"Maybe a little, but more angry than scared, and maybe more determined than angry. It was that man wanting the money again, wasn't it?"

"Different man, but still wanting the money. Has Allison's response always been the same when he calls?"

"Yes. I can tell she hates the calls. They really mess up her life. Normally, she would rely on Joe, but…"

"But Joe isn't here."

"No. Frank?"

"Umm?"

"You know, I'm beginning to think maybe you're her substitute for Joe. You're about Joe's height. How much do you weigh?"

"One eighty-five."

"So, six feet, two inches, one hundred seventy-five pounds, and are your hair and eyes dark brown?"

"Yes, both."

"And you're what, thirty-five, thirty-six years old?"

"Thirty-seven, to be exact."

"Well, Joe just turned thirty-five last month, so he's a couple of years younger than you. Otherwise, you might be twins, or at least brothers." She leaned against me. Her hair felt like cotton candy without the sticky. "What do you make of all that? A little? A lot? Nothing?" she mouthed into my shoulder.

"Hard to say. We need old Thoth to help us out."

"Who?"

"Thoth. He was an ancient Egyptian god I read about somewhere. Probably in the *Smithsonian*. He was the scribe of all the other gods. I guess because he was supposed to have invented all the letters. Old Thoth was considered to be the god of wisdom, learning, and magic."

"We could sure use a little of all three right now." She snuggled in more tightly against my shoulder.

"Amen. The sooner the better." I kissed the top of her blonde, cotton candy head. Her body molded against mine, warm and soft.

~ * ~

Lunch was tuna fish on whole wheat, paired with a fancy frozen fruit salad that was only slightly cooler than the atmosphere. I figured the stress and strain were getting to Allison. She was quiet, almost morose, through the meal. Lindsey tried to carry on with chit-chat about the weather and local news, but Allison's mood gradually infected her as well. I hadn't been talkative to begin with. My mind was occupied by what we would do when the next call for the one hundred and twenty-five thousand came. I can't say my thinking did me any good.

After lunch, nobody hung around for coffee and dessert, so I grabbed a cup, strolled into the den, and commandeered the telephone. I punched in my home number and then hit the three-digit code to retrieve my messages.

I had three. One was from Mick wanting to know if I wanted to meet him for lunch at the pizzeria. Sorry, Mick, too late. Number two was from a Mrs. Weatherby wanting to know if I could help her locate her granddaughter. She sounded legit, so I copied down the number she left on the machine. The third was from Fat Tony. Actually, he referred to himself as Tony D'Angelo. He wanted me to call him about the matter in which he and I had a mutual interest. I knew he meant Joe Dubronski.

I hung up and thought things over. I couldn't see where I had anything to lose. I punched in the numbers Tony D had left.

"Hello." The voice was flat, impersonal, essentially void of life. I could have been talking to a machine. I knew I was talking to Al.

"Al, let me talk to Tony."

"Who is dis?"

He reminded me of a movie Mafia hitman. A hitman he was. Mafia maybe. Movies never.

"Frank Quick."

"Hang on a sec." The phone clattered loudly on his end. I could hear muffled conversation, too indistinct to understand. A few heartbeats of silence, then, "Hey Frank, thanks for calling me back. Was hoping you would do that today."

"What's your hurry?"

"What hurry? I was just wanting to have a little chat with you. You know, a little heart-to-heart."

"I didn't know you had a heart, Tony."

Tony thought I was funny. At least he laughed. Perhaps a little forced, maybe a little phony, but a laugh nonetheless.

"You're funny, Frank. A real funny guy. But seriously, I want to have a little talk with you." A brief pause, then in a much more serious tone, "I need to have a little talk with you."

"About what?"

"About a certain party in whom we are both very interested." His knowing tone implied there could be no doubt about whom he was speaking. To tell the truth, there really wasn't much doubt, but I had to aggravate Fat Tony just a little more, especially when he was miles and miles away.

"You want to talk about yourself? Sure, that'll be fine, although undoubtedly you know many more intimate details and exciting real life stories than I."

"Cut the smart-ass comedy crap, Quick. If I wanted a comedian, I'd have hired one. I want to talk seriously with you, very seriously, about Joe Dubronski."

"Why all this interest in Joe? Thought you guys were just sometime business partners."

"Let's talk in person, Frank." Tony backed off one notch on his concern meter, trying for friendly again. Friendliness wasn't his forte.

"Sorry, Tony. I'm on the move right now, so it'll have to be on the phone. My line should be clean." At least I hadn't detected any bugs when I'd done a search earlier in the day.

Tony took his time making up his mind. I realized I wasn't making Tony D'Angelo very happy and that might not advance my career prospects, but then I wasn't in the business to make Tony D happy. For that I gave thanks.

Finally, he gave a long, sad sigh to let me know he was very disappointed in and very unhappy with me. Tony could say a lot with a sigh. "All right, Quick, go ahead, tell me what's happening with Joe. You know, by the way, you make me very unhappy with your uncooperative attitude. I thought we could be friends, cooperate you know, go along and get along. I am very disappointed."

"Life is full of disappointments."

"What?"

"Never mind. I was overstating the obvious. Sorry to disappoint you further, Tony, but there just isn't a lot going on with Joe right now. He isn't here and lots of people, especially his wife, are wondering where he is."

"Who else wants to know?"

"You, for one."

"Besides me, asshole." Tony was forgetting to be friendly again.

I started not to respond at all, but then figured what the hell. I might as well make something positive out of a negative, if I could, even a relationship with Fat Tony. In this life you truly never know.

"All right, Tony, you tell me who fits this description? Big time English accent, more curly white hair than a French poodle, thinks he's pretty, but isn't even close. Got a real nasty attitude and some bad muscle boys to back him up."

"Eddy Lloyd!" Tony D. didn't bother to hide his surprise or his disgust. "What's that little, slimy, gay-wad turd have to do with Joe Dubronski?"

"He's another guy who is very interested in Joe's present whereabouts."

"Why?"

"Well, Tony, it appears that English Eddy is also doing business with your partner, Mr. Joe Dubronski."

"How much business?"

"About one hundred twenty-five big ones is what Eddy claims Joe needs to come through with to cover his part of the deal, and Eddy wants his money right away. Acts like he means business. You want to tell me how much business you and Joe are doing?"

"That's none of your business, gumshoe. I don't need you or anybody else as a go-between for me and Joe Dubronski. I'll find him, but if you happen to find him first, remind him that he owes me and I ain't never going to forget."

I didn't have to be there in person to be convinced. I'll say this for Tony D, he was able to express his feelings, with great clarity.

"Tony, Tony, calm down. You're not paying attention to me. Nobody knows where Joe is right now, not even his wife. She hired me to look for him. I'm looking for him. If and when I do find him, I'll be sure and let him know of your concern."

"Come on, Frankie boy, wise up. Get your head out of your ass, or maybe I should say get your hands off your dick. Of course, that blonde Hollywood nymphet knows where he is. That bitch is a pure ballbuster. Hell, she probably masterminds half his deals. You'd better watch it, private eye, or she'll use you and lose you like a busted rubber."

"Hello, Tony. Come on in out of the twilight zone. Joe Dubronski is AWOL and nobody I know has any idea where he is. So if you have a message you want relayed, you'd better pass it on to me now."

"Frank, I'm very disappointed in you. Thought we were a couple of upright guys. That we could talk straight with each other, work things out. However, I see now that I was wrong. You're not the first good man who's lost his head over a piece of tail. You won't be the last. Don't say I didn't try to talk sense to you."

"Hey Tony—" I started to argue a bit further. Perhaps I could convince him of my sincerity. Probably it would have been a lost cause. Not that it mattered. Tony had hung up.

Twenty-four

The call came before I was ready. I didn't have a plan. Hell, I didn't have a start on a plan.

It was five minutes after eight in the evening and the three of us were playing at being a cozy family at home. We were in the softly lit library, sitting in easy chairs, with the flickering fire crackling on the other side of the stone hearth.

Allison was sitting on the corner of a green loveseat festooned with intertwined white roses. Her golden head gleamed softly in the lamplight as she looked over the latest issue of *Cosmopolitan*. I sat in a high-backed companion chair that had broad, thickly upholstered arms which wrapped around the width of the seat cushion. It was like sitting on a padded throne. Lindsey sat on a footstool before the fire.

After sitting and thinking unproductively for several minutes, I roused myself to action and began to clean my gun. Reflected flames flicked disdainfully on the barrel and the smell of gun oil seemed foreign to this room. Allison had jerked her head up when I popped the cylinder and I thought she was going to comment. However, she merely gave me a long, unfathomable look instead, then went back to her magazine. Lindsey shifted so that her back was to the fire. She wore a Walkman with headphones and CD box lay open beside her.

The first ring was one of those short half beeps you get once in a while. I sensed Allison's eyes on me. Our glances met as the phone rang for the second time. Maybe it was my imagination, but I thought I read fear in her eyes. It wasn't going to be a walk in the park for any of us. I grabbed the phone on the third ring.

"Hello."

"Allison Grant, please." Cultured tones with an English accent.

"Hello, Mr. Lloyd. This is Frank Quick and I am authorized to speak for Ms. Grant with you."

"Well, well. *The* Frank Quick. Do hope the world has been treating you well lately. Rumor has it that you've taken a couple of rough knocks lately."

"The world has probably been treating me better than I've been treating it, but then I doubt you called to inquire about my health."

"No, no indeed, I dare say." Sir Eddy chuckled boyishly. Even over the phone, the chuckle sounded phony. I had a sudden urge to smack his smirky face.

"Actually, I called to make arrangements for the delivery of a certain sum of money Mrs. Dubronski's husband owes me."

"Ah, the infamous one hundred twenty-five thousand dollars."

"Yes, the one twenty-five."

"Eddy we need to chat. You see, he's not here and she doesn't have that kind of money."

"Then she had better get it."

"Are you going to come and get it?"

"No, she can bring it to me. Perhaps I'll collect a little interest from the little lady." The sneer in his voice made me wish I could get my hands on Eddy's neck.

"I don't think so. She'll get what she can and *I'll* bring it. Where do you want to meet?"

"How about where we did before?"

"Ha ha. You're about as funny as a broken leg. Let's make it the zoo, behind the monkey house."

"Too public."

"Not at midnight."

"No way to get in there."

"Sure there is. Either come early and stay late or use the break in the fence over on Malpharin."

"No way, old chap. Doesn't sound like my cup of tea." Half the time Eddy Lloyd's accent sounded as phony as a cheap counterfeit twenty. I didn't give a damn about his accent or whether we met at the zoo. I hadn't figured he would go for that. It was too easy a place for me to set a trap for him. He was right...access was very limited. All I'd wanted was to get him thinking along the lines of a meet at a location where I stood half a chance of coming out alive. Not good odds, but it beat the hell out of him taking a pot shot at Allison.

"What about the back parking lot behind the old Sears over in Greenbrier?"

A huge, vacant, old parking lot. Yards of asphalt and no cover. No thanks. "I don't think so. That one plays all your way. There I'm just a sitting duck for you and your thugs. You know you'll have me outnumbered, Eddy, so why don't we at least agree on a neutral site. Let's say Camden Park."

I could hear him let out a long breath. Lord, let him bite on this one, please.

"Where in the park?" A current of suspicion underlined his interrogative.

I took a gamble, guessing he wouldn't agree to the first place I suggested. "Behind the horse stables."

"Too noisy with all those fleabags around."

"The maintenance sheds over where they park the trucks?"

Seconds ticked by slowly and noisily in my mind. I imagined I could hear him thinking. Finally, when he couldn't think of a reason to say no, "Okay, make it midnight tomorrow."

Bingo!

Twenty-five

"But I might get shot!" Billy Donlevy whined. Billy was fighting a cold and swiped at his long, thin nose with a tattered tissue.

"Nonsense. You'll be up in your cab, way out of the line of fire. Plus, you'll have your head down. All you have to do is listen for my cue and pull the light switch on. I only need a diversion. These guys will have me outnumbered, and if I'm going to get out of there in one piece, I've got to have an ace in the hole. That's you, Billy boy. You're my ace in the hole."

Billy looked more than a little surprised at my description of him. Undoubtedly, it was the first time he had ever been referred to as an ace in the hole. Most of the descriptions of Billy Donlevy I'd heard were far less flattering.

It wasn't that Billy was so awful; he was just nondescript. Not a bad sort, simply not especially talented or attractive. Key point was—he owed me a big favor. Last year I'd pulled him out of a tough jam with the wrong sort of gambling companions in the alley behind Archie's. I was calling in my chips.

Billy drove a maintenance truck for the city. All I needed for him to do was stick around after work and hide his scrawny carcass in the cab of his vehicle. Later, when I gave him the signal, he would flip on his lights, thereby distracting, and maybe temporarily blinding, Eddy Lloyd and his companions. Then I'd get the drop on them. At least that was the plan. It might not have been worthy of Hannibal at Cannae, but it was the best I'd been able to come up with.

Billy wasn't one bit enthusiastic about the idea. "But Frank, I'm going to freeze to death in that truck!"

"You won't have to stay in there the whole time. After the rest of the crew leaves, you can ease back inside the shed, then slip out later. Just make damn sure you're in the cab before ten."

Actually, I didn't figure Eddy Lloyd would get there before eleven, especially when we both knew he held almost all the good cards, but safe beat the hell out of sorry. Besides, a little inconvenience wasn't going to kill Billy. I wasn't the least bit sorry about his long night. He owed me big time, plus his whining was getting on my nerves.

It took me another ten minutes to address all his concerns. Then, before he could change his mind, I quickstepped down the sidewalk. Halfway to the corner, I glanced back. His shoulders slumped in resignation, Billy was dabbing at his nose with the tissue and slowly shaking his head.

As the afternoon had gradually worn out its welcome, the clouds had begun to thicken and pile up until they looked like a dirty layer of snow pushed to the curb of the sky by giant snowplows. A light mist had begun to filter through between the branches, and the temperature was dropping sharply. Light snow by dark wouldn't surprise me. The weather lent an atmosphere of foreboding to the late afternoon. The ride back to Allison's was a somber one.

Twenty-six

Supper had been Lindsey's homemade chili, flavored with chit-chat. Both of the women were full of nervous talk. They told me the recipe was Lindsey's own and she'd done most of the hard work, but Allison had helped by fetching ingredients. They told me the Dow-Jones was off forty-three points. They told me the president had a cold. They told me to be very careful tonight. They told me to take Rico with me.

I told them the chili was good, that I'd be extremely careful tonight, but that I'd go alone. I explained I didn't need even a fraction of my mind occupied with worrying about someone else's safety. I would borrow the car, which was going to upset Rico anyway.

In one way, it was stupid meeting Eddy at all. I didn't have the money and wouldn't have given it to him if I had. His bone to pick was with Joe Dubronski, not his wife. Who knew whether Joe really owed Eddy anything anyway.

Still, Eddy Lloyd had to be dealt with. He impressed me as the type of person who would stop at nothing until he got what he felt was owed, or wanted. A violent man who didn't care who was on the receiving end of the violence.

Looking at it from a realistic viewpoint, Allison couldn't draw a safe and secure breath as long as Eddy Lloyd felt the way he did. What the obnoxious Eddy had done to me might be mild compared to the permanent damage he could inflict on Allison. Rape and scarring both crossed my mind. I planned to have a very full and frank discussion with one Mr. Lloyd tonight. However, there are those who will argue that I have been known to overestimate my powers of persuasion.

Twenty-seven

The clock on the Lincoln's dashboard read 11:07 as I pulled to a stop at one of the scenic loops that branch off from the main park road. The city had taken to closing the park at dark during the early '80s, but cabbies and others citizens of the night had complained so vociferously—it caused them to drive an extra six blocks—that the road was reopened. There had been several muggings, rapes, and car-nappings in the park since then, but what the heck, it was sure more convenient for friends of the mayor. Anyway, the reopening suited me tonight. There are days it pays to take what the Lord gives you.

My spot was about one hundred and fifty yards as the crow flies from the maintenance barn where I was scheduled to meet Eddy. If I'd stayed on the road with its twists and turns, it would have taken me ten minutes to get there. Instead, I cut through the light growth of trees that populated the hillside as it sloped to the barn. The underbrush had been cut away by the city work crew and the footing was good, the traveling easy. In less than three minutes, I was quietly where I wanted to be.

As low man on this particular totem pole, I needed to do some reconnoitering. Before any confrontation it never hurt to determine the lay of the land. Plus, I wanted to make damn sure brother Billy was in position. Without him the odds were way too long for my setup. Even with him there, they weren't exactly stacked in my favor.

What I had planned wasn't totally on the up and up. Hell, it wasn't on the up and up at all. Violence was almost certain to be an element of this night, and I'm not a man who loves violence for violence's sake.

Desperate times demand desperate measures, however, and, while we might not be at desperate times just yet, if we allowed ourselves to be at the mercy of Eddy Lloyd life could be very desperate indeed.

Eddy took what he wanted out of life. Took it violently, without shame, without remorse, without care or concern for how his actions harmed others. There's a lot of truth in what some call the Good Book—I'll grant you that. What you sow, you'll reap, sometimes.

I scrambled the final yards out of the brush and onto the black asphalt. Three large spotlights were set in a half circle at the rear perimeter of the maintenance area. They gave off substantial light, presumably for security reasons, and the area was brighter than I'd figured. As I started over to Billy's dark green truck, I caught a glimpse of snowflakes falling from the black sky. They were few and far between, but large and wet when they landed on my cheek. Winter was coming. A chilling breeze ran through my light jacket.

I meandered over to Billy's truck, stopping twice along the way. Once, I paused to set down my briefcase, as if it was full of heavy money and my arm was tired. The second time I knelt and untied, then retied my shoe, taking a long look as I did so down the avenue of darkness between the two rows of parked vehicles. Both stops were planned, and were purely camouflage. I didn't figure Eddy would be here this early. He held all the good cards and could come late, but life had taught me a long, long time ago never to assume anything.

I was glad to locate Billy's truck. I'd seen him in it a few times when he was out on his rounds, and he had given me the number that was painted in white on the door panels, so I was able to find it easily. My goal was to make it appear my path had been randomly chosen. I'd looked hard for Eddy and any evil companions he might have brought along, but I could have missed one easily enough in the windy, snowy darkness.

As casually as I could, I leaned against the driver's side of old number 1207 and whispered, "Billy, you in there?"

"Yeah. That you, Frank?"

Like who else would it be? Sometimes Billy could be a real butthead, but tonight I needed him. So I tried to keep the sarcasm out. "Yeah, it's me. How you doing?"

"Man, I'm about to freeze to death. Should have brought me some coffee."

It was cold, I had to grant Billy that. I was starting to get the shakes myself. Of course, some of that was nerves. "Coffee would only make you need to piss. Didn't you wear your long johns?"

"Yeah, but I'm still freezing. It's colder than crap here in the cab. Plus, I ain't getting to move around hardly at all."

"Won't be long now. You all set?"

"Yeah, I'm ready."

"What's your cue?" I'd told him a half dozen times already, but it never hurt to remind a guy like Billy.

"You say, 'things are tough all over,' and then I pull the switch on the lights."

"And duck."

"Yeah, and duck." Billy laughed, but the sound was mostly fake. I didn't blame him for feeling the way he did. I wasn't crazy about being here myself. I leaned against the truck and wished I had a cup of coffee. Then again, I sure as hell didn't need the caffeine. My nerves were already screaming. Raw fear tends to affect me that way.

"Frank, you really think there will be shooting?" A wistful air to the question, as if he could wish and it wouldn't be so.

Sorry, Billy boy, wishes are only wishes and facts are facts, and that's the way it is and always will be. "'Fraid so, Billy. I'd say the odds were good there will be."

Time crept on and the cold worked its way inside my coat. Long before the appointed hour it had gone through my flannel shirt and undershirt and made me wish I were somewhere warm. I decided I'd start in Florida and work my way south. Billy had to be cold, too, up there in the truck. At least he was out of the wind, and I'd told him to be sure and bring a blanket. I hoped for once he'd listened.

I stomped around a lot and occasionally walked in tight little circles to combat the cold and try to relieve the boredom. I didn't stray far from the truck in case Eddy got here sooner than expected, and I never quit looking and listening. Snow came in showers, heavy, blinding, and whipped to a mini-blizzard by the wind, then dying off completely the next minute. I hadn't factored weather like this into my calculations and it served to heighten the nerves.

In the end he came. He came without fanfare or secrecy. He simply drove up at a moderate rate of speed and pulled smoothly to a stop just outside the maintenance compound. He came in a big dark Cadillac, a year or two old. I couldn't remember whether they had changed the front headlights with this year's model, or the year's before. I'd been watching the car for some time. It had been a lone wolf all the way. That wasn't to say somebody else wasn't creeping up on my backside. If they were, they were doing a damn fine job of keeping quiet.

Eddy stepped out on the passenger side, front door. At least two other guys got out of the back seat. The one who got out on my side was tall and looked skinny even under a heavy navy pea jacket. He wore a baseball cap. The logo looked like *Yankees*. The man on the far side of the Caddy was shorter, with a dark blue sock cap pulled tight against his skull. That was all I could tell about him. Whoever was driving stayed behind the wheel. The motor kept running.

I took all that in at a glance, then focused on Eddy Lloyd. He wore a light beige trench coat and his hands were thrust deep into the big slit pockets. Even with the freezing night air, he was bareheaded and the breeze ruffled his white curls. Once, I saw him shiver beneath the trench coat. I wondered if it was the cold or his nerves. He had a big, confident smile on his face. I could see him staring resolutely at me, but he was too far away to read his eyes.

The snow had been light, but now large flakes started to fall. I noticed, the way you notice the craziest things at the really important moments of your life, the cell phone antenna on the Cadillac had one of the Mothers Against Drunk Driving ribbons tied to it. The ribbon flapped forlornly in the wind, its ends frayed and tattered as a last place team's pennant hopes in mid-August. Funny, I hadn't picked Eddy as an anti-drinking kind of guy.

Eddy strolled forward a few steps, hands deep in his pockets, the wind whipping at his hair. I figured he had to have a gun in at least one pocket. I knew I did, and it felt very reassuring. Despite the snow, which seemed to be intensifying with every step he took, Eddy kept his smile in place. I kept my back against Billy's truck.

"Hello, Frank. World treating you all right?" Making conversation as though we were simply two old friends passing in the dark of a snowy evening.

"Better than I deserve."

Ten yards away he stopped. I still couldn't read his eyes. He didn't say anything, as if he expected me to say more. He might be waiting a while. After a long moment, he must have come to that conclusion.

"You bring the money?"

I knew he had to be able to see the briefcase at my feet. "What money?"

"The one hundred and twenty-five thousand dollars Joe Dubronski owes me." Eddy spoke patiently, as though to a child.

"You need to talk to Joe about that."

Eddy barked a short laugh. "Joe doesn't seem to be around much these days."

"That would seem to be your problem, Eddy."

"Afraid not, old soldier, it has become Mrs. Dubronski's."

"Two points that you need to understand. One, Mrs. Dubronski doesn't owe you anything. Two, she doesn't have access to that kind of cash."

"Ah, come now, Frank. This is the age of equality…a wife certainly can be held accountable for her husband's debt. As to the money, who are you trying to fool? Mrs. Dubronski, aka Allison Grant, has been a name in the media for years. News, talk shows, even the odd movie or two. Don't tell me a little cash hasn't found its way into her perfumed pockets."

"After taxes, not near as much as you think. Besides, she hasn't really worked for over two years. She has lots of expenses. Plus, what funds she has are tied up in investments."

"She should have been un-investing them. I've given her almost a month."

"She has been trying to find her husband. That's who your beef is with." I glanced at the other men, then back at Eddy Lloyd.

"Look, Eddy, she hired me to find him. What would it hurt you to give me a couple of weeks to see if I can locate Joe? If he does owe you the one hundred and twenty-five G's, then you can take it up with him. What do you gain by harassing a woman who wasn't involved in whatever kind of deal you and Joe had set up? Give me just a little time."

Eddy took another step forward. The smile was gone from his face and his eyes looked as cold as the night.

The wind had picked up, changing direction in the process. Now, it was coming in off Eddy's left shoulder, driving the snow—more pellets than flakes—into my face. They stung like tiny bullets of ice. My fingers tightened on the gun in my pocket.

"She's had plenty of time. I've been calling her for over two weeks. Ms. Golden Panties needs to come across with some cash."

"Now…"

"Don't 'now' me, Quick." His voice, rising on the wind, overrode mine. "I don't need to hear any excuses from that tight-legged bitch. She is one of those prissy cunts who think they are so much better than the rest of us."

"What does that have to do with a damn thing?"

"It has to do with that slut needing to pay me the hundred twenty-five thousand her deadbeat husband owes me."

"She doesn't have it. She doesn't owe it. Why should she have to pay it?"

"Because it is owed to me, don't you see, old boy?" Back to the clipped English accent, with a heavy sarcastic emphasis on the "old boy." He made it sound like "dumb dog."

Out of the corner of my left eye, I could see tall and skinny sliding to my left. The third man I couldn't see. I didn't dare take my eyes off Eddy long enough to pick him back up. The Indians were everywhere, and I didn't have any wagons to circle up.

"Come on Eddy, give her a little slack. Big man like you can surely spare her a couple more days."

"No. I've waited long enough, as long as I am going to. Now what's in the briefcase?"

"Not enough."

"I'll be the judge of that."

Snow filtered down the back of my neck as I squatted to pick up the briefcase. I heard the click before I saw the gun. It looked absolutely huge in his fist. My insides felt full of rocks. I swallowed hard, or tried to swallow, anyway. A knot the size of a hen's egg seemed to have formed in my throat.

"Slide it over here, Quick. Carefully. Very carefully."

The voice was still smooth, the mannerism still cool. He came first one, then another step closer. I could see his eyes well enough now, too well as a matter of fact. In the security lights, they looked hard as blue ice. For the longest minute of my life I stared at them. It was like looking into the eyes of death. I felt suddenly young and weak, almost too feeble to push the briefcase to him. I leaned forward a bit to get leverage and felt the pressure of my gun digging into my leg. I put one hand behind the briefcase and said a little prayer.

"You won't like it, Eddy. It's not what you are hoping for. However, it's all we have right now. Why don't you give us just a few more days?" One last chance for Eddy to give both of us a very big break.

"Slide it over here. Now!"

Anger and frustration were fueling the words, emotions were riding high, coming to the surface. High enough, I hoped, to distract him from my actions, make him one-tenth of second slower in his reaction. That tenth of a second I so desperately needed. A tenth of a second that might determine whether I lived or died.

"What if it's not enough?" I tried to put a whine in my voice. Let him think I was pleading, weak. Such misconception of the situation on his part couldn't do anything but help.

"Tough shit. That bitch better have it there." He didn't have to add "or else". We both knew the end of that sentence. I also knew my cue.

A million thoughts flash across your mind in those final seconds before you think you might die, forming a kinetic kaleidoscope of all the memories of things that had been, transfused with all the dreams of things that might yet be. I deliberately shut my mind down and pushed the briefcase hard across the frozen asphalt toward Eddy's feet.

"Things are tough all over." My voice was as loud as a cannon in my own ears. I grabbed for my gun, pulling it upwards as the lights from the truck flashed on behind me.

I heard Eddy scream, "You bastard," as I pulled the trigger. The gun fired through my coat pocket and I felt the recoil hammer against my side.

Eddy clawed at the night, staggering forward a step, his head falling on his chest. One of the others opened up with what sounded like an Uzi. I was already dropping and rolling for cover. Bullets pounded the front of the big green truck, sounding, for all the world, like hailstones hitting a tin roof.

Blood pulsed in my head and a slick sweat covered my skin. Fear flowed like water over a dam as screams rattled in my ears. Some of them might have been mine.

Illuminated in the glare of the truck's headlights like a spotlighted deer, Eddy forced his head back up, swayed, a stunned, glazed look on his face, then stumbled forward. I caught a glimpse of a dark stain on the upper right portion of his torn overcoat. His gun dangled from his left hand.

I watched as he brought it up and swung it in my general direction. The barrel seemed to be zeroing in on me. I squeezed the trigger again, aiming better this time.

The left side of Eddy Lloyd's face exploded. Blood, bones, and brains splattered across the snow slick pavement.

Bile rose in my mouth, foul and nasty. I scooted across the asphalt until my shoulders and head were resting against the inside of one of the truck's big front tires. I longed to puke my guts up, but vomiting was a luxury I couldn't afford.

A spray of bullets streaked across the pavement in front of the truck and slightly to my right, sending up a chorus line of sparks as they ricocheted off the asphalt before pinging against the truck's grille.

I rolled back over on my heaving stomach and tried to pick up the other two. All I could see was falling snow and the sprawled body of Eddy Lloyd. Then I caught a glimpse of movement off to my left. I opened my eyes wide and unfocused, concentrating on picking up movement. Details I could worry about later.

Two seconds and I caught the movement again out of the far left quadrant of my vision. This time I caught enough to stay with him. It was the tall, thin man. He was still wearing his baseball cap. I steadied my trembling right arm with my left as I wormed around to get him in my sights and squeezed off another shot. The bullet didn't hit him, but it must have caught his attention because he half turned and unleashed another spray of bullets at the truck. It sounded like a dozen of them hit the truck.

As they ripped through the outer skin of the vehicle, I prayed they were either stopped by some heavier metal inside or were too low to hit Billy if they made the cab. The second of my hopes was smashed when one of the windows burst. Shards of glass rained before me in the night.

I couldn't pick up the third man, so I forced myself to concentrate on the shooter. He ran to his left in an awkward, crab-like motion. I couldn't see clearly enough to be certain, but it looked like he was trying to jam another clip home. I slowly expelled air I hadn't realized I had been holding, and tried to lead him just enough.

The big gun jumped in my hand. Under the truck the sound of the firing was magnified. My ears rang and my eyes watered. Through blurred vision I saw the thin man jerk like a puppet suddenly reaching the end of his string. Then he stumbled forward, head-on toward the truck. I pointed the round opening of the gun at his chest and pulled the trigger. He staggered backward when the bullet smashed into his torso. Pirouetting ever so slowly on his right foot, he lifted his hands toward heaven, then pitched facedown on the snowy surface of the parking lot, arms flung out like the hands of a broken clock. As I watched, a pair of massive tremors ran the length of his body. Then a final jerk of his left leg, and he was still.

The Cadillac was rolling. Rolling fast in front of Billy's truck. The right rear window was down and as I watched, a gun suddenly protruded from the black space and opened fire.

A bullet smashed into the tire by my head and it blew, accompanied by my screams. I pulled the trigger again and again until there was only the click of the hammer on an empty chamber. All I hit was the Caddy, dead center of the rear quarter panel and one taillight. I lay on my belly and watched its remaining taillight dwindle, then disappear in the dark.

Shivers rippled through my body. My hands shook so badly the gun was useless to me. I let it slide to the pavement and curled myself up tight in a big ball against the blown tire.

I was very glad there was no one living to see me. I knew it was just a reaction to the guns, the violence, the death, but fear is a deformity few men are brave enough to admit.

After a minute, I was all right. At least I was able to get my own body back under some semblance of control. I retrieved my gun and rolled out from under the truck, reloading. I'd have to lose it later. Brushing off snow, I heard the rise and fall wailing of a police siren. Time to move.

I grabbed the door handle on the driver's side of the truck and pulled myself up on the running board. Weakness settled on me suddenly and the big green door was outrageously heavy as I tugged it open. Billy lay there, curled into the fetal position with a blanket over his head. I couldn't tell at first glance if he was dead or alive, but I didn't see any visible damage.

The cab of the truck was a different story. The big front windshield had caught one or more bullets and shattered glass covered the bench seat and floorboard as though a glass-spewing volcano had erupted.

Pulling the blanket from him, I whispered, "Come on, let's move." I have no clue why I whispered. Eddy and his fallen companion weren't ever going to hear anybody again.

My voice sounded strange in my ears, hoarse, cracked, and pitched higher than normal. I shook Billy's shoulder with a primitive vigor.

To my intense relief, Billy's eyes opened and he began to sit up. I expelled used air and said a quick prayer of thanks.

"That you, Frank?"

"Yeah. Let's move, Billy. Police are on their way."

I'll give Billy credit. He rolled out of the cab faster than I'd rolled out from beneath the big green machine. He had the shakes himself and went to one knee when we hit the ground, but I pulled him upright and we stumbled off.

I'm sure we were a pretty sight. In my mind's eye, we looked like a couple of drunks trying to take up jogging. I know I was weak, weak the way you are after a long illness.

"Goddamn, Frank! Goddamn! Shit, Frank! I thought for sure I was going to die."

"I know, Billy. It was bad. Look, man, we've got to move faster. The police are coming."

We soldiered on the best we could, stumbling on, intent on leaving the parking lot of broken bodies and busted glass behind. Blood stained the snow as though the earth had cut herself.

As we jogged by, I caught a glimpse of Eddy Lloyd at the edge of my peripheral vision. His face presented me with a dichromatic view. The right side appeared peaceful, one might even say serene, in the soft glow of the parking lot lights. The left side was a gaping, open wound, oozing blood spreading over exposed bone and brains, mixing with the falling snow. Eddy wasn't so pretty anymore, and I was suddenly centuries older.

Billy and I jogged up the slope to the car. He slipped once in the snow, but quickly righted himself. My hands trembled on the wheel. Billy sat propped up against the door, shaking like a palm frond in a hurricane.

The motor turned over the first time I twisted the key. I jammed the gearshift into drive and we were rolling. At the edge of the park, we pulled into traffic and dropped in between a bus and a Mercedes coupe blacker than the night. In the distance the wail of the police siren rose and fell.

Twenty-eight

I sat on the couch in the den, a *National Geographic* open on my lap. I turned the pages, glancing at pictures, skimming words. The morning after the night before, and my mind was still too turbulent to allow me rest. Even two hours of playing zombie on the couch after I got back, a sizeable slug of whiskey, and the security of the Dubronski castle hadn't completely calmed ravaged nerves. I'd told the women some of the truth.

A hand, soft and warm, appeared without notice on my shoulder and gently massaged my deltoid. I looked up to find Lindsey. She wore a white gown and a tentative smile.

"Hi." My voice sounded like someone had my larynx in a vise and was slowly turning the handle.

"Good morning. You all right?"

"I'm still kicking."

"Sometimes that says a lot."

"It does this morning."

"Was it very bad?"

"About as bad as it gets."

"Would it help to talk more about it? You didn't say much last night." She came around the arm of the couch and slid in beside me. I could feel her warmth and softness against my side. They reminded me that it was indeed very nice to be alive.

"Not right now. Maybe later. Perhaps you could sit here with me for a few minutes?"

"I believe that can be arranged." She nestled in against my side, the smile spreading across her face.

"I was very worried about you last night. I...er...well...er...I was afraid that you might not come back."

"Only the good die young. I figure to live to be at least one hundred."

Lindsey laughed, a good strong, happy-to-be-alive laugh. It made me want to laugh, too, something I hadn't been doing very much of the past couple of years. It also brought back an old memory.

"I used to have an old professor in college. Said he planned on dying in bed on his one hundredth birthday, shot by a jealous husband. I wonder what ever happened to him. He was a scraggly old varmint when I knew him and that's been over fifteen years ago. At that time, he wasn't married and lived alone in what was rumored to be some of the nastiest bachelor quarters the town had ever seen. His pants were always stained and you could tell what he had for lunch by checking out his tie. What *was* his name? Taught sociology...Dr. Gale. That was it, Dr. Gilbert Gale."

"What did you major in?"

"Life, you might say. I took a number of classes, studied a little, partied a lot. Was there on a combo basketball and baseball scholarship. Played all four years. Made just enough grades to stay eligible. If I remember right, my major was supposed to be history. In the end, I quit going to class. Never bothered to graduate."

I took my right index finger and ran it along her right eyebrow and down her right cheekbone and along her jaw line. "Thought about going back to school a couple of times, but something has always come up."

"Were you good?"

"In basketball, you mean?"

"Uh-huh." She snuggled in close to me. Her cheek was silky soft against my rough fingers. I could feel the swell of her breast against my side. I leaned over and kissed the top of her head. Her hair smelled clean and full of sun, just like the shampoo commercial on TV was always promising.

"I could shoot." I left the rest unsaid: that I was an inch too short, a step too slow, and had no jumps. Baseball had been a different story. "What about you? Where did you go to school?"

Her little pink tongue came out and licked her lips. I couldn't swear to it, but it looked like she had lipstick on, even at this unholy hour of the morning. "I went to three schools. Started out at the University of Illinois, went to NYU when Allison was modeling in the Big Apple, and finished up at UCLA. Moved out there when Allison tried the movies."

"What did you major in? No, don't tell me, let me guess." I pulled her face around so that we were head on to each other. Our noses were no more than two inches apart. I looked long and hard at her. She had her sightless eyes closed tightly, as though she thought I might be able to see through them into her past. I ran my right thumb along the sides of her nose, first left, then right. "Psychology."

She giggled. "Are you always this intuitive?"

"Sometimes I get lucky."

"All right, what am I thinking now?"

I let my fingers slide down her cheeks, like raindrops drifting down a window pane. I didn't say a word. I just bent my head and gently pressed my lips to hers. They were soft, warm, and yielding. Her slim arms slipped around my shoulders. It felt damn fine to be alive.

Twenty-nine

The papers didn't make much of it. Oh, it got some press. "Double Death in the Park," they called it, and for a time one of the writers, Michael Dennison, tried to put some mystery into it. However, the parking garage scandal broke the next day and my little adventure faded to the back pages.

The police figured it for a drug deal gone bad. I'd left the empty briefcase in the middle of the bloody bodies and they took it from there. It was cheap, standard issue Wal-Mart stock, and I'd picked it up at a garage sale ten years ago. The briefcase had been wiped thoroughly before I headed to the park, and I'd worn gloves after the wiping.

Of all the descriptions written about Eddy Lloyd, the one I liked best was Dennison's. He called him a lone wolf living on the wilder side of life with no visible means of support. All the writers seemed to agree that Eddy frequented gambling establishments and was often accompanied by a beautiful woman. I was sure some people would miss his flashy money and love of excitement. I was equally sure I would never forget him.

I had a couple of contacts on the police force, guys I'd done jobs they couldn't do for themselves because of their position. I never took any money for my special services, preferring to trade them for information.

Both my sources confirmed what I'd surmised, Eddy Lloyd indeed was a one-man operation. If he needed backup or someone with special skills, he contracted out, otherwise he took care of things himself.

That was good news for us. No one else would be after us for the mysterious one hundred twenty-five thousand and, therefore, I could get back to finding Joe Dubronski. At least that was the way I had it figured. Allison Grant had different thoughts on the matter.

"No, Frank, I would really feel better if you stayed here with us for a couple more days." She leaned forward as she spoke, letting her pleading eyes work on me. We were sitting in her kitchen, drinking coffee. Sunlight filled the room, the coffee was a special grind, a combination of Brazilian and Columbian beans, and the vibrant blue of her gown matched her eyes. It was a lovely scene straight out of *Vogue*. None of that helped make any sense out of her insistence on my presence.

"But Allison, Eddy Lloyd has gone away for good. You haven't had a call or threat since his last telephone call. I can't find Joe hiding here in the house with you and Lindsey. Can't you see that?"

She took a moment to answer and, before she did, she ran a single, slender figure down my left forearm. "I hear the words you're saying, but something in here tells me that I need you in the house." She gently tapped herself on her swelling left breast as if it held the secrets to the universe. She gave me a smile that promised a lot. I reminded myself that promises were easy to make.

I pushed out of my chair and strolled to the window. The frustration I was feeling swelled up inside of me and threatened to spill over. I didn't trust my tongue not to say something hateful. A cardinal flew hard and fast for a big holly tree that grew up tight against the house, its branches brushing the bricks. The bird was a red blur as it flashed by the window, a blood-soaked bullet speeding toward its target. I shook my head in an effort to clear the image from my mind.

Allison's voice brought me back to the room, the moment. "Frank, can't you see that Lindsey and I need you here with us?"

"But you hired me to find your husband."

I hadn't meant to use an accusatory tone, but Allison's face took on a sorrowful expression and her eyes found the bottom of her coffee cup suddenly of great interest. When she spoke, her voice was so low I had to strain to hear.

"I know, and I do want you to find him. It's not that, it's just that it's been so bad of late, all those phone calls and no one around that I can really rely on."

I'd suspected it for some time—Allison Grant was one of those women who never really felt whole unless they had a man around. Successful, yes; complete, no. I tried to redirect her attention. "There's Rico."

"Rico can't think. "Her eyes came up and she must have seen something in my face, because she quietly added, "Don't get me wrong. Rico is a good man to have around to do things. He's always willing to try to do what you want done, and he does his best, but he has no..." she searched for the word, "independence of thought. He's not someone I could have a conversation with."

I wondered if she had ever really tried, but I curbed my tongue and tried another tactic. "Look, Allison, I'm not a bodyguard and this is not a Kevin Costner movie. There are lots of guys who would jump at the chance. I know several and could put you in touch with some of the very best, but that line of work is out for me. I need to be on the move too much. Been by myself for way too long for domesticity. There are times when I need to be on my own."

She rose from her chair. From habit or intention, her body angled itself so that the light accented her curves. She moved across the room with a languid grace. Her journey took her to the far side of the room, as though she deliberately wanted to put distance between us. At the doorway, she paused and gave me a long, knowing smile, one hand posed provocatively on her hips. "Then I guess you'd better get busy and find my husband, Mr. Quick." If there was any warmth in either her words or her smile, I couldn't find it.

Thirty

Back when I played a season for the Richmond Braves, I once caught a sinking line drive that seemed to spin directly from the center of a glaring sun. I caught the flu once on a rainy, chilly night in Detroit. I caught my break in the Dubronski case while I was eating a bagel at the Westminster Club.

The Westminster Club is an overpriced, trendy, yuppie bistro down in Widener Grove. Widener Grove is a section of town that had been one of the in places back in the 20s. Its time in the sun had faded in the 30s and 40s and disappeared during the 50s and 60s. The 70s had brought discos, and an aborted rebirth for the area. Disco had mercifully died, and Widener Grove had lain fallow during the 80s. However, there is always someone out there ready to try and make a buck, and in the decade of the 90s a trio of young, ambitious developers had done that for Widener Grove. The Westminster Club was an early effort, full of black and white art deco, live jazz, and nouveau cuisine that was as badly cooked as it was overpriced. The chef had a solitary redeeming feature—he baked a damn fine bagel.

It had been for me, as the Beatles once sang, a hard day's night. I'd spent the hours of darkness frequenting the establishments Joe Dubronski used to frequent, where I showed his picture to the young and old, the beautiful and the ugly, the strong and the weak, the right and the wrong, the movers and losers. Nobody had seen him.

Now I was sitting at my own black and white checkered tile table. The table rose high off the floor on spindly wrought iron legs, and three stools were spread around it. I perched on my seat and let my feet rest on the black iron ring that ran around the circumference of the three legs about a foot and a half off the floor. I had nothing to show for my efforts but a greasy picture, aching legs, and eyes that felt like they were rapidly filling with sand. I gnawed tentatively on my bagel and watched steam rise from my coffee cup. I'd turned off the thought process and was strictly into scan mode. Snatches of conversation drifted by. Some I waded out and pulled in, others I let slide. There was no rhyme nor reason to my process; I was functioning on about three cylinders. A couple next to me chatted, their voices pitched loudly enough for me to hear.

"So you did see the play last night?"

"Yes, and we had great seats. We were in the balcony, but dead center, only five rows from the rail. It was like being on stage." The woman's smile was rapturous as she remembered the evening. If she noticed the scowl on her companion's face she didn't let on.

A tall, bald black man and a short, heavy white guy were standing at the espresso line. The white guy was doing most of the talking. The black guy sipped his espresso, stroked his goatee, and nodded sagely from time to time. From the few words that drifted my way, I gathered that they were talking finances. 'Zero coupons bonds' I recognized, but 'synthetic GICs' and an 'irrevocable benefit commencement date' meant zilch to me.

From behind me, someone said something about a trade he thought the Knicks should make. His companion remarked that the Bulls had never been the same without Jordan. They agreed that Dallas needed a coaching change.

The stray word 'Clinton' drifted through my ill-defined space. A dark-haired woman with black mascara above and below her eyes gave me a long cool look across the room. Her hair hung far down her back and spilled out in rebellious bangs from under a red band. The bangs kept falling into her eyes, giving her a furtive look as she looked out between them, like a wild animal peering from the edge of the forest. I looked away and took another bite of bagel.

The unhappy young man couldn't let the theater tickets alone. His unhappiness was evident from the scowl that clouded his face and marred his good looks. "Where did you get the tickets?"

She flipped a long wave of ash blonde hair away from her face. "From Tony."

"Tony who?"

"Tony D'Angelo."

Hearing that name drove my weariness out and I inclined my head in their direction.

"Tony D'Angelo? *The* Tony D?" He sounded quite surprised.

"Yeah, the man himself." The blonde added a nervous little laugh. Some of her companion's displeasure was finally soaking through.

"I didn't know you knew Tony D." He made the words mean she had been keeping secrets from him. His black eyes sparkled accusingly.

"I didn't until last night."

"Well, how did you meet him? One of his parties?" His furrowed brow and sarcastic tone hinted at a Roman orgy. "Or did he pick you up at a bar?"

One hand drew back and I thought she was going to slap him. Maybe in private she would have, but she was in public and she didn't want a scene. After giving him a dirty look, she let it slide.

"No, I met him through Al. You know Al?" The smile had vanished and a look as hard as lacquer covered her face.

"Yeah, I know Al. Known him for years. Face like a manhole cover, flat and full of craters and scars. Used to chain smoke Camels and lust after Betty Jo Vinduci. Didn't he drive for Joey Cardello? You know, Joey the Card?"

"That's him. Only now he works for Mr. D'Angelo."

"Doing what? No, don't answer that question. I don't want to know." He looked down at his espresso cup with a look that was half distaste. I wasn't sure what the other half was. I wondered if it was fear.

The blonde did the flipping number with her hair again, then let her lower lip slide out at least half an inch in a pout she'd obviously practiced before. She was an obvious attention consumer. Her demands would exhaust men in short order, unless they were strong enough to ignore them. Her current companion was a prime candidate for the used man lot.

He either sensed her unhappiness or caught a glimpse of the pout on her otherwise lovely face, because his eyes slid away from his cup to her face as if they were drawn by a magnet.

"What was Al doing with tickets? He never seemed like the kind of guy who got into Broadway plays."

"Al's a lot deeper than you think. In some ways deeper than you are." She shot him a hard look. I watched his face wilt before it.

"Anyway, it was Mr. D'Angelo I went with, not Al. Al just knew Mr. D had these tickets, and he knew I liked plays and shows, all the fine arts. Anyway, those tickets were supposed to be for someone else, but they became available at the last minute, and Mr. D'Angelo just hates for things to go to waste. So Al put two and two together, and that's how I got to go."

She beamed triumphantly as though she had explained a difficult algebra problem to a slow class. I began to suspect her culture was no deeper than a veneer.

Her companion rolled his eyes in a way that led me to believe he shared my viewpoint. I noticed he did it when she glanced toward the kitchen where someone has just dropped and broken a fair sized portion of the day's profits. I suspected experience had taught him the value the blonde placed on his opinion.

When she turned back around, he asked her, "Who were the tickets supposed to be for?"

"Oh, some associate of Mr. D'Angelo that he's on the outs with. The way Al tells it, this guy and Mr. D did a lot of business together, but then this guy stiffed Mr. D some way on one of their deals. Al tried to explain it all to me, but it was awfully complicated. Anyway, some way this guy got Mr. D'Angelo involved in this really big project, then switched at the last minute and did the deal with someone else. From what Al said, Mr. D'Angelo's *so* mad, and you know what happens when he gets mad."

Red lacquered fingernails drummed at the rim of her cup. "Now what was that guy's name that Mr. D was just totally hacked off at? Some kind of Pollack name…Du something or other, Duvonki, or, no, maybe it was Dubronski."

"Piss on them both, Camille, what about us? Or are you getting too high and mighty for me?"

I pushed the last of my bagel in my mouth, swung off my stool and headed for the door. As I walked by them, the blonde was telling her admirer that of course she still cared for him, but the look on her face belied the words. She was already moving up to bigger things, more money, and more powerful men. I left them to their deceitful games and went to look for my old buddy Al.

Thirty-one

A dozen hours later I was still looking for Al. He hadn't been at his usual haunt, Michael's. I'd tried there first. Yeah, they knew him, but he wasn't there now. Sure, they'd let him know that Frank Quick was looking for him. I heard this in a couple of other joints and drove halfway across town looking for a development project where Mr. D'Angelo was supposed to be conducting a walk-through inspection. Either my informant had his story wrong or Tony D was a no show. I waited an hour beyond the scheduled time. After that point I was tired of watching guys in hard hats look at blueprints and point with their fingers at steel beams suspended in mid-air, so I went home.

My place was cold and dirty, but I ignored the elements and flopped down in my favorite reclining chair, complete with cracked brown leather and coffee stains, and flipped on ESPN. Waves of tiredness washed over me. I hadn't slept in over twenty-four hours and I nodded off still in my clothes.

I should have slept like a rock, but it was a fitful sleep, full of twisting, turning dreams that forced a hazy, twilight sleep frequently punctured by half-opened eyes and snatches of wakefulness.

Once, when I was partially awake, a female body-building show was on. Remember watching it for a few minutes. Now, I certainly like a well-muscled female physique, but women with breasts like slabs of concrete are not my passion.

Actually, I think men ought to develop their bodies to the degree the ladies have. There was a tall, thin-faced redhead from Columbus, Ohio who was ripped to shreds. She was my choice for first place, but I faded out before they completed the call backs.

When I woke it was after midnight and the telephone was jangling on the spindly black table beside my chair. My head was clouded with remnants of a dream about my dead cousin Charlie, and my tongue felt thick and fuzzy with sleep.

"Hello."

"Hear you've been asking about me."

No mistaking those flat tones, so devoid of feeling. That man was a vocal wasteland. I wondered if he ever experienced, or expressed, passion.

"That's right. I want to talk with you."

"About what?"

"Joe Dubronski."

"We had that conversation."

"Not really." I waited for a protest, a denial, an exclamation of surprise. None came, only Silent Al on the other end of the line.

He was still there. I could hear him breathing. He whistled faintly through his nose.

"We only talked a little about Dubronski. I told you he was missing and that his wife had me looking for him. You told me you two had a drink on occasion and you both like to wager on sporting events. Remember that conversation, Al?"

"Yeah, I remember. So?"

"So you told me Joe and Tony D'Angelo did some business together."

"They do."

I pushed out of the chair and wandered over to the window, dragging the phone with me. My knees and ankles ached and one knee popped in protest. It sounded like the shell of a peanut cracking open, but there was no pain. I am simply getting old.

"Yeah, well, I hear there's a little more to it than that."

There was a sudden upswing in the volume of noise and I couldn't hear his response. There had been background noise all along, as though he were at a bar or restaurant. The band must have returned from break. I asked him to repeat himself. He did, louder, and this time I caught at least every other word. Something to the effect that you could hear anything out on the street. While true, that comment wasn't pertinent.

"Later, Al. I can't hear half of what you say. Tell me where you are and I'll come over and talk with you in person. Make it a lot easier on both of us."

I half expected a 'no,' but after ten seconds he intoned "okay."

The mini-blinds were up and I could see Debi patrolling her turf. Her skinny legs looked bizarre sticking out from an oversized rabbit coat. Even from my angle, I could see that she wobbled on her stiletto heels like a baby learning to walk.

"Where are you?"

"Michael's."

"Is that reggae I hear?"

"Yeah, they're having some kind of fucking Bob Marley festival."

"Sounds good to me. You know some people call me the White Jamaican."

"I've heard some call you Butthead."

The click of the phone was sharp in my ear. After the blasting of the band, the silence seemed enormous. A smile drifted across my face; maybe old Al did have a sense of humor.

~ * ~

I grabbed my coat and headed for the car. The winds were calm and if a man dressed right it would be a nice night to be out, a fine night for a run. I was tempted.

"Hey, Frank, where you going?"

I let go of the door handle and stepped back from the car. Debi minced forward on her six-inch heels with steps that promised danger for both of us. I shook my head as I watched the bulky, fuzzy coat wobble toward me. However, as oversized as the coat was, a potential customer might think Debi could be hiding a figure under all that fluff and pay the price of admission to find out. Knowing Debi, she was counting on that.

In addition to the coat, she was wearing oversized glasses that covered half her face. I'd never seen her wear anything but sunglasses. Under the street lamp, the glasses looked thick enough to be prescription.

"Out on business. What's with the glasses, Debi? Trying for a new look?"

"Got to where I couldn't tell the men from the women. Doctor said I needed glasses."

"Why not contacts?"

"I'm not sure. Something about the curve of my eye and astigmatism. Anyway, glasses are in this year, especially the style I got. Don't you think they make me look sexier, Frank?"

"They're very attractive. Well, I'd better push off, Deb. Got business to attend to."

"Let me ride along with you?"

Some of my negative reaction must have reflected in my face. "Ah, gee, Frank, come on. I just want to ride with you. I'll stay in the car. Listen, business is really slow tonight and I'm going to die of boredom, if I don't freeze to death first. Come on, just one little ride. Please, big guy, give a poor little hooker a break."

Her brown eyes, magnified and distorted by the lenses, pleaded with me.

"Hey, I know you are like, yeah, like a big crime fighter. You can think of it as doing your part to get prostitutes off the streets."

"All right, hush up and get in, and none of your idle chatter on the drive. I need to do some thinking. Remember now, you promised to stay in the car. You'd better do it, or don't ever aggravate me again."

Smiling broadly, she stumbled around to her side of the car. In any number of ways, she reminded me of a woman who still carried a touch of little girl inside her. In any case, she sure as hell presented a unique look on the street. Never let it be said that the great Frank Quick wasn't a sucker for unattractive hookers in wobbly heels and thick glasses.

Thirty-two

A spotlight lit up a long white banner with blue lettering that fluttered half-heartedly in the light breeze blowing through downtown. Between flutters I was able to make out the words: "**Michael's Presents:** (in letters smaller than what followed) **The 3rd Annual Bob Marley Festival**."

Then below in smaller letters: "*Featuring the Reigning Kings of Reggae: Rorschach Jamaicans*." Definitely sounded like my kind of night.

I left Debi leaning up against my aging Chrysler, trying to fire up one of her skinny, dark cigarillos. She looked ludicrous, but then so had a lot of folks I'd seen on my journeys.

Smoke and sound battled for supremacy inside the heavy, twin oak doors that monitored the front of Michael's. The smoke was a curious blend of cigar, cigarette, pipe, and something that threatened to crack the linings of your lungs. The noise was abusing, syncopated reggae that made me instinctively want to move my body to the beat. Bob had been gone since '81, but his music and influence still lived.

I must have instinctively moved in response to the rhythm, because an overweight woman with frowzy brown hair and huge tortoise-shell glasses suddenly appeared at my elbow. "Looks like you're really into the music. Would you like to dance?"

"Thanks, but I'm here to meet someone. Maybe later."

She gave me a 'Yeah, sure' look, turned abruptly, and merged into the heavy traffic headed toward the dance floor. I felt bad about telling her no. I'd been turned down often enough to know how it felt.

In all the chaos, it took me a few minutes to locate Al. Finally, just as a song about the sun of the islands ended and the dancers left the floor, I caught a glimpse of him at a table in the back. He was sitting on a raised platform I hadn't noticed on my earlier visit. I picked my way through the throng. The band was making noise about taking a break and management was making an announcement that there was a Volvo station wagon in the parking lot with the lights on.

Al glanced up as I approached his table, the implication being that he had just noticed me. I figured otherwise. Al was a noticing kind of guy. In his line of work if you wanted to stay alive you tended to be a noticer.

His table companion was a thin-faced blonde with bare shoulders and bored eyes. Al jerked his head and she got up. She did it slowly, making an elaborate procedure out of picking up her cigarettes, lighter, and drink. Al's expression never changed. I pretended not to notice. The blonde was showing a lot of cleavage, pushed up nicely as though she were presenting it for inspection. The legs, which I watched as she walked slowly away, looked equally nice. I could understand Al overlooking a minor display of emotion.

I took the vacant chair. "Didn't figure you for a reggae man, Al."

"I'm not."

"Yet you're here tonight and you were here the other night."

"Business interests. None of your business."

I sat and watched the milling crowd. They reminded me of the chickens on my Uncle George's farm, looking for a place to scratch. I'd spent a couple of teenage summers on the farm, yet hadn't thought of it twice since.

"You said you wanted to talk. So talk." Al's lips moved only fractionally. The Camel in the corner of his mouth barely jiggled and the mirrorless eyes never left the dance floor.

"Okay, I want to talk with you a little more about your boss and Joe Dubronski."

"Why do we keep having this same conversation? Answer me that, Quick."

The smoke from his cigarette drifted into my eyes. I blinked away my irritation, telling myself I needed answers, therefore I had to put up with the pain known as Al.

"We've talked all right, but not enough. Word is that Joe and Tony did a lot of business together, that they were like big-time partners."

"You can hear anything. You know that."

"I know. That's why I'm here. I want to hear it from you."

"Hear what?"

I wasn't sure if he was deliberately avoiding conversation, or just being obtuse. "The real story on Tony and Joe. What I hear is Joe influenced Tony to spend major bucks on backing a development that ended up going to somebody else. Story on the street is that Joe set Tony up all the way."

Al slowly turned his head toward me and dragged the Camel out of his mouth. His eyes were like two chunks of granite. I couldn't read a thing in them. They might as well have been dead.

"Now why would he want to do that?"

"Somebody made him a better deal?"

Al shrugged. His sports coat hung on him like cloth draped over wire. Under the fabric, I figured him for skin and bones.

"Business." He said the single word as if it covered a multitude of sins. Maybe he was right.

"No businessman likes to lose money, especially when his partner cuts somebody else in on the deal. Don't figure Tony D as a guy who likes to lose anything, certainly not big bucks, which I hear he dropped two ways."

"Two ways?" Al looked puzzled.

I glanced at the bar. The blonde was leaning against the polished wood, one long leg posed provocatively on the brass rail. She had one hand around a drink the color of rubies and was staring at us. The expression on her face was not a happy one. I turned back to Al.

"Yeah, two ways. One, he spends a bundle buying up property and developing the site. Two, he doesn't get any profit when the construction deal goes to someone else. I doubt that made Tony very happy, especially when one of his own men is such a drinking buddy with the guy who screwed him."

A light flickered in Al's eyes. That shot had hit home. He stuck the Camel back in his mouth and took a long draw, blowing a ribbon of smoke out between thin lips. He studied the smoke as if it were writing his future.

"You don't have to worry about Mr. D'Angelo. He can take care of himself. You'd better be watching out for yourself, Quick."

We looked at each other for an elastic moment. The light that had flickered in Al's eyes had gone out. He was a good man for keeping secrets. Time to go. I pushed my chair back.

"Enjoy the music, Al." He never even blinked. I turned and headed for the door. All the way across the dance floor I sensed eyes boring into my back, Al's and the blonde's.

Thirty-three

Morning sunshine spilled softly through the windows and tumbled across Lindsey's shoulders, highlighting her hair, providing a backdrop for her face.

We were just finishing a fashionably late breakfast at Two Worlds. Allison had actually set this early morning meeting up to discuss the case. However, Lindsey had told me her sister had received a last minute phone call and sent her on ahead with Rico, along with a promise to get a cab and join us later. I'd sent Rico back, promising to drive both ladies home.

Rico hadn't been enthralled at the idea of waiting through the breakfast meeting and greeted my instructions with a wide grin. That had been an hour ago and Lindsey was finishing her pancakes. Still no Allison. That must have been some phone call.

Lovely in an azure blue silk blouse and darker blue wrap-around skirt, Lindsey had blue and silver combs in her hair, long dangling earrings, and a drop of syrup clinging to the corner of her mouth. I had an urge to kiss it away. Instead, I told her about it.

I expected her to blush a bit and dab, ladylike, at it with her napkin. Instead, she laughed and slipped the tip of her tongue out of the corner of her mouth and licked it off.

"You must think I'm a mess," she said, lips still slightly parted in a half smile.

"No, no. That was much cuter than using your napkin, and more practical." I was smiling myself.

"It seemed more efficient that way and Allison is always telling me that to be successful in this world I've got to be more efficient."

"In what field have you chosen to be successful?"

She laughed again, the sound rising over the gentle hum of conversation at the other tables and the muffled clatter of dishes from the kitchen. A woman in a gray pin-stripe and a long strand of pearls gave us a hard look until she caught me staring back at her. Then she quickly averted her eyes. Lindsey sipped tea before she answered my question.

"Lately I seem to have been majoring in dependent sisterhood. I tell myself I'm helping Allison by being there, and maybe I am. I've got a double major in French and Music, and a lot of good that seems to be doing me now. I've given some thought to a singing career, but to be honest, I'd have to make it more on my handicap than my ability. I've got a nice enough voice, but nothing special. You understand why I don't want that."

One hand lay on the white linen tablecloth. I slid my hand over it and gave a gentle squeeze.

"You really are beautiful, you know. Ever consider trying to make it as a model?"

She laughed like I was the hottest star on the Comedy Channel. "Me?" More laughter. "Me, a model? Never! Never in my wildest dreams."

"Your sister did."

"Allison is incredibly beautiful, and she isn't blind. Who would want a model with eyes like mine? I mean, I couldn't look into the camera, or focus, or anything like that. That's the most absurd idea I've ever heard."

A touch of anger began crawling up my neck. For a moment, I was glad Lindsey couldn't see my reaction. Then I was ashamed of myself for such a thought. Still, I was peeved at her.

"So, you've never seen your eyes since you became blind. I'll bet no one has. Besides, I see models in sunglasses all the time. You could model for convertibles, jeans, swimsuits, even sunglasses themselves. As for your sister, you are every bit as beautiful as she is. In fact, in subtle, genteel ways, perhaps a shade more lovely."

Lindsey turned a few degrees in her chair and twisted her face up in a way I found strangely appealing. I knew she couldn't see, but I got the impression that she was, in some fashion, seeing through all the obstacles and getting an unobstructed view of my soul. It was a disconcerting moment. I wanted to say something clever to break the spell, but everything I thought of seemed childish, rude, or condescending. For once, I was smart enough to keep my mouth shut.

"You're a strange man, Frank."

"I won't deny it."

"A strange and silly man."

"Silly? I don't know how to take that. Silly in what way?" My face was suddenly hot.

"Silly in that I think you mean what you say."

"I do mean what I say."

"You're really sweet, but I realize you're only trying to be kind."

I rose, unsteadily, from my chair and reached my right arm across the table. Blood sang in my ears. For a heartbeat, maybe two, I thought of Mona.

Then I softly took her round, upturned chin in my hand. My reflection came back to me from her sunglasses as I bent my head.

She was as still as stone.

I placed my lips on hers.

She tasted of butter, syrup, and promises. For a second her lips were resistant. Then they melted and parted and yielded to the pressure I gently applied. Deafness came over me in an instant. It was as though we been sucked into a giant vacuum. A smooth, slender arm slipped across my shoulders and fingers etched an unknown design on the back of my neck.

Thirty-four

Allison never came and Lindsey and I got lost at a Hampton Inn on the way home. By the time I piloted the Chrysler between the gate posts and down the long, winding drive, the afternoon had grown old.

My expectations of being greeted at the front door with an explosion never materialized. Rico and a rail-thin youth were the only ones in front of the big house, and they were thirty yards away under a huge, ancient maple, raking up the dead and dying leaves of autumn. The boy paused in his efforts and gave us a long look. Rico kept raking.

Lindsey drifted off in the direction of the kitchen to try to find Allison or the maid. I wandered around the vestibule. In addition to the Edward Hopper on one wall, the Dubronskis had what looked like a Remington bronze on a three-legged table butting up against the opposite wall. I meandered over to give the bronze cowboy a closer look.

The day's mail lay beside the sculpture and, out of habit, and a touch of curiosity, I gave it the once-over. There was what looked like a bill from Allstate, the latest issue of *National Geographic* still in its brown slipcover cover, a postcard of a Royal Caribbean cruise ship sailing on an incredibly blue ocean, and a business-sized envelope with Allison's name and address typed on it. The envelope was postmarked Prescott, Arizona, and the postcard was signed in lime green ink by someone who called herself Midge. Midge was having a good time, but eating too much.

"Juanita said Allison left about nine for a meeting and hasn't been seen or heard from since." Lindsey's voice startled me, and I almost dropped the postcard. I slid it back on top of the pile, wondering if she'd heard me fingering the mail.

"You want me to wait? Or should I go on home?"

Lindsey seemed to consider the question for a moment. "Allison didn't give Juanita any indication how long she might be gone." She paused and the tip of her tongue probed the top of her full bottom lip. "She's been trying to handle some of Joe's business affairs since he's been missing, and some of those meetings can go on for hours. Why don't you stay, if you don't mind?"

"Sure."

Lindsey moved closer and eased her head against my chest. The softness of her hair as it brushed against my cheek was like silk on sandpaper.

"Why don't you go to the den and start a fire, while I change out of this dress and heels?" I told her that sounded like a fine idea and kissed the top of her blonde head.

~ * ~

Blue and gold flames danced before my eyes as I stared into the fire. Dreams wandered across the wasteland of my mind. Lindsey snuggled in against my side, soft and warm. Her fingers pressed against mine.

"This is nice," she murmured drowsily into my chest.

"Sure is." I was so comfortable it was a strain to talk.

"Today was wonderful."

"Wonderful barely hints at a proper description."

"Well, isn't this a cozy scene?"

Allison's voice cut through the romantic atmosphere like a razor blade through overripe fruit. Intent on our own thoughts, neither of us had heard her come into the room. Lindsey half jumped off the couch as I felt my body involuntarily stiffen.

"My goodness, Allison, you scared the daylights out of me." Lindsey twisted her body and turned her face toward her sister.

"You two look quite romantic snuggled up before the fire."

The words were a statement, a statement with a bite. I glanced at Lindsey. A faint blush had formed on her white neck and extended to her cheeks. I couldn't imagine her ever being successful at poker.

Silence invaded the room, bringing with it a certain tension. I formed the impression that Allison Grant was very much on edge. Lindsey squeezed my knee, an action I took as a warning to hold myself in check. A fleeting thought that there had been similar moments in the past involving these two zipped across my mind. Lindsey seemed to tense and grow more rigid as the silent seconds ticked.

Then Allison broke into a funny, depreciating laugh and walked slowly across the room to look out the tall, thin window. It framed her well as she peered into the inky blackness. I wondered what she was seeing.

"Sorry, it has just been one of those days. Long bastard of a meeting and then traffic was pure hell all the way home. Some fool absolutely pulled out in front of us about Algonquin. Must have been drunk. It was all the cabbie could do to miss him. God, I need a drink! Where is Juanita?"

She turned from the window and strode back across the room, her heels clicking firmly on the polished wooden floors. Her body seemed to strain against the blue serge suit that encased it.

"Juanita! Juanita!"

It was a long, tense minute until the rather plump, middle-aged maid arrived. She was slightly out of breath and paused just inside the door to gather herself.

"Juanita, bring me a rum and Coke. Easy on the Coke. Lindsey? Frank? What will you have?"

"I'll have the same, but please go easy on the rum," Lindsey said.

"Coffee, please. Instant is fine."

"Are you sure? That's not much of a drink." Allison's voice seemed to cast doubt on my manhood.

"I'm sure. I'm a touch low on caffeine right now."

She shrugged her padded shoulders. Her breasts rose and fell with the movement.

"Okay. To each his own poison. Bring the drinks right away, Juanita." She dismissed the maid with a nod of her head. Juanita scurried away on thin brown legs, putting me in mind of a chubby robin chasing after a bug.

Allison came across the room to stand in front of the fire and turned to face us. In the shadows cast by the flickering flames, she was indisputably a beautiful woman.

I thought she also looked like a troubled one. She opened her mouth, but paused, before shutting it again without speaking. A moment later, she turned her eyes to the fire. She placed one hand against the rough cut stones that formed the fireplace and leaned her weight on that arm. Whether she did this for warmth or support I wasn't certain; it struck me as a slightly mannered pose.

Time seemed to move carefully and slowly within its allotted parameters. The clock inside my mind loudly ticked off the seconds. Lindsey stirred uncomfortably on the couch. Once, she cleared her throat, but didn't speak. In a moment she scooted toward me and took my right hand in her left. Only the crackle and pop of the fires broke the silence in the room.

It was an unpleasant wait until Juanita's footsteps could be heard coming down the hall. She balanced a silver tray dotted with our drinks before her. She served the ladies first. Steam still rose from the lip of my cup. The pattern I recognized as Billingsley Rose. I stood to take my cup from the tray, then sat on the arm of the couch.

"Thank you, Juanita, that will be all for now." Allison's voice sounded clear, hard. The maid turned and quietly left the room. Perched precariously on the couch arm, I sipped coffee. It was strong and, for instant, surprisingly full-flavored.

"Hard day, Allison?" Lindsey's voice was low and soothing. She was behind me now. Since I couldn't see her anymore, I lowered my eyes to experience her world, if only for a moment.

"God, babe, they are all hard right now. I miss Joe more every day. This not hearing anything is killing me."

"Want to talk about today?"

"No, it was only business. Joe has a lot of projects going on all at once. It's so difficult to keep them all straight."

I kept my eyes closed, heard her sigh, but had to imagine the rise and fall of her shoulders. It was definitely a different sensation. Maybe it was my imagination, but I seemed to be gathering more of the sounds around me. The crack and pop of the fire seemed to have instantly increased threefold in volume.

I had a question of my own. "Any of the business have to do with Tony D'Angelo?"

A quick "No." Then, a half second later, "Why?"

Probably just my imagination, but something in her voice made me think she already knew the answer to the question. I took a sip of coffee to give myself time to think what words I wanted to say. I took a small comfort in the aroma.

"Like I told you before, my investigation reveals he's a man who has a number of business dealings with your husband."

"What sort of dealings?"

"From what I've found out, they've formed a partnership. One that develops projects, if you will. Apparently your husband has good connections and the brains to put them to use. He gets a line on a project the city or another developer is planning, then figures out a way to get a piece of the action."

She must have moved away from me, for when her voice came it sounded fainter, more distant, as if she were across the room. "Where does this Mr. D'Angelo come into the picture?"

"He seems to supply a significant percentage of the working capital. Was hoping you might be able to tell me a good deal more about both Mr. D'Angelo and these projects."

I heard the rustle of her clothes as Lindsey shifted on the couch. I took another sip of my coffee. It was cooling rapidly.

"I'm sorry, Frank, but Joe really keeps me in the dark about his business dealings."

A log popped with extra vigor in the fireplace. The sound startled me and my arm jerked. I could sense the coffee sloshing inside my cup. I opened my eyes and glanced at Allison.

Allison Grant met my gaze with one of her own, or one she remembered from some play. Her perfect blue eyes were clear, and utterly without guile, the look on her face was as innocent as a newborn would wear. I reminded myself that she was an actress, and that lots of women who weren't actresses were very good at keeping dirty family linen hidden.

Lindsey's left hand pressed against my back. I could feel it moving up and down, gently massaging my flesh through my clothes. There was a surprising strength in those slender fingers.

"That's too bad," I said, as I tried to penetrate the mask that always seemed to be in place before the face of Allison Grant.

Blue-shadowed eyelids tightened marginally. "Why is that too bad?" She sounded like the television hostess she'd once been, interviewing some poor schmuck.

"I've stumbled across certain indications that in recent months your husband made some business decisions that cost D'Angelo a considerable sum of money."

"You mean one of their business deals didn't pan out? Really Frank, in business that happens all the time."

She gave me a smile that made me feel like she was a member of a very select club.

"To be honest about it, I do know that Joe made some rather, shall we say, bold investments in the past, and that not all of them panned out. Surely anybody in business must realize that there are no sure things. Any deal could go sour for a number of reasons. Don't see why you are so interested in this one project that didn't make it."

"It is not quite that way. The project is making it, and making it big. From what I can learn, and I'll admit that not all my sources are disinterested parties, it seems that D'Angelo and your husband were supposed to be partners on this one. D'Angelo spent big-time bucks on the groundwork, but then your husband cut a deal with somebody else for the lion's share of the deal."

I studied her face, and learned nothing. I shrugged and said, "So D'Angelo spends a lot of money and now has a challenge just recouping his expenses, let alone realizing the profit he was planning on."

Skin tightened over her cheekbones. Tiny patches of white stood out on either side of her nose. One dangling silver earring twisted in response to an imperceptible movement of her head.

"You don't think he's done something to Joe, do you?"

I felt Lindsey's hand stiffen, then flutter spasmodically against my back. The tension that lay coiled around the room seemed to tighten a notch.

"No, I don't. From what I can gather, Mr. D'Angelo is simply extremely interested in Joe's whereabouts, at least for the moment. My guess is he wants to collect on the debt he feels Joe owes him."

Allison didn't respond. Inside my mind, I could hear the clock ticking again. I started to count. When I got to twenty-six, she slowly turned and stared into the fire. Two minutes later Lindsey and I left the room, hand in hand. If Allison noticed us leaving, she didn't say a word. She simply kept staring resolutely into the dancing flames as if they held a special message for her.

Thirty-five

Sleet popping against my bedroom window, woke me the next morning. The fast-moving front promised by the forecasters had arrived on schedule. Lindsey's image drifted across my mind. For the first time in years my battered brain seemed empty. Unfamiliar pangs of loneliness tweaked at my heart. Mixed in were a few pangs of guilt. There had been no one since Mona. I wondered if I was ready.

I curled up and debated with myself whether to get up and do my run now or wait until later and see if the weather cleared. Sleet battered more urgently against the glass as the morning aged, and waiting was ahead on points when the telephone jangled on my rattan bedside table. I grabbed the receiver, knocking over the long-faced Baby Ben in the process.

"Hello."

"Good morning, Frank Quick." Allison Grant's mellow tones were soothing.

"Morning."

She chuckled. Yes, maybe we had just better start with 'morning' today. I don't know that good is particularly apropos. "Have you looked outside?"

"Yeah, the sleet woke me earlier."

"Lousy weather. Nearly as lousy as my mood last night. That's one of the reasons I called, to apologize for last night. I'm sorry, it was a long hard day and your news really hit me hard. I just kind of went inside myself. Do that sometimes when I'm under a lot of stress. I didn't even see you and Lindsey leave."

"No problem. Believe me, I understand about rough days, and nights."

"Thanks. The other reason I called is related. At least it has something to do with this lousy weather and, to be honest, my lousy moods."

I propped myself up on one elbow. "What do you mean?"

"Well, I got to thinking how cool the weather had been and the forecast was only for colder and nastier and I knew how much strain we've all been under the past few days." She paused, as though uncertain how to proceed.

"Yes?"

"And I decided that we all needed to get away for a few days. You know, a change of scenery."

"Get away to where?"

"Jamaica." Allison put a lot of self-pride in the word, as though she had discovered the island herself.

"Jamaica?"

"Yes. I have a friend who owns a travel agency. She got us the most wonderful deal. Just a quick break, you understand. Three days and two nights at this very elegant, very private club outside of Kingston. Naturally, I'll cover all the costs."

"What about finding your husband?"

"From what you say, things are at a standstill right now. Maybe we're all just too close to the picture. It used to happen to me when I was in a movie. I'd get so involved in the filming, the actual production, that I'd lose track of how I really wanted to bring the role to life. I'd have to force myself to step back and rediscover my character. So, it occurred to me that if we were to step away for a day or two and relax, then look at everything with fresh eyes, one of us, probably you, might well come up with a more productive approach."

Her voice sank to a conspiratorial whisper. "Besides that, Frank, I'm beginning to get worried about Lindsey."

"Worried about Lindsey?" I sounded like a parrot. "Worried in what way?"

"You've only known her for a few days, so there is no way for you to judge, but she hasn't been the same girl since the day Joe turned up missing."

The sleet, which had abated, pounded against the window panes with renewed vigor. It sounded like some small animal desperate to gain entry. Suddenly it seemed to be inside my skull, battering furiously at my brain. Concentration was difficult.

"How is she different?"

Allison didn't respond immediately. Perhaps it was too much fancy thinking, but I had the sense that she was being careful about how she formed her response, as though she didn't want to upset me.

"She just hasn't been herself. Her appetite has been off, her moods have been much more somber, she's kept very quiet and very much to herself. Her entire personality has suddenly become introspective, as though she were under a great deal of strain. I keep getting the feeling she is keeping something bottled up and if she doesn't release some tension soon she will simply explode. I don't mind admitting to you, Frank, I'm very concerned about Lindsey."

"What about yourself?"

"Sure, what girl couldn't use a couple of carefree days in the sun and sands of Jamaica?"

Allison's voice sounded exactly like the voice-over on a commercial that had been running on the tube the last few weeks. I smiled to myself...she was good enough to do it herself. Then I realized she probably had.

"Why don't you two go and I'll stay here and keep working."

"No way, big guy. A couple of ladies like us definitely need an escort. Besides, you've had a few pretty stressful days yourself, and I know it would mean so much to Lindsey. What do you say? Reggae?"

"Reggae, baby!" I chuckled at my own foolishness as I listened to Allison giving me the details of our trip. Sleet still pounded against my window, only now there seemed to be a pattern to the pounding, and a message in it for me. But I wasn't sharp enough to discern it.

Thirty-six

Sunlight glinted off the wing of the jet as I peered out the elongated oval window, blinding me for a second. I averted my gaze, closed my eyes, then watched dozens of pinpricks of light dance against the insides of my eyelids. After the gray, fog-laden skies I'd left behind, all the sunlight seemed strange. I felt as though I were playing hopscotch with the seasons, jumping directly from the sleet and snow of winter to the sunlight and warmth of summer. Spring had been completely passed by.

Lindsey was in the aisle seat beside me, half-curled into a ball, twisted so she was facing me. Her golden head was on my shoulder, and when I turned my head from the window her hair brushed against my face as softly as the fronds of the green ferns my Aunt Enid kept in huge, twin clay pots on either side of her porch steps in Columbus, Ohio. As a boy I'd spent several summer vacations there. As a man I'd watched her die slowly of the cancer that ate away her liver. I wondered if anyone still tended the ferns?

Lindsey made animal sounds in her sleep and snuggled closer to my side. Her perfume smelled faintly of lilacs and hinted at midnights.

Her breath came in soft little puffs. Always a lady, even in her sleep. A stray stand of hair had fallen across her forehead, and I took one finger and gently pulled it back into place.

I was amazed that she could sleep. We were flying a charter full of happy souls going on vacation, all looking forward to sun and fun. They'd begun to celebrate their furloughs from the working world as soon as they hit the cabin door, and hadn't stopped since.

The stewardesses had sold an impressive number of miniature bottles of whiskey and rum. A large young man sitting across the aisle from Lindsey, sporting blue sunglasses that hung from a yellow string around his neck, was well on his way to polluted. A trio of empties stood at parade rest atop his pull down tray.

Out of the corner of my right eye I could see his stubble covered face. In a loud voice he was sharing all the successes of his last vacation. According to him, he'd won several thousand dollars playing black at the roulette wheel at the Princess Casino in Freeport. He said he'd already been to the Bahamas twice, so he wanted to experience a different island this year. His goal was to hit all the islands in the Caribbean by the time he was thirty. This seemed to favorably impress the young lady to whom he was talking. She was having trouble keeping her hands off him. At the moment her left hand was running up and down his well-developed right forearm. From time to time she would pause her caressing long enough to palpitate his muscle, as though she were testing the meat before making a final decision to buy.

The plane did a long, slow bank to the left and started drifting downward. The captain turned on the "Fasten Seatbelts" and "No Smoking" signs and a tall, thin, dark-haired stewardess with great legs and a bored voice urged everyone to return to their seats and fasten their seatbelts. Lindsey stirred, then pressed her lips against my chest.

"Are we there?" Her voice was little-girl-lost.

"Approaching the airport now." The ground was coming up fast. Houses were visible and microscopic cars moved down miniature roads. Sunlight bathed Kingston and glinted off blue Caribbean waters.

"I'm so glad we're here," Lindsey said in my ear, her head propped on my shoulder, incoming sunlight caressing her skin. "That sun feels so good. Still, I wish Allison had come. She needed to get away for a couple of days in the worst kind of way." Her soft white right hand rubbed down the back of my roughened left hand.

"Said she would join us later, didn't she?"

"Yes. Something about a deal going through at the last minute and that it had to have her signature."

"Couldn't they have waited a couple of days?"

She shrugged, and I felt her breasts slide up and down against my chest.

"She hasn't really come out and said it, but I'm beginning to think their financial picture has not been so great of late. From what I gathered, this deal was important. Allison and Joe always lived well, but she hasn't done much in the way of a paying job in quite some time. I know I told you Allison and Joe were doing well, but, based on what I've overheard the past few days, I think a couple of Joe's big deals might have gone sour. And, now that I've been thinking about it, I suspect they have a cash flow problem, which is why Allison started doing commercials again, and accepted a part-time talk show gig."

The plane made a sharp turn left and increased the degree of descent. Cars looked nearly life-sized now and I could make out people instead of scurrying black dots. I tracked ancient scratches on the plastic window pane with my right index finger. "Does Joe gamble?"

Lindsey took a second to answer. With some people I'd have suspected they were formulating an evasive response. With Lindsey, I knew she was simply making sure she gave me a complete answer.

"Some, for sure. I really don't know how much. They've made a couple of trips to Las Vegas and one to Atlantic City in the last year, but I think that was more for the shows and to get out of town. I've also heard Joe mention his bookie a time or two." She paused as the ground rushed to meet us.

"They have had a couple of shouting matches about it. I didn't particularly want to hear, but you couldn't be in the house and not hear. They were both quite loud."

The wheels of the plane bumped once, then settled on the tarmac. Jet engines roared as the brakes engaged. Passengers began to stir restlessly in their seats, gathering their belongings, starting to stand. The stewardess with the bored voice was saying something about local time and temperature and wishing everyone a memorable stay in the islands.

Thirty-seven

They hustled us through customs and into the main terminal. We fell in line with our fellow passengers as a representative of the charter firm led us through the swirling crowd to our bus. As we crossed the main lobby of the terminal in a single bobbing, weaving line, I was struck by a boyhood memory of seeing a covey of quail scurrying across a highway. The birds had been anxious to get to the other side. Our fellow vacationers seemed excited about the promised sun-and-fun.

Lindsey squeezed my hand as we paraded across the tile floor. A pair of other airliners had recently disgorged their passengers and we had to pick our way through a substantial inflow. Reggae music playing over the loudspeaker competed for supremacy with the excited babble of humanity. I wondered how all the noise and excitement weren't overwhelming for Lindsey.

She seemed to be thinking along the same lines. "Isn't this exciting? I didn't figure on so many people."

"There is a good crowd, mostly tourists. Believe I heard them say our charter had fifty-five people. Look out!" I grabbed her arm and halted her as two young boys, about nine or ten, raced through our group. One was slightly taller and chased the other. They screamed with pent-up energy. I didn't envy their parents.

The charter people were taking care of the baggage as Lindsey and I scurried to catch up with the group. A short blonde with blue-tinted sunglasses directed us with a clipboard as we popped out the door. After the muted light of the terminal, the full sunshine nearly blinded me for a moment. Hand in hand, Lindsey and I stumbled down the sidewalk toward the red and gold bus with *Island Tours* scripted in white paint across the side.

We were behind a middle-aged couple dressed in jeans and checkered shirts of blue, green, and red. The jeans flattered neither of them. The man lugged a black carry-on bag and complained how heavy it was. He made some comment about wanting to know what was in there and she told him that she was paying for this vacation and he could just shut up and carry the damn bag.

Our bus was parked in the middle of a half-moon pull-in that broke off from the main road as it curved in front of the terminal. A soft breeze accompanied the sun and blew gently through flower beds containing brilliant red flowers that were foreign to me. From its hiding place in one of the thickly branched trees that stood between the sidewalk and the terminal, an unseen bird fussed at us. Reggae spilled from the speakers mounted on the walls of the building. Traffic was light on the road to our right and the temperature was mild. I was with a beautiful, sensitive, passionate woman and the islands seemed very nice. Joe Dubronski was nothing more than a nagging pinprick at the very back of my mind. Perhaps Allison had been right, after all.

Lindsey squeezed my hand and flashed me a brilliant smile and Old Frank felt just about as happy as he ever had in his life. In a white silk blouse and navy skirt that hung just a couple of inches below her knees, Lindsey looked smart and sophisticated. Swelling like hidden fruit, her breasts pushed against their silken stricture.

There was a flurry of confused sounds off to my right near the building. I didn't pay much attention to them as Lindsey was saying something about the island breezes being wonderful.

Suddenly, she coughed, a short, funny little cough, and an expression of the utmost surprise covered her face.

She stumbled against me and I had to catch her to keep her from falling. She was heavy and awkward in my arms. Her legs no longer seemed capable of supporting her weight. My right hand, tight against her rib cage, felt sticky and wet.

I looked down and saw that it was bright with blood. The whole right side of her blouse was turning crimson. Her lips were parted, but no words came.

Behind me a woman screamed and I turned with Lindsey in my arms. Between two gaudily painted buses were three gunmen. Two were black men, who I figured for natives. The third, I didn't have to guess about. His flat expressionless face needed no re-introduction. I blinked and looked again. It was like a nightmare that wouldn't quit.

In their hands the guns looked huge. The crowd, its carnival atmosphere shattered, parted before them like the Red Sea before Moses and his staff. I couldn't move quickly with Lindsey in my arms and she couldn't go anywhere without me. Desperation fueled my muscles and I half-drug, half-carried her toward a baggage cart piled high with suitcases and golf bags.

Like giant firecrackers, guns went off behind me. A bullet screamed by my ear, its song heavier than the island breezes. It was a song of death and forever. I was trying to shelter Lindsey's body with my own, but I felt her jerk as another bullet found its mark. I couldn't tell where and I didn't dare stop to look.

The cart was still ten feet away. A poor little grandmotherly type stood frozen in my path. I tried to dodge her on the run, but Lindsey was awkward in my arms and I stumbled into the woman, knocking her to the ground. The impact, combined with the slickness of Lindsey's blood on my hands, almost tore her from my grip. I paused to regain my hold and felt a slug smash into my left thigh. The force tore my legs out from under me and we fell heavily, awkwardly, to the sidewalk. Blood and blackness washed across my eyes in waves.

Screams filled my ears. Airport security was missing in action. Slipping in our own blood, I scooted down the sidewalk, dragging Lindsey toward the baggage cart, now only five feet away.

The gunmen pushed their way through the stampeded crowd. Lindsey jerked as another shot struck home. Its cousin crashed into my left shoulder and my body was on fire.

My injured arm was useless and I couldn't hold Lindsey with one blood-slickened hand. A bullet singed my belly and for a moment I was conscious only of a burning pain. Lindsey's face swam up to me from the concrete. Her darkened glasses lay smashed and broken. Her sightless eyes seemed to plead with me for help.

I pressed my right hand against her cheek. When I pulled it back, it left my bloody fingerprints. From somewhere, I summoned the strength to raise her head and kiss her lips. Still another slug tore into her, twisting her beneath me. Blood bubbled up through her throat and smeared our lips.

"God Damn! Stop!" I screamed. My god, why wouldn't they stop shooting!

The rising-falling wail of a police siren rose in the distance.

Inches above my head a giant bird circled.

Slowly the bird turned into a shadow.

Then the shadow turned into Al's flat face.

I tried to curse him, but could only manage a "damn you" that sounded weak and pathetic even to my ears.

He was so close I could reach out and touch him, so I did. He shook off my ineffectual grip like a giant tossing aside a child. Al had a most peculiar expression on his face. To my pain-distorted mind, he looked seriously puzzled. I wondered what the hell was wrong with him. Lindsey and I were the ones who were dying.

"Quick?" To my battered ears his voice sounded incredulous.

My blood pounded in my ears and stained the Jamaican sidewalk. Reggae music still poured forth incongruously from the speakers attached to the outside of the terminal. I wanted to tell Al to go fuck himself, but couldn't summon the strength.

"You're not Dubronski. You're supposed to be Dubronski. Why the fuck aren't you Dubronski?"

He was screaming now, anger lifting his voice. I couldn't make sense of it, couldn't figure out why he was mad. Hell, I was the one who'd been shot.

"She's not Allison Grant, either, is she? Goddamn! Goddamn! Nothing is right, freaking nothing at all. The whole damn thing's a setup. Shit, shit, shit."

Al's words seemed to hover in the air above me. I kept getting them all mixed up with that huge shadow that wanted to be a bird. I could feel my life seeping out of my body as the shadow bird rose directly above me and blocked out the sun.

Thirty-eight

As though from far off, I could hear the swirling of a great confluence of water, while close to me I could hear the precise drip, drip, drip of liquid as it fell from a high place. All that water put me in mind of a hidden spring I'd discovered by accident as a boy hiking the Appalachian Trail.

That day had been hot and steamy, with a full summer sun beating down without remorse. Along in the dead of the afternoon, about three o'clock, I'd given up hiking and gone to lie down in the promising shade of a white pine. The shady spot hadn't been as cool as it had looked, but at least I was out of the direct sunlight—a blessing in and of itself.

I'd taken off my shoes and socks and laid aside my pack and replica French Foreign Legion cap, and soon began to feel less queasy. Under the pine, the air was still, merely a breath of breeze occasionally whispering through the uppermost branches, and quite warm. Amid the stifling silence of the afternoon, drowsiness overtook me and I drifted toward sleep.

However, in that fluid moment, seconds before I crossed the final valley into sleep, I heard a faint drip, drip, drip of water. I'd listened, suddenly alert, for I was very thirsty and my canteen was perilously close to dry.

In a minute I'd fixed the position of the drip—below me in an outcropping of limestone, a few yards off the trail on the sloping side of the ridge. It took five minutes of crawling through climbing vines, choking weeks, and thorny brambles to get there.

I could still taste that clean, cool water. This current drip sounded much like that earlier one and I longed to go find the spring, but I couldn't make my legs move. Which made me quite angry.

Once I felt a soft, feathery touch and wondered if it was the giant bird that kept blocking out the sun from me. If it was, it was very gentle. All feathers and down, with no talons or sharp beak.

From time to time an unsummoned reggae beat popped up inside my head. I felt the urge to dance, but there was no one to dance with me. I sensed other dancers moving on the floor, just beyond my field of vision, and I tried to call to them, but my tongue seemed thick and heavy, dry as an old Conestoga wagon that had lain abandoned in the desert for a hundred years.

I missed Lindsey suddenly, incredibly. Her name was on my lips, but my throat rasped like sandpaper and I was forced to be content with silence. I couldn't figure out where she was and I began to worry.

Worrying seemed to make me extraordinarily hot and I felt sweat begin to form. Soon, sweat ran off my body until I was certain that beneath my skin I was as dry as a mummy in his wrappings deep in an Egyptian pharaoh's tomb.

A sharp pain jabbed my arm and a silent golden circle formed inside my skull. I existed, that was all. No thinking, talking, dreaming—merely existing just this side of a great, rushing light.

~ * ~

It was very dark. My eyes were open, but it was very dark. Gradually my eyes came into focus and I could see the room was not totally without light.

Tiny light slivers formed vertical strips in the blackness as though some giant had taken his knife and cut slits in the soul of darkness. For what seemed like halfway to forever, I lay perfectly still and quiet, watching the thin grooves of light.

It was so quiet I could hear myself breathe. Once I even thought I could hear my brain working inside my skull, flapping gently like some old worn conveyor belt as it pulled information through the system.

The silence in the room seemed to be so fragile I was afraid if I even whispered the entire world would shatter. So I lay, unmoving and silent as concrete. Without my noticing, sleep slipped into the room and I drifted into the blackness

~ * ~

The next time I awoke, the room was much lighter. My vision was clear, and I could see two men sitting in cracked brown leather chairs. The man closest to me was white, with a neatly trimmed mustache the same light brown color as his carefully groomed hair. He wore a tan blazer over a white shirt that was open at the top. The blazer bulged under the left arm. Something about him, perhaps his attitude, said American.

The other man, large and dark, fit my concept of a Jamaican. His broad brow, long sturdy limbs, and skin as black as the inside of a huge, cast-iron kettle gave him an air of authority. He wore white duck pants, a multicolored shirt with an indecipherable pattern of swirls and connecting lines. A white linen jacket lay across one arm of his chair. He sat upright, as though he didn't want his back to touch the chair.

I figured them both for law enforcement. I wondered if they were there to protect me, or to make sure I didn't get out of bed and totter off. Neither possibility satisfied. I started to sit up, but a sheet of pain tore through my body and I fell back, moaning like a wounded animal.

Sweat broke out on my face as I turned my head on the pillow. The white man watched me from his chair. Blue eyes, gleaming like polished marbles, were set deeply in a small, well-formed face. I had the eerie sensation that those eyes could see right through my skin. A small pale scar puckered the flesh at the edge of his right eyebrow. The man seemed to change position without obvious movement, always bringing his face more directly into line with mine. I found myself hoping he was here to protect, and not to persecute.

"Awake are we, Mr. Quick?" He ran the palm of his right hand over his mustache. "It is Mr. Quick, isn't it? Mr. Frank Quick?"

I tried to say "Yes," but the syllable sounded like the last croak of a dying frog. I nodded my head and that was worse. A giant bell began tolling inside my skull. Pinpoints of light danced in front of my eyes, so I shut them and kept my head motionless on my pillow. Appeared my rock-and-roll days were over forever.

"Good, we were almost certain." He noticed the question forming in my eyes. "Your billfold, Mr. Quick, we took the liberty. Didn't think you would mind. All kinds of nice identification. Then, just to make sure, we checked your fingerprints."

"Thorough," was all I could rasp out.

"Yes, well, we had to be, you see." He looked American and his accent was mid-western, Iowa or Minnesota, that slice of geography, but his phrasing and mannerisms were out of sync with the rest of the image; linguistically, almost British. Which made me wonder if he was a diplomat, rather than the policeman I'd first projected. However, the bulge inside his sport coat belied that notion. Maybe he was a diplomatic policeman.

"Why?"

"Because, you being a foreigner and gunned down on Jamaican soil, we had to quickly establish with whom we were dealing."

The image of Lindsey's bright red blood soaking her white blouse flashed across the screen of my mind like a subliminal message. "What about...?" The question trailed off my lips, a whisper fading in the wind at dusk. I couldn't bring myself to say her name.

He knew where I was headed and gave me his version of a sympathy smile. "Your companion, Ms. Grant?"

I nodded, carefully.

"I'm sorry. She didn't make it."

Hot tears stung my eyes and I turned my face into the pillow. I kept my head turned for a very long time. I hoped the two men would be gone when I looked again, but they were still there. The white man leaned forward, his left elbow on his left knee, his chin in his cupped left hand.

"You were lucky to make it yourself."

"Really?" I felt like hell and knew I'd been out for quite a while and undoubtedly had lost some blood, but, judging by my bandages and the location of my wounds, I didn't see how the damage was life threatening.

"Really. According to witnesses, the gunman put his gun to your head, but for some reason he never pulled the trigger. At least the gun wouldn't fire. Weapon might have jammed. Never liked those machine pistols myself, especially the cheap crap you pick up on the islands."

He studied me intently, then grinned. "You are one lucky mother." He suddenly seemed to be as tired of the phony diplomatic charade as I was. I liked him much better as a good-old-everyday American Joe.

I didn't really know what to say; doubted if I could say much of anything—not with the lump in my throat. Simply thinking about Lindsey being dead made my head and heart ache. I expelled a non-committal grunt and closed my eyes. The hospital room seemed to be spinning, along with the rest of the world. Lindsey was gone and nothing else much the fuck mattered.

"Seemed to upset the old boy when he saw your face. Did you recognize him?"

Since I didn't know where the man with the blue marble eyes was headed, I merely shrugged.

"Might help us locate him if we had a name."

"Think he's still on the island?"

The white man reached down into the inside pocket of his blazer, extricated out a toothpick and stuck it in his mouth. I glanced at his partner. Only his black eyes glowed like two live coals. I hadn't the first clue what the man was thinking.

"Don't know." Marble-eyes paused to consider either the question or his answer. "No evidence, but I don't think he is, although his accomplices may be. Anyway, it doesn't matter where he is, there are several people who would like to track him down."

"Such as?"

His turn to shrug. "Why don't you help us?"

He waited for me to respond. I had nothing to say.

"You must know who he is. He said your name."

"He did?"

"Yeah. Seemed like it pissed him off mightily when he discovered it was you. At least that was the impression our witnesses formed. Was he expecting someone else?"

"How the hell should I know?" Now the nightmare was flowing back to me, carrying with it the memory of Al seeming very surprised to find the man he'd shot was me.

Certain aspects of that awful morning were still hazy, but one thing reverberated as clearly as a church bell on Christmas morning. Without warning, a stray gray bird of a thought soared the currents to the ionosphere of my mind and, between one breath and the next, I distinctly remembered Allison insisting I wear a bright yellow and blue shirt that belonged to Joe. His "lucky island" shirt, she had called it.

A lot of notions, probably all of them wild and crazy, were running like barbarians down the corridors of my mind. Arguably, I should have shared them with the policeman, or whatever he was, but I was out of my territory and I didn't know him. Trust, like love, had to be earned.

"Sorry, but my head hurts like hell and I'm more than a little tired. So, if we could maybe do this later?" I gave him a weak smile and turned my face against the pillow.

For a long time, I could see Lindsey's face imprinted on the wall of my mind. Then it was joined by Allison's. They metamorphosed into one and thick red blood bubbled brightly from between its parted lips. When I woke, I was drenched in sweat and the room was dark. A large black nurse with gentle hands dabbed at my face with a sponge. Both men were gone.

Thirty-nine

Boredom had begun to set in by the next morning. There was no television in my hospital room, no newspaper, no magazines. My stitches had begun to itch and I found my own company depressing. I kept thinking about Lindsey and how happy she had been as we got off the plane. And how she would never smile that special little smile for me again. And how I would never again kiss those soft lips or feel the warm, smooth touch of her hand.

After a while, I thought about Mona, and suddenly life was too much with me and I wanted to cry, but I'm a big boy now and big boys don't cry. At least that's what I kept telling myself.

About two o'clock in the afternoon, a young doctor, accompanied by an unsmiling nurse, paid me a visit. He took my temperature, checked my pulse, gently examined my wounds, and studied my charts. Finally, he looked up and stared into my eyes. I found his bedside manner a little disconcerting.

"Something wrong, doctor?"

"No, no. Quite the contrary. You seem to be progressing very well, Mr. Quick."

"Good. You seemed to take a long time looking at my chart. Was concerned something might be wrong."

"Not at all. Yesterday, you had a fever, but none today. Already, your body has begun to heal."

"How long before I can get out of here?"

He didn't answer, but ran a slender finger up and down the bridge of his long nose. He wasn't white, but he wasn't black either. More of a light tan, with facial features similar to those I'd noticed belonging to the Norwegian ski jump team at the last winter Olympics.

"My answer depends somewhat on what you plan to do when you are released."

"Haven't gotten that far yet with my thinking. First thing is to see about my friend's…" I'd planned on saying "body," but the word stuck like a fishbone in my throat.

"Your friend has been flown home for burial."

"When? Who claimed the body?"

The surprise in my voice registered in his eyes. "They came two days ago. You weren't conscious. An aunt and uncle. From Iowa, someone said. Forget the name of the town. Perhaps it was Dubuque." He gave the word a French twist.

"She has a sister, what about her?"

"I do not know. Perhaps the authorities were unable to contact her."

My thoughts were black as a moonless Jamaican night. "When will I be released?" was all I said.

The young doctor merely smiled at me and shook his head.

Forty

About noon the next day, the same unsmiling nurse returned. I'd been alone with my thoughts throughout the night and morning. Except for an orderly who brought me a late breakfast and a brief visit from the night nurse, it was as though I'd been in solitary confinement. Anyway, I was glad to see a familiar face, even one as unsmiling as hers.

"Where's your buddy?"

"You mean Dr. Robinson?" Her hands moved smoothly along my bandages. Her voice was accented with the lilt of the islands.

"Yes. Is he going to pay me a visit today?"

"Perhaps later. He had some unexpected surgeries today, so who can say." She shrugged. Inside the white uniform, her big body was firm.

"Anyway, your condition is much improved." Her gentle hands paused at their work. For the first time on either visit, she looked directly into my eyes. Her skin put me in mind of vulcanized rubber stretched across the flat planes of her face. Her chin looked as big and hard as a man's fist. She struck me as a formidable woman with something on her mind. I asked her a question with my eyes.

Her strong fingers were gentle as they pulled the IV from my hand. "Forgive me for being personal, Mr. Quick, but did you know that when you leave officers of the law will be watching you very closely?"

"Why do you say that?"

Her head was bent over her work and I could see ridges of muscle where her neck merged with her shoulders. At some point in her life, she had known hard, heavy work. When she spoke, her voice was so low I had to strain to hear her words.

"I overheard your countryman talking to Dr. Robinson. He told the doctor he thinks you know much more about the shooting than you are telling. He made it clear you would be watched."

"Why are you telling me this?"

She looked up, the IV tube dangling unnoticed from her fingers. "Your lady, she was very young?" I nodded. "And very beautiful?" I nodded again.

"The policeman, he joked about her."

"Joked about her? What do you mean?"

"She was blind, no?"

"Yes."

"He said she never knew what hit her, couldn't see what was coming. He said he supposed a blind piece was better than no piece at all. He laughed at her," she paused, "and you."

"Me?"

"Yes. He said if you were there to protect her, she would have been better off with a seeing-eye dog."

Hot anger, tempered with a hint of the shame of failure, flashed through me. "Did the doctor laugh too?"

"No. He threw the policeman out."

Forty-one

Four long days later they set me free.

The tour company Lindsey and I had been with offered me a room for as long as I wanted it. That seemed generous, but they probably figured having their tour members shot and killed wasn't particularly good for business.

I told them not to worry—I wouldn't be suing them, and thanks, but no thanks. All I wanted was to get home. Certain matters there needed my most personal attention.

I spent one final night in Jamaica, staying at the Queen of the Coast, ordering grilled swordfish via room service. Everyone was friendly and the service was first-rate. My room had a splendid view of the ocean and the sheets were clean, starched, and white as the snow that never fell here. If the police wanted to watch me, they were welcome to have at it. I found the situation infinitely sad.

I gave a brief thought to going to the bar after supper when I'd gotten some strength up and listening to a little reggae. Even washed my face and put on a clean shirt. Then, it seemed as if the whole effort was simply too much. Maybe I wasn't as fully recovered as I'd thought, but the weakness seemed to me to be as much of the will as of the flesh. I slipped off my shoes and lay across the pink and yellow polyester bedspread. I lay there, watching the lights of the city invade my room, allowing the brain waves to smooth out. The last of the White Jamaicans all alone in his hotel room. All alone in an island paradise. All alone in hell.

~ * ~

I awoke to morning sunlight streaming brazenly through the window. Lindsey's name was on my lips and my eyes were suspiciously damp. I'd slept uninterrupted for ten hours and the rest had done me good. I eased out of bed, washed my face, and brushed my teeth.

I still had on the clothes I'd planned to wear the night before, but I didn't bother to change. I took the elevator to the lobby and caught a cab to the police station. I'd given them an official statement the day before, but they had a typed version for me to sign and a few more questions to answer; the whole process took about twenty minutes. After that, I went straight back to the hotel and checked out. The same cab I'd used to go to the substation took me and a fat lady in a loud orange and yellow print dress to the airport.

Forty-two

The cab crawled to a stop and let me off in front of my brownstone. The day was overcast and cool, with a hint of rain. Already, I missed the Jamaican sunshine.

The cabby was short and dark, with thick glasses held together on one side with adhesive tape. He was also wonderfully silent, a trait for which I was grateful. Outside of "Where to?" when I got in, he hadn't spoken a word. Even better, he hadn't played his radio. I welcomed the solitude and tipped him better than I otherwise would have. He set my bags on the curb and pulled away with a roar in his butter-yellow chariot, which sounded like it was developing a major hole in the muffler.

I slipped my flight pack over my shoulder and half-scooted, half-drug my suitcase inside the front door. Until I healed, it was far too heavy for me to lift. I left a note on it, promising ten bucks to the first neighbor who would bring it up, then hauled my weary self up the stairs.

The key hung in the lock for a second before it twisted, but the door swung open easily, too easily. In my absence, I'd had a visitor or two. Whomever had been there hadn't worried about the mess they left behind. Broken dishes and scraps of paper littered the kitchen. The door to the refrigerator stood wide open. Every shelf had been taken out, even the ice trays had been dumped. The inside of the couch and easy chair in the living room had been gutted.

The bedroom was even worse. My meager wardrobe was slung everywhere. The pockets of the pants were turned inside out, the linings of the jackets slit. All of the drawers were pulled out of the chest of drawers and turned upside down on the floor. The mattress had been pulled off the bed and ripped open.

I felt a wave of nausea wash over me, followed by a swell of anger. This had to be the work of Al or some of his honchos. Oh, it could have been burglars on a destruction binge, but I didn't think so. They'd have been more malicious, but less thorough. But what had Al, or whomever, been looking for? I had no important secrets, at least none that I knew, and certainly none on paper. Plus, they'd known where I was if they wanted to talk to me.

The anger passed and I felt my legs go weak and start to tremble. I pulled an undamaged blanket from a pile and spread it on the floor. I lay down slowly and with care, like a ninety-year-old man afraid of falling.

~ * ~

I was dreaming of clouds, great masses of purple and black thunderheads, building on the far western horizon. At first they were the height of skyscrapers, then mountains. Then they dwarfed even the highest peak. Still they kept building, higher and darker, until they merged and blotted out the sun and traveled above the earth like a threatening giant.

The giant loomed closer and closer until it was so close I could reach out and touch it. Nearer and nearer it came, until I felt it would suck the air from my lungs. I tried to twist and turn away, but I was trapped against a wall of stone. I choked back the rising scream of fear.

"Hey, man, wake up. Frank, what happened here? Man, oh man, somebody really trashed your place."

Without opening my eyes, I knew who it was. That voice could only belong to Debi. Company I could do without right now, especially her.

"What the hell are you doing here?"

"Hey, now. Is that a nice tone of voice to use on your old friend, Debi?"

She flipped the switch on the bedside lamp. Miraculously, unfortunately, the bulb had survived the trashing. Bright light, unencumbered by the shade, threatened to burn through to my brain.

"Wow! What happened to you? Damn, Frank, you look like death warmed over."

"Yeah, Debi, I feel like it too. Listen, don't want to hurt your feelings, but it is a long, sad story and I'm simply not up to it tonight. Do you mind just sliding back out the way you came? We can have this conversation another time."

"But I brought your suitcase up."

"Okay. Thanks. I'll give you the ten bucks."

"No, that's all right. Just did it to be friendly. I don't want money from you." Hurt stood out on her face like a smashed grape on a pure white Persian rug.

"Hey, I'm sorry. Didn't mean to hurt your feelings."

"Just shut up, Frank. I got the message. I'm going."

"No, listen. You don't have to go."

"Yes, I do, Frank. I really do."

I watched her step rapidly to the door. I knew I needed to say something—she'd only been trying to help—but I only lay there. Sometimes I really fuck things up. I sent her a silent apology, for whatever that was worth.

Forty-three

The physical body heals faster than the soul. A visit to my own doctor, some American food, and a few nights under my own roof, wreck though it might have been, did me a world of good.

It wasn't hard for the police to find out I'd been working for Allison Grant, so naturally they came around to see me. Not that I helped them much. Oh, I was sympathetic to their job and gave them all the detailed information I could on both Allison and one Joe Dubronski. Him, I was beginning to reclassify from a missing person to a figment of my imagination. But I couldn't tell them what they really wanted to know—which was exactly where Allison Grant was at present. Oh, I had an idea or two, but I didn't know, so I didn't tell. Besides, an insanely large urge to find the gorgeous Ms. Grant-Dubronski myself was blossoming inside my battered brain.

Allison, it seemed, was truly and totally gone. I'd been unaware that her talk show contract was up several months ago and she'd been continuing her duties under a series of thirty-day extensions. She hadn't bothered with the last extension offer and station management simply viewed her vanishing act as a ploy to get more money. Allison's ratings had been off noticeably the last two Arbitron's, and her temporary replacement was a younger, oriental woman with bigger breasts and longer legs. With her arrival, there had been an upswing in the overnight ratings. Suffice it to say the talk show executives were in no hurry for Allison to reappear.

Allison's friends were used to her sudden absences: trips to the West Coast, vacations in the Caribbean, photography shoots in the Colorado mountains, gambling junkets in Vegas.

I gathered, from checking with some of them, that she often stayed away for weeks at a time on these irregular trips. Her friends, at least the ones I talked with, were all deeply involved in their own lives. Whatever gaps Allison made in the fabric of their existence by her sudden absences were slight and soon mended. I formed the impression they would be no more than mildly shocked if she never returned. Certainly no one I talked to was organizing a search party.

In the end, I spent a long winter alone, recuperating physically, hanging on emotionally, and remembering—remembering the good times, and the bad. I also did a great deal of thinking, and a bit of planning.

It was a hard winter, a cold one. The only thing colder than the weather was my heart.

Forty-four

It was late February and the snow that covered the ground had a dirty, used look to it. I was standing by the living room window, thinking about Jamaica and watching the world pass when the phone rang. I jerked involuntarily—I hadn't gotten many phone calls lately—and went to answer it.

I picked up on the fourth ring. "Hello."

"Quick?"

"Yeah."

"You don't sound like yourself."

I didn't need to ask who was calling. Some voices you never forget.

"It's been a tough winter. Why the hell are you calling?"

"Heard you were feeling rough and thought you might like to hear a friendly voice."

"I don't ever need to hear your voice again."

"Now, is that anyway to talk to your old buddy, Al?"

"Why don't you do the world a favor, Al, and shoot your brains out?"

"And to think I called to tell you good-bye."

"So you are going to shoot yourself?"

"You're not funny, Quick. No, I'm leaving town and thought you'd like to know. Just in case you wanted to look me up sometime."

"That's an idea."

"Forget it."

"Where you going?"

"Don't worry, I'll get in touch with you if I need to."

"So why waste my time?"

Al cleared his throat. I could hear street traffic in the background, and now and then a snatch of a roving conversation as people passed by.

"Just passing along a little bit of info to my old partner."

I'd never been, and never would be Al's partner, but I let that slide. I wanted to hear what he had to say, not that it was likely to be important.

"Such as?"

"Such as the hit wasn't supposed to be you and the blind girl. We had good info that it was Dubronski and his wife. Tony D got the word himself, straight from a reliable source. I swear to God we thought it was them. Hell, you know I'd have never not finished a legit job. But when I seen it was you and not Dubronski, I didn't pull the trigger. You might say, in a certain way, you owe your being alive to me."

"And who the hell shot me in the first place?"

"Damn, Quick, I told you the hit was on Dubronski. Tony D had verified info that it was going to be them getting off that plane. You and your woman weren't in the picture. We never had nothing against you."

He paused, waiting for a response, I figured. Only I didn't have one to give him. I'd been wondering anyway and Al sounded like he was telling the truth, or as close to the truth as he was ever likely to get. In a way it made sense—Al wouldn't have had any reason to shoot me. I was the one who was looking hardest for Joe. But Tony D was a man who played all the angles—he'd have had others looking.

"Anyway, I wanted to let you know that, as far as I know, Joe's wife is still kicking. At least, she was last time I saw her."

I felt the adrenaline kick in. "And when was that?"

"At the airport, right after, well, you know. Now, I couldn't swear in court, but I'm ninety-nine, point nine percent sure it was her. See, I was getting ready to board my flight, and took a final look around, out of habit, you understand, and there she was—hot footing it across the concourse, as big as life. Only her hair was colored, see. Had kind of a reddish tint to it, see."

"Was she getting on or off a flight?"

"Off, I'd say. She was headed straight for baggage claim."

"Okay." I probably should have asked more questions, but my brain was whirling.

Maybe I zoned out for a minute, because the next thing I heard was Al's flat voice.

"No thanks necessary, but I figure we're square now."

"Not quite."

"Yeah, well some folks are hard to please. Anyway, here's a bit of news that will brighten your day, I'm sure."

"And what's that."

"Tony D has the big C. Bad. In the colon. Doctor's giving him six months, tops."

"Couldn't happen to a nicer jerk."

"You know, you're kind of a jerk yourself, Quick."

"Fuck you," I said, but I was only speaking to silence. Al was gone and I was back to being alone. Only now I possessed one more piece of the puzzle.

I stood there holding the phone, trying to make all the pieces fit smoothly, until the operator told me to hang up. Not every piece fit yet, but I was beginning to see the picture.

Forty-five

Six months after I sent Debi out into the night, I went out the front door myself, loaded my bag and body into the Yellow Cab 407 and rode through the blackness to the airport, where I got on Delta Flight 1089 and headed west. A couple of time zones and several hundred miles later, we touched down outside of Phoenix.

I stumbled down the ramp behind a fat lady with hair a color never found in nature. She had a large red boil on the back of her neck and the collar of her blouse rubbed against it with each agonizingly slow step. At the first opportunity, I double-stepped around her. She wore a most unhappy look on her face, for which I couldn't blame her.

The night baggage crew was fast and efficient. My single bag was waiting for me. I grabbed the canvas strap, slung it over my shoulder, and headed toward the Hertz counter. A bleary eyed clerk with bad breath and a woebegone air rented me a nearly new Ford Taurus with air, power steering, and anti-lock brakes. It was a nicer car than any I'd ever owned.

Soft, dry air drifted in off the desert and caressed my face as I strolled out the automatic door. Granted, it was tainted by the smog and smell of Phoenix and the surrounding urban sprawl that bordered on hideous. Still, it carried a breath of something wild and exotic. The trace of a promise hung in the air. I strolled west to meet it.

The road rolled north out of metropolitan Phoenix. I drove through Peoria, Sun City, El Mirage, and Hot Springs. Asphalt spread out under a full moon like the bare naked soul of a man on an earthen cross.

Rock, sagebrush, and cactus flowed by the window. Under the moonlight, their distorted shadows spread across the dull, brown, dusty landscape like seaweed on the ocean floor. The arms of the cactus seemed to wave at me as I blasted by. Only I didn't know if they were waving hello or goodbye.

I drove through the night under the full moon that bathed the sands in silver. As I left the lights of the city behind, stars began to appear. First, they came in ones and twos, then in sudden handfuls, as if a playful god had thrown a sack full of cotton balls across the black of the desert sky.

This patch of earth struck me as extraordinarily beautiful. It was also so quiet as to border on the silent. At sixty miles an hour the desert is an exceedingly quiet place. The whooshing of the car and the muffled hum of the engine drowned out the small cries of the living creatures of the sand and rocks.

Somewhere in the middle of the night, sleep began to overtake me. It had been a long, hard day, and I was a couple of time zones out of sync, traveling fast in a body that wasn't quite back to full strength. Sounds of wind and desert began to consolidate, meld. Cactus seemed to sway and dance before me. I eased the pressure on the accelerator and started to look for a place to pull over.

The sand directly adjacent to the road appeared to be packed solidly, but I didn't want to take any chances. Traffic was light along this stretch of road and it figured to be a hell of a long way to help. I slowed even more and actively looked for a safe pull-off.

Even at reduced speed, I almost missed my opportunity. In the daylight I'd have seen the building easily, but at night it was a different story. The long, low, ramshackle wooden *Trading Post* sat about thirty yards off the road and, solely because I was looking for something like it, I caught a glimpse of the main building at the edge of my peripheral vision and hit the brakes hard.

Still, I slid forty yards past it and had to make a cautious U-turn in the road. I rolled back slowly and this time saw the crushed gravel driveway that led off the highway. I eased around a couple of giant potholes, but the drive was basically firm. I pulled up alongside the front porch of the wooden building and killed the engine.

A rail, for the cowboys and pseudo-cowboys of bygone days to rest their boot heels on, ran along the front of the wooden-planked porch. A single straight-backed, cane chair lay on its side under the glow of my headlights. A pair of outbuildings and three or four rusty, metal cages were scattered about the grounds. I figured some entrepreneur had set up a combination general store and wildlife exhibit here at one time. Must have been years ago, as the buildings and grounds had the dusty air of desertion and the atmosphere was rank with the sour scent of failure. I shut the headlights off, locked the doors, and stretched out as best I could across the front seat.

I lay propped up against the seat and the door and let the waves of tiredness wash over me. I recognized I might be on a wild goose chase of epic proportions, but I had to start somewhere. The haunting memory of blood bubbling between Lindsey's lips wouldn't let me do anything else. Besides, for two weeks I'd been remembering that certain conversation in front of the fire. Allison Grant and Prescott, Arizona had become locked together in my mind.

Forty-six

The sun rose like a huge ball of fire over the hood of the Taurus and the chill of the nighttime desert was soon gone in my glass and chrome bedroom. As I sat up, stiff, sore muscles protested every inch and I realized I was getting too damn old to sleep in the front seats of automobiles.

Once I found my bearings, I twisted the ignition key and lowered the side windows. Morning was still young; the stillness of the daylight desert had not yet fully taken hold. Small dark birds chirped at me from a huge cactus a dozen yards to my left and a small creature scurried about in the loose brush that had drifted against the porch.

In the clear morning light it was easy to see that the entire compound had been abandoned to tumbleweeds and Gila monsters long ago. The porch had begun to sag in the middle and one of the larger outbuildings had collapsed in on itself. The whole dreary vision was a pathetic reflection of someone's long dead dream.

I shut the motor off, stepped out, yawned, then wandered around the main building, partially to stretch my legs, but more to satisfy my curiosity. Most of the windows were caked over with grit and grime, but around back one pane was completely broken out. Standing on tiptoes, I could peer inside.

It wasn't worth the effort. All I could see was dust and cobwebs, a few empty shelves decorated with what looked like mouse droppings and an old baseball cap so greasy I couldn't even make out the lettering above the bill.

Directly above the baseball cap, a faded sign hung askew on the dusty wall. It read, *He Who Hesitates Is Lost*. I wondered if *Look Before You Leap* might not have been a better choice. I contributed my small part of the annual rainfall and headed back to the car.

I had come farther last night than I'd realized. An hour and a half, which included a greasy breakfast and a gasoline fill up at the first town I rolled into, put me on the outskirts of Prescott. If my guesses were correct, here was where I had to be cautious. I had no idea of Joe and Allison's standing in the community, whom they knew, or where they might be living—if they were even here. I eased down the main drag, keeping one eye open for them and the other for a likely motel.

I found the motel first. It fronted the highway on the far side of town, twenty yards inside the city limits. A series of long, low cabins with blue-green awnings were set in a semi-circle in a courtyard flanked by a swimming pool about the size of a school bus. A pair of pinion pines stood sentinel. The pines appealed to me, so I wheeled the Taurus off the highway and onto the dusty gravel driveway.

Dust was still settling when I walked into the office. The man behind the Formica-topped counter put down his magazine. It looked like a *National Enquirer*. He gave me a lopsided grin.

One big tooth in the front was broken off short, and he had a jagged scar running south a good inch and a half from his left eyebrow. His close-cropped hair grew in tufts, with bare hide shining through between paths of hair. He put me in mind of an old tomcat who had been in too many fights.

"Can I help you?"

"I'd like to rent a room."

He took a look at a row of keys on the fake walnut plaque behind him. "I can let you have number seven. That one is close to the pool."

It looked to me like he could have let me have just about any of the dozen rooms. Only numbers two and four didn't have keys hanging from their hooks. But it made no difference to me. "That will work just fine. How much?"

"Thirty-five dollars per night for a single."

I read the question in his eyes and nodded. I gave him my American Express card and, while he did his paperwork, I filled out the registration card. I took the key he offered along with directions to the ice machine, but before I left I eased the newspaper photo of Joe and Allison I'd copied off the microfiche of the newspaper file back home out of my shirt pocket.

"Seen this handsome couple?"

He let out a low whistle between his teeth. "Quite a babe, but no, ain't never seen them." He cocked his head to one side and gave me a quizzical look from half-averted eyes.

"Why are you looking for them?"

"Oh, I need to transact a little business with them."

He started to say something, then thought better of it and gave me a skeptical look instead. I waited a moment, but he sealed his lips and picked his magazine up. Tossing the key from one hand to another, I meandered back to the car.

The day was already a warm one, with the promise of being stifling. The weather man had prophesied a heat wave for the desert southwest. By the time I pulled up in front of number seven, my shirt was wet between my shoulder blades. After the chilling air of home, I wasn't accustomed to the heat.

Number seven was virtually indistinguishable from its neighbors, except for the facts that it was closest to the pool and its number was askew. I hoped these were good omens.

The room was Spartan in design and furnishings. A faded green bedspread covered the double bed, while a single brown, ladder-backed chair stood in front of a small desk missing a chip off the left front corner. An old-fashioned Tiffany style lamp, one that looked like one my aunt in Philadelphia had used for years, provided the only light in the room. An early version of indoor-outdoor carpet covered the floor. The carpet was a faded green and had seen plenty of hard use. I got the feeling that if I spent much time in this room I'd feel as though I were doing hard time.

I put my suitcase down and stepped into the small bathroom. Actually, tiny might be a better word. I'd seen bigger closets. Somehow they'd crammed in a mini-sink, a commode, and a shower stall. The window-unit air conditioner, which I'd flicked on when I came in, would have to struggle to push much cool air back into this oven.

Sweat slid down the middle of my back and a spreading stain formed under my armpits. I felt hot, sticky, and nasty, altogether disagreeable. I slipped out of my clothes and into the shower. It wasn't a clean, cool mountain stream, but it was wet and there was soap.

Five minutes later, I emerged cleaner, cooler, and extraordinarily tired. I rustled clean underwear out of the suitcase and put them on. Then I lay down atop the ancient bedspread.

I dreamed I stood with several other people at the entrance to an ancient Greek temple located high on a rocky precipice. The temple was open on all sides—really just columns and roof—and a strong wind was blowing. I could feel it working its way through my hair.

As we stood there, the wind became stronger and stronger, until finally we had to cling to the columns to keep from being blown away. Soon the muscles in my arm began to ache with the strain of hanging on.

The wind only intensified. It never slackened or stopped. Ultimately, the constant, ever-increasing pressure proved too much, and the weak, the very old, and the very young could no longer hold to the columns. The relentless wind bore them away, along with their fading cries for help.

I wanted to help them, but I knew I couldn't let go of my own column or I, too, would be borne away by the powerful wind. My arms began to feel like lead, heavy and aching as they strained against the storm. Soon I was the only one left on the platform struggling against the wind. I felt my arms weaken and my fingers slip from the column.

I woke with a scream stillborn in my throat. My entire body ached like I'd gone fifteen with Ali in his prime and my head pounded as though it were a drum being beaten by some mad giant. Reality couldn't be much worse than dreamland, so I rolled off the bed, dressed, and went to look for Allison Grant Dubronski and good old Joe.

Forty-seven

I started at the local newspaper, where I told the plump redhead at the front desk a lively tale about looking for my estranged wife. When I mentioned a possible reconciliation, her eyes moistened. She let me look at the microfiche without another question.

I spent a long hour and a half scanning the front page, local news, and society pages, going back a couple of years. After the first twenty minutes, I was wishing desperately for an index. By the end of an hour, my eyes were starting to burn. I wondered if I was beginning to need glasses. When I finally gave it up, I had a terrific headache, but no leads. The redhead gave me a sorrowful look when I shook my head on my way out of the room.

I showed my pictures of the dynamic couple to a handful of real estate agencies, a trio of bartenders, and a cab driver parked at his stand in the shade of an abandoned Western Auto hardware store. I got the expected comments on Allison's attributes, and the cabby, a wizened old man with a face as hard as a green apple and ears like the handles on an old-fashioned glass milk jug, expressed seemingly genuine envy over Joe Dubronski's luck. Nobody had seen either of them.

By the time I'd listened to the story of the cabby's uninteresting love life, I was tired, hungry, and thirsty. I got back in my rental and drove in search of a McDonald's.

Unlike people who want to stay missing, Ronald McDonald wants to be found. I found him a block from the high school, between a book store and a Jiffy-Lube. Classes must have just let out for lunch as teenagers filled the restaurant and parking lot. A few of the bigger boys, football players from the looks of them, got Big Macs and fries, but most merely bought a drink. Watching their weight, I figured.

Not being overly concerned with my physique, I went for a grilled chicken sandwich, fries, and a large coffee. Then I strolled outside and sat at one of the plastic picnic tables. Each table was equipped with a red and white beach umbrella. A soft breeze was blowing out of the southwest and it was comfortable in the shade thrown by the umbrella.

Table space proved to be at a premium. Before I finished my chicken, which greatly resembled cardboard, a tall, well-built boy came up and nodded his head at my table. I nodded back to the unspoken question.

The boy sat down, but before he got his ketchup package open he was joined by a girl with long black hair and eyes the color of the desert sky just after sunrise. She smiled at him sweetly, but he concentrated on his fries. I half recalled a quotation, I couldn't remember to whom to attribute it, something to the effect that youth was wasted on the young.

She asked him about his plans for the weekend. He gave her an evasive answer, one that led me to believe he might be doing something with the boys. He stumbled over the words as he said them, leaving me doubting he meant them. I could sense that she shared my lack of total belief. Her blue eyes began to mist and she hung her head.

I stuffed the last bite in my mouth and stood. Time to roll, for more than one reason. Walking to the car, I hoped I'd never acted like the muscular young man. Deep down, however, I had the sneaking suspicion I had, and more than once, and maybe worse. I thought of the way I'd treated Debi and mentally harangued my sorry self.

Six hours later, I chalked up a useless afternoon to looking for Joe Dubronski. I bought a box of the Colonel's original and drove back to the motel. The chicken was greasy but tasty, and I spent a dreamless night in lucky cabin 7.

I awoke to the rumble of a big rig on the highway and the twittering of birds in the pines. I lay still and listened to the music of the morning as I watched daylight squeeze in through the cracks in the blinds. When the birds fell silent and the room grew warm, I rolled out of bed and faced one more day.

The sky was cloudless that Friday morning in May and the unobscured sun blazed down with force on Prescott. The parking lot asphalt felt soft and squishy beneath my feet and my car was like an oven.

I started the engine and powered down the windows to let the captured heat escape and give the air conditioner a chance to do its job. A block down the street, the time and temperature sign said it was 91 degrees at 10:47.

All the chicken I'd eaten the day before still sat heavily in my stomach and sweat trickled down my back. I stopped at a gas station and bought a cup of coffee the color of used motor oil. I meandered back to the car, sipping and ruminating on the situation. My thoughts were darker than my coffee.

At the moment, my trip to Prescott didn't seem to be such a bright idea. After all, I was only guessing Allison and Joe were out here, and I could see clearly I hadn't given near enough thought on to how to find them. The task loomed larger than the butte to the west.

Still, they had to be somewhere, and it figured after their time spent apart they would have gotten together. In addition, my hunch ran strong that they were in the Prescott area. I kept remembering Allison's words about where she would go if she had a chance.

Besides, it was the only game in town. If they weren't here, I had no clue where to start. I had enough in my savings to cover a week's worth of Prescott. I resolved to give it that long, then see where I was. No reason to head home now, so I fired up the engine and rolled on beneath a cloudless sky.

Forty-eight

My first order of business was to get a lead on their whereabouts. I considered trying the police, but rejected the idea because I had no hard information to give them, and because they would ask questions I couldn't or wouldn't answer.

I thought about trying to sweet talk my way into a telephone number for Joe and Allison, then realized they wouldn't be stupid enough to have a phone in their real names. Still, I figured I had a chance, unless they had totally gone to ground in a remote cabin deep in the mountains, or in another town, state, or country. Allison Grant was simply too striking a woman to go unnoticed for long. I simply had to find the right girl-watcher.

Half a mile down the highway I hit a major intersection and for kicks hung a left and began to travel north. I drove past a series of small businesses: a one-hour photo drop-off, a taco place, a baseball card shop, a hamburger hut, and a dozen more of the same ilk. The commercial district gave way to a lower middle-class section of older suburbs. Tract houses, leftover from the 50s, look uninviting even when they have nicely manicured lawns and shade trees. It was the sameness of design I found so unappealing. I often imagined a vulgar giant had constructed them all from the same box of Legos.

Apache Way, the road I was traveling, gradually bent to the east. Civilization began to fade, with vacant lots interspersed between houses. Soon rock-strewn patches of sandy soil topped by scrub and cacti predominated. For lack of a better plan, I kept going.

In less than five minutes I was outside Prescott proper. One ridge beyond the city limits, a Wal-Mart sign appeared on my right. That great symbol of a certain class in early twenty-first century Americana rose like a blister on the Arizona landscape, surrounded by nothing but asphalt rimmed by desert sand. Large, squat, and butt-ugly, it sat temporarily triumphant under the boiling afternoon sun.

The parking lot was better than half full and shoppers moved with surprising speed in the heat, as though afraid they were going to miss the bargain of the day. I pulled in and parked the Taurus next to a Winnebago with Ohio license plates. I counted seventeen bumper stickers on the back of the trailer and tried to ignore the chartreuse octopus curtains in the window.

I got out and strolled toward the brown building. Maybe it was the color, or perhaps my mood, but the Wal-Mart put me in mind of a large pile of cow dung molded into a rectangle and left to bake in the Arizona sun.

A pair of wooden benches fronted the entrance. The paint on them was cracked and peeling, making it hard to read the bus schedule block-lettered in yellow on the back of each brown bench. They looked hard and uncomfortable, but they were in the shade. One was unoccupied and I sat, prepared to watch the world go by for a while as my mind settled into freefall. I was tired of the searching road and you never know.

Within a minute, a couple came out the pneumatic door. Unfortunately, not the right couple. He was tall and straight with a beautiful head of white hair. She was smaller framed and bent at the shoulders. Her hair was thinning and gray, yet she moved more forcefully than he did. After they eased past me, and the angle of my vision changed, I could see he was resting part of his weight on her.

Over the next fifteen minutes I saw a broad chested man in his thirties wearing an auto mechanic's uniform and carrying a case of oil, a slender woman with two small, silent children holding to her dress—their eyes large and blank like pools of dark water in their round faces, a teenage girl with peroxided hair, and a man and wife with three wild boys.

I put the boys' ages between six and twelve. They ran screaming into the parking lot, throwing punches and insults at each other. I couldn't believe their energy level in this heat. Their parents trudged reluctantly along behind. They slogged over to the Winnebago I'd parked next to and called the boys to them as though the youngsters were mischievous puppies. Mother and boys climbed into the back of the vehicle. The father walked around and got in behind the wheel. He started the engine and pulled away with a grim look on his face. Shouts, loud enough to be heard over the motor, emanated from the back of the camper. Not one iota did I envy that gentleman.

The bench beside me had been occupied by two old men. The one with the portable oxygen tank struggled to his feet and dragged himself and his air supply inside. The other rose from the bench in stages, fingered another pinch of snuff out of the can and slipped the snuff in his mouth. He put the can back inside his shirt pocket, picked up the Wal-Mart coffee cup he was using as a spit cup, ambled over and sat on the far end of my bench. He hadn't shaved for a couple of days and fragments of snuff were caught in the iron gray stubble on his chin.

"Hot enough for you?" He had a squeaky, old, high-pitched voice, as if his vocal cords had tightened during the aging process and now he had to squeeze out the words.

"Sure is." I kept my eyes on the parking lot. A blonde had pulled up in an El Camino.

"Weatherman says it'll get up to ninety-five tomorrow."

"Is that right?" The blonde had opened the door and was getting ready to get out. She was a long way away from me but it was possible. Maybe Arizona was my lucky state. I was overdue.

"Aren't from around here, are you?"

"No." I scooted up to the front edge of my bench.

"This is the first real hot weather we've had. It's come early this year. Usually doesn't get here till June."

The blonde slid out of the El Camino. Her door opened away from the Wal-Mart and when she stood the body of her vehicle was between us. For a second my heart jumped up in my throat. Then I could see it wasn't Allison. The beating of my heart slowed to more moderate levels and I turned and looked at the old man. A thin stream of snuff juice leaked out of the corner of his mouth.

"Man on the radio said it's going to get even hotter later in the week."

"Yeah." He gave me a grin that revealed his brown-stained teeth. "Only supposed to get up to ninety-three today. That's how old my daddy was when he died. His dad lived to be eighty-six. I plan on pushing it to one hundred. Only got fifteen more to go."

He turned his head and spat a muddy stream into his cup. "They're both buried less than ten miles from here as the crow flies, on the home place. Our place backed up against the McIver place and Nick McIver, well he's the one who sold this property to our man Walton's gang to build this damn Wal-Mart. Guess old McIver made some money, but not near as much as they are." He nodded toward the building behind us.

"Lots of dollars change hands in there."

"Lot of people think they're getting happiness at a bargain."

"There's no free lunch."

He looked over at me, gave me a brown-toothed grin and said, "We sure are full of shit, ain't we?"

"Damn straight."

After that exchange, we sat there in the broiling Arizona sun and let sweat drip off us. After about a half hour of fruitless watching, I felt my attention span slip a cog and my mind began to wander.

Two old buzzards perched on wooden benches in the heat watching the afternoon drift on to a slow, certain death, that's what we were. My eyelids became heavy and a slow stupor inhabited my body. Unprotected skin on my face began to burn, but I didn't have the energy, or the ambition, to do anything about it.

The flow of people in and out of the Wal-Mart faded to a trickle, then stopped. I roused myself enough to change positions, exposing a different part of my face to the sun. Sweat slid down my sides and my spine. Heat rose from the asphalt of the parking lot like it was the middle of a giant pizza oven. Time lost all meaning and I drifted into sleep.

First flickers of an early evening breeze roused me. Shadows, mercifully, had fallen across me as the afternoon wore on. Even with them, my cheeks were burning and tender to the touch.

I glanced over at my fellow observer of things large and small at the Prescott, Arizona Wal-Mart. His head lay against the top rail of the bench as if it had grown too heavy in the afternoon heat for his scrawny, wrinkled neck. One deep-water-blue eye was half open and a thin brown stream of spittle ran from the left corner of his mouth. I had to smile—we surely were two old sunburned buzzards. Aching muscles protested as I sat up.

The sun hung low in the western sky and it was cooler than when I'd first planted my carcass on the bench. Hunger pangs rumbled in my stomach, reminding me it had been a long time since the Colonel's original.

I glanced at my Casio. 5:43. My arm was sunburned. My mind said it was time to call it a day. My heart agreed. I forced myself up from the bench. The parking lot had filled considerably while I dozed, but I had no trouble locating the Taurus.

"Damn, what a looker!" Eagerness invaded his raspy, old voice, rendering him a self-fulfilling prophecy. His face was split in an evil leer. His eyes were twin pools of smoldering lust.

My fellow buzzard was looking over my shoulder at the flower and garden center. I turned my head to follow his gaze. A statuesque redhead was walking away from us with an armful of begonias. Had to agree with the old prospector, she was indeed one good looking lady. In the sunlight, her close-cropped hair shone like a cap of hammered copper. Her round bottom swayed with each step. Shapely legs extended from her shorts.

Somehow she seemed out of focus, or, to more accurately state it, out of context. It was as though I'd seen her before, only she didn't belong in this scene. She paused before a three or four-year-old Ford Ranger pickup. Already its red paint had begun to blister from prolonged exposure to the elements. As she put the key into the driver's side door lock, she turned her profile to me.

In that instant it felt like a ton of bricks slammed into me. Allison Grant, or her stand-in, was alive and well and shopping at Wal-Mart. Red hair notwithstanding, she was my missing woman, or someone so similar I couldn't tell them apart across the shimmering parking lot.

"Hey, where you goin'? Figured you and me was going to have a good chat?" The old man's querulous voice trailed after me as I jogged across the parking lot.

Asphalt was soft beneath my feet, giving way like beach sand. It took a surprising effort to pull my feet up and take the next stride. Dancing in water must be something like this, I thought as I dodged a crack the pothole patrol had missed.

It seemed to take an inordinately long time to get to the Taurus. I unlocked the door and tugged it open. A wall of heat flung itself into my face. Ignoring the blast, I slid behind the wheel and twisted the key.

The steering wheel was as hot as the handle of a pot left too long on the stove. I jerked my handkerchief out of my right hip pocket and slid it under my tender left hand as I wheeled the car through the squishy parking lot. The pickup was a red blob, already at the intersection of the main road. I powered around a fat fool in a clanking Plymouth van that wasn't doing thirty and tried to close the gap.

By the time I got to the main road, the truck was a blur of red paint at the outer horizon of my vision. I jammed my foot down on the accelerator and pulled out in front of a slow moving Olds before it could get in front of me. The driver had to brake hard and he blasted his horn in defiance, but I wasn't making any backward glances.

I had a reason to go very fast and the driver of the red pickup didn't. Almost immediately, I began to gain on her. We were traveling away from town and there were no traffic lights to impede me. Within a couple of minutes after I'd pulled out in front of the Olds I'd gained so much highway that I began to ease back on the gas. I didn't need to come up on her too quickly and arouse her suspicions.

The country wasn't mountainous, neither was it perfectly flat. There were frequent dips and rises and I worked on keeping a couple of those between us. I needed to stay close enough behind her to see when she turned off, but not close enough to create an impression. Even though the sun was still glaring off the windows and I doubted she could see my face, I was still concerned.

Given what she was trying to accomplish she would be naturally wary, and Allison Grant was not a stupid woman. That I knew from bitter, first-hand experience. Now, I wasn't positive she was the redhead in the pickup, but my instincts told me it was Allison driving across Arizona before me.

Traffic was light, and in the daylight it was difficult to alter the image of the car. If it had been nighttime, I could have changed from high to low beam, or, if the moon was full and the sky cloudless, I might have chanced turning the lights out altogether for a few seconds. Anything to alter the image and reduce the possibility of putting Allison on her guard.

A black Dodge Viper appeared in my rearview mirror, running hard. I eased back another notch and hung to the right hand side of my lane to facilitate his getting by. The driver didn't need my help. He was in a hurry in a car with an engine packing major horsepower, and he had the guts to use it. He blew by me on an open stretch beyond the sign warning of blowing and drifting sand. Swirls of dust sprang up on the side of the road in his wake. Less than half a mile ahead, I could see the red pickup clearly.

A long finger of bare rock descended from a butte and ran across the ground like a line drawn in the sand by a child. At the point where the rock met the road the ground dipped and the asphalt bent sharply right. First the pickup and then the Viper braked and curled into the turn. Seconds later I did the same. It was a mean curve, especially at this time of day, because when you came out of the turn, you were facing directly into the sun hanging low in the western sky.

I went into the curve faster than I should have, and the combination of too much speed and the sudden direct glare of the sun gave me one long, bad moment.

I squeezed the brakes and tried to keep my eyes on the road and away from the sun. Within seconds, the black stars had quit dancing in front of my eyes and the Taurus was behaving. I studied the asphalt before me. The Viper was just a black profile running on the horizon. The red pickup had vanished.

Unsure whether she had pulled off or speeded up, I jammed the accelerator to the floor and gave chase. For the next couple of miles, I broke the speed limit and accomplished nothing. Even at ninety, the Viper pulled farther away from me. Eventually, the blacktop bent back to the left and I could see the open road for miles in front of the black blur of the Viper. I began to brake and swung into an illegal U-turn in the middle of the Arizona outlands.

I carefully retraced the miles, keeping one eye on the road while the other maintained a lookout for the pickup. I was all the way back to the bad curve before I found the turn-off.

It wasn't much, more a path than a driveway. Years ago, someone had put down a few truckloads of gravel, most of which had by now sunk into or been covered by the desert sand. Scraggly weeds fought for life between scattered stones. An air of desertion—of death, hung about the place.

However, there were fresh tire tracks and wispy curtains of dust still hung in the air. It was easy to see why I'd missed the turn-off. It was a sharp left where the curve had been a sharp right. And it occurred precisely in the final bend of the curve. That combination created an exceedingly dangerous turn-off for anyone coming from Prescott, as you had to zip blindly across the other lane. Undoubtedly, it was good for the safety record of Yavapai County that traffic was light and the turn-off seldom used.

Half mile ahead a small cloud of dust rose over the sand humps and scrubby mesquite, moving like a small army advancing slowly on the enemy.

The road was rough and rutted and the washboard effect jarred both the Taurus and my insides. I realized, perhaps too late, that if she was throwing up a dust cloud, I'd do the same. I slowed to a crawl and hoped Allison's vision was obscured by her own dust.

Without warning, the road dipped, then made a sharp right into a small arroyo, where it degenerated to two ruts traversing rough and uneven ground. The way out of the depression was ever steeper. It looked as though you had to go almost straight up the far wall of the arroyo. The pickup had obviously made it. I seriously doubted the Taurus could.

I braked to a stop, shifted into reverse, then backtracked until I came to where a natural, open space sprawled beside the road. There I got the Taurus turned around, nose pointed toward the main road. I shut the engine off, pocketed the key, took my revolver out of the glove compartment, slid out from behind the wheel, and started walking.

In less than two minutes I was drenched in sweat. Heat still lingered, though the sun lay low in the west. A thin border of clouds hung in the western sky, colored red by the fire behind them.

I picked my way carefully down into the arroyo. Even then, halfway to the bottom, the ground suddenly gave way beneath my left foot and I slid down the rest of the way like I was trying to beat the throw from left field.

I ended up propped up against the side of the gully, my feet on the dry bed. I dusted myself off, crossed the floor, and began the climb out the other side. Flowing right, the path actually was more on an angle than it looked from the other side. Still, it was a steep ascent. Even with the pickup, I doubted if Allison wanted to make the trip to town and back more than once or twice a week. Only a few adventurous spirits would ever come this far on an exploration.

By the time I'd climbed out and made the far side dust and dirt clung to me like a blanket. Sweat ran in crooked streams through the grime. I felt as if I hadn't showered in a week.

Evening was starting to fall and twilight was painting the earth a soft purple. I wondered about the moon—was it a full one? I couldn't remember. I longed for three things I didn't have, and had no way of obtaining in the middle of this empty land: a drink of water, a flashlight, and a partner for backup. I sat between smooth boulders and surveyed the battleground.

Forty-nine

The cabin was a dark hulk set against the larger, darker hulk of the hillside. Weathered planks, a roughhewn door, light spilling through ill-fitting windows were all I could make out.

I was pleased to see a nearly full moon rising between the trees. Moonlight lit the branches and a rambling path that led to the cabin. The pickup was backed in beside the cabin. Beyond the pickup, an older, larger vehicle with a long bed sat rusting on flat tires.

The engine of the pickup was still cooling, the knocks and pings of the engine loud in the first hush of nightfall. A small tree or large bush appeared to be growing up through the broken hull of the more ancient vehicle.

Night comes quickly in the southwest. In twenty minutes, not even a glimmer remained of the sun that had burned so brightly at noon. I crept as silently as I could through the soft, shifting sand that lay like fine powder over loose rock and gnarled tree roots that conspired to upset my balance. Twice I stumbled and once I fell, catching my shirt on a thorny bush and opening a gash on my sunburned left cheek courtesy of a rock.

I choked back a groan and lay silently for a long minute. No one came to the door, no one called, "Who's there?" I wiped my bloody cheek with a sandy hand, forced myself upright, and soldiered on.

She was there. Highlighted for a moment in lamplight, profile perfectly framed by the opened window. A glistening copper colored skullcap of hair, turquoise choker tight against the lovely throat. That special gleam in her eye that set Allison Grant apart from the ordinary.

Unique, lovely, powerful, and willing to sacrifice her own poor blind innocent sister so she could live on stolen money, Allison Grant personified evil for me.

Only a dozen feet of Arizona wilderness and a wavy pane of glass separated my hands from her throat. In that moment, in the hot angry rush of blood that beat against my temples, I wanted badly to pull the trigger. Yeah, maybe it would have been a coward's shot from ambush. But then, Allison was more deadly than the tarantulas that crawled across the desert southwest. Still, the urge for her to realize who was killing her was strong. By the time I'd made up my mind, it was senseless to speculate—she'd already stepped away from the window.

I eased tighter against the cabin. The wood had probably been rough and full of splinters when it was built. Sun and wind had long ago worn the planks smooth. I ran the palm of my left hand along the wood. It was almost as though I were touching Allison herself. I was that close. She was there, breathing, smiling, enjoying life only a few feet on the other side of this weathered wood. I heard her silvery, lilting laugh and hatred blinded me.

I took a deep breath and suddenly I could taste the sweetness of Lindsey's lips. I gagged as they turned to the coppery taste of blood.

I heard a bird scuttle across the undulating ground before the cabin. Then he rose, a black whirl in the night. I caught a glimpse of a dark image against the lighter leaves of a low scraggly bush that grew between two long, low outcroppings of rock. It gave a sharp, shrill cry from the branches of the bush. From the hillside opposite came an answering cry.

I edged away from the cabin and let my eyes grow accustomed to the dimly lit ground. Soon, I could see enough to make out a mound of earth about fifteen yards to the left of the bird's bush. The mound ran parallel to that bank, rising sharply five or six feet into the air. While it wasn't dead in front of the window, it still afforded a better angle of sight into the cabin. Moving cautiously, I eased across the ill-defined yard and came around behind the mound.

I took my time…an empty lifetime stretched before me like black Arizona asphalt. It wasn't any task to scramble to the top. Once there, I lay down and surveyed the landscape. The gun in my hand felt heavy and comforting.

The cabin stood unevenly on the darkened ground, moonbeams falling on it helter-skelter. It was tilted to one side, leaning tentatively into the darkest patch, as though there was supporting strength to be found in the blackness.

Allison moved back and forth in front of the window. She appeared to be setting the table for a fashionably late supper. I could see what looked like a bucket of Kentucky Fried Chicken on a wooden table. The Colonel was a bit hit in Arizona.

A vase brimming with wildflowers stood beside the bucket. Allison began to split a cantaloupe open with a long-bladed, wooden handled kitchen knife. Light glittered off the blade.

Someone turned on a radio and soothing sounds, a blend of violin and piano, joined the crickets who'd begun to chirp in the underbrush beneath the juniper to my left. It was homey and touching and ran through me like barbed wire.

It was almost anti-climactic when it happened. All those months of looking for Joe, thinking about, dreaming of Joe Dubronski, then finally, undeniably, he was there. He'd been simply a picture in my hand for so long I'd almost begun to believe he was a figment of my imagination.

Old Joe was real, though. Dark hair, longer than in his picture, salt and pepper beard. Half leaning against the window, his profile unmistakable. I was less than twenty yards from the cabin, and, though I hated like hell to admit it, he did look a lot like me, or I like him—however you wanted to say it.

My evil, darker brother whom I had never met. Partner in the plot that had sent Lindsey to her untimely, undeserved death and had me knocking on death's door. Hate rose like bile in my throat.

With darkness came a chill and a faint breeze. There was a bite to the night air now and I shivered as I watched the golden lamplight hover around the people behind the window as though they were hypnotic. Moonlight covered the cabin like a blanket of freshly fallen snow.

Lindsey was out here with me in the dark. I could sense her presence, smell her perfume, feel her soft smooth hand in mine.

Funny how a broken heart can keep on beating.

My mind felt as though it had been cleaved in two. Teardrops formed, but a man can't cry—not if he is a real man. At least that's what I told myself.

Fifty

Months ago, I'd promised myself I wouldn't stoop to this level, that I'd only locate them, then let the law take its course. Maybe I'd meant those words when I'd said them. But logic and reason didn't always signify.

What I can swear for certain is that, even in my most vivid flashes of imagination, I'd never conceived of the pain and rage generated by seeing Allison and Joe together. I shook until I wondered if my body was going to break. Finally I got the logical side of my brain engaged and brought myself under control.

Hunkered down in the darkness like an ignoble savage, I stared at them, hatred running through me like electricity. Night breezes carried their laughing voices to me. Half of me wanted to throw up, the other half voted for screaming.

In the end, I passed on both options and crept through the darkness, trying to move like a coyote, struggling to maintain focus. Al was gone somewhere—him I could find later—and Fat Tony was, according to Al, looking death between the eyes. In any case, I could deal with them another time. Tonight, however, opportunity had arisen and I aimed to grab it by both horns. I kept my eyes on the light.

As I neared the cabin, I could smell fried chicken and Allison's perfume. Joe's laughter mingled with the sound of a violin concerto pouring forth from the radio. Night air was cool and smooth against my face. It was all so lovely I felt like puking my guts out.

Smart would have been to retreat and return, complete with sheriff and posse. Stupid meant going in uninvited and unwelcomed. Never have I claimed to be the brightest bulb in the pack.

Suppose it all boiled down to there are times when a man simply has to act. At least if he wants to live with himself. Sure, I could have gone for reinforcements. But what if Allison and Joe vamoosed while I was gone? In the end, I decided there were some chances worth taking—only the chance of losing them wasn't one of them.

Choking back the rising bile, I gently placed one hand on the door knob and took a deep breath, trusting the desert to guard my rear.

I ripped the door open and their heads jerked toward me like puppets on amphetamines. Their eyes opened cartoonishly wide and their mouths flopped open. Grinning, I stepped inside, waving the gun in their direction.

"Guess who's coming to dinner?" I made my voice soft, but kept my eyes hard.

Leaning casually against the wall, I watched their faces change.

Dubronski's eyes narrowed as he stared at me like I was a stranger. Seconds later, I realized to him I was. The man had never seen me in person.

I gave him the once-over. From across the room he looked enough like the reflection I saw in the mirror each morning to be a cousin, perhaps a brother. Twins we weren't, but the resemblance was uncanny. No wonder Allison had figured passing off a dead Frank Quick as a dead Joe Dubronski wouldn't be a problem. With her identifying the body, it would have been a cinch. No fingerprints would have been necessary if the grieving widow was certain, and

Allison Grant Dubronski would have been certain. She'd have given an Oscar worthy performance. Of that I had no doubt.

Noise came from my left and I angled my head in time to catch Allison edging away, taking small casual steps, as though she were going to powder her nose. Only she was keeping both eyes on my face.

Expressions rippled across her face. They were impossible to read comprehensively, but my impressions were surprise, followed by fascination, followed by repulsion. Her lips were separated, but she wasn't making a sound.

My legs were trembling, but I thought of Lindsey and forced my body off the wall. I took a step into the room, then another. Dubronski half-rose from his chair. Allison took another step toward the darkness beyond the room.

"Now Allison, aren't you going to ask me to join you for pie and coffee?"

Her head was as still as stone, half-turned away so that shadows lay across her face in irregular swatches. One eye was visible, glittering like blown glass.

"Well, guess not. Then how about introducing me to this handsome fellow?" I nodded at Joe.

His eyes flicked toward her, then back to me. Then he finished standing. His arms hung loosely by his side, but his hands formed fists and muscles in his bare arms knotted, running thickly just below the skin like high-grade manila rope.

"You." Allison spat the word out like it was a worm lodged in a half-chewed slice of apple.

"Me," I said, giving her my best egg-sucking, hyena smile.

"But how…" She paused and ran a hand through her short hair that shimmered in the light like polished copper. "How did you find us?"

"Oh, I'll admit it took me too long. From the day we met I played the sap. I should have figured out your little scheme months ago, but then I never was very smart. Fact is, it wasn't until I remembered a game of 'if I could go anywhere' the three of us played one night that things started to fall into place. That, and an envelope in your stack of mail after Joe went MIA postmarked Prescott. You remember the three of us, don't you? And of course you remember when I stayed with you, with you and Lindsey." I nearly gagged on her name.

"You bastard," she said softly, yet distinctly. "You son-of-a-bitch."

"Allison," Joe said.

"You're the bitch," I said, "planning to kill your own sister and a stupid PI just so you and Joe could get off Tony D's radar permanently. You should have handled the details better, though. Letting Al be part of the killing crew wasn't smart. He knew me, you know? And once he saw my face, well, then everything slid sideways. My guess is he and Fat Tony will lay low for a bit, then start looking for you again. Looking real hard." I didn't say a word about my phone call from Al. Years ago I'd learned that it wasn't always smart to tell everything you knew.

The cabin fell silent, the aftermath of my words hanging in the air like smoke from cheap cigarettes. A coyote yelped in the night.

Lindsey's face rose like a new moon in my mind and I wanted to cry. Instead, I blinked and swallowed. For a heartbeat, the room swirled out of focus.

When it spun back in, Joe Dubronski was already around the table and coming hard.

"Kill him, Joe," Allison screeched. "Kill him. He knows everything."

I turned to meet Joe, but he threw himself on me and drove me against the wall. I felt the gun fly from my hand.

I tried to pull free, but Joe's grip was firm. My right arm was pinned, so I hammered a left at his head. Allison screamed as he drove the top of his head against my face. Stars swirled and I tasted warm blood, my own.

As though from a great distance, I could hear myself cursing. Joe had a grip like a python and with his right hand on my throat it was becoming difficult to breathe. I tried to jerk my right arm free, but his hold seemed unbreakable. My strength wasn't what it was before Jamaica and I should have factored that in my planning.

Panic rose, and I pushed us off the wall and we stumbled across the room, smashing against the table, grunting like two wild boars. Over the grunting, I could hear plates and silverware crash against the floor.

I caught my balance first and drove my left fist into his gut. His grip eased and my right arm swung free. Pivoting, I drove a straight right against his left temple.

Joe groaned and stumbled backwards. I moved in on him, swinging with both arms. He ducked and bobbed. My left grazed his forehead, while my right smashed against his left shoulder blade.

He jammed his head into my gut and we fell to the floor, rolling, cursing, punching, and gasping for breath.

Without knowing how, I ended up on top. For a second, we were frozen, like figures in the Bayeux tapestry, then I drove a right for his jaw.

He was too quick, though, jerking his head to the side, then grabbing my head and pulling me down.

Our heads smashed together and the world spun into a darkness splattered by a thousand dancing lights. Blood gushed from my nose. His fingers tightened around my throat and I gouged at his eyes as we rolled across the floor. Broken dishes and dirty forks jabbed at my back.

We thudded into a wall and I pulled my head free, grasping for air. Then he jerked me down again and his body began to rise over mine. I lifted my head but he kept a hand pressed against my throat. I struggled upward against the pressure, getting both shoulders off the floor, then my strength suddenly gave way and I fell back, pulling him down with me just as the room exploded.

I was deafened, and wondered for a moment if I was dead.

Then Joe was falling off me and the world roared again. Something burned the right side of my face, branding me.

I rolled free and kept rolling. Hearing was coming back as I scrambled to my feet.

The gun roared again and something incredibly hot and hard smashed into my left thigh—the same damn leg that had taken a bullet in Jamaica. I could hear my screams as I crashed into the counter. Then I was falling.

The floor was hard, but I rolled and reached for the top of the table, trying to pull myself up. The pain in my leg dragged me down into dirty dishes, scattered utensils, and greasy fried chicken.

At first there was only pain.

Then the room slowed its spinning and I scooted away and got my back up against the sink. I only had time for one quick look before she started moving. She was coming to make sure.

My right hand clawed for a weapon and I felt my fingers close around a smooth wooden handle. I prayed I'd grabbed the right thing.

I sat on the floor, feeling washed out, fighting off the blackness. I made myself think of Lindsey and the resulting rage helped. The room swam back into focus.

Directly across the room, Joe Dubronski lay on the floor. His mouth and eyes were open. Blood pooled on his chest and ran in a thin stream across the wooden planks. His dark eyes stared at me. Lights flickered in them. Moving awkwardly, sluggishly, he struggled to crawl toward me. As I watched, the lights in his eyes dimmed.

I turned my head, trying to find Allison again. The room kept alternating between light and dark, and for what seemed a long time I couldn't find her.

Then she was there, ten feet away, smiling. Her eyes looked bright and shiny, like newly minted coins. In her hand my gun looked huge.

Placing her feet with care, she walked toward me, slowly, the gun leading the way. Her eyes never left my face.

I didn't say a word and I didn't move. I simply sat with my back against the sink, feeling blood dripping out of me, watching her come, trying to gather strength, my fingers gripping the handle. Getting her close was the only hand I had left to play.

It seemed to take her a long time to get to me and I felt my mind drifting in and out of consciousness. In the end she made it, so close the smell of her perfume mingled with that of my blood. The barrel of the gun was warm against my temple.

"Well, well, well. You big, dumb bastard. You just couldn't leave it alone, could you?"

I forced myself to stare into her eyes, trying not to cry, or piss all over myself.

"And now Joe is dead, thanks to you. Why the hell did you have to move just when I pulled the trigger? You've fucked things up all along, you son-of-a-bitch." She was so close her features were blurry and her breath washed warm against my face.

"And now, well you're going to have to die." She smiled at me, a clown's sad smile. "In a way it seems a waste. You really are rather handsome, and actually, in some ways, more of a man than Joe. But, you've left me no choice, Frank. So this will be our final goodbye."

I opened my eyes wide and tightened my grip on the wooden handle. Her finger was on the trigger. Then it eased back, ever so slightly. She leaned even closer. Her lips brushed my bloody lips, very softly, her tongue flickered in my mouth.

I whispered Lindsey's name into her open mouth and drove the smooth wooden handle of the butcher knife upward. Everything I had left, all the rage and shame and pain, went into the thrust.

Allison grunted and I felt her teeth bite into my lip. Then her face swung away and she sat down on the floor in front of me.

She looked very surprised.

The gun still dangled from her fingers. One finger quivered on the trigger, but she couldn't quite close the deal.

For what seemed like a prelude to forever, we simply sat and stared at each other. I kept my eyes on the lights in hers. When they started to dim, she looked down at the knife buried in her gut, then her eyes drifted back to mine. I only sat there and watched. Time was what I had left in this world.

Her lips parted and she whispered "Bastard."

Then her eyes rolled up and she fell back as the gun roared.

Fifty-one

Can't say how long I sat on that bloody floor. My strength rose and fell like primordial ocean tides. Finally, with a high tide rising, I made a tourniquet out of a kitchen towel and wrapped it around my leg above the bullet hole in an effort to stop, or at least slow, the bleeding.

Shock slowly ebbed and some elemental strength returned. I told myself I had to move or I was going to sit there and bleed to death. For a time, death seemed the better alternative.

Then I remembered Lindsey and tried to stand. I couldn't make it. After three tries, I aborted that maneuver and began to crawl. I crawled through Allison's blood, and Joe's, and, I expect, some of my own.

I kept slipping in and out of consciousness, but finally reached the open door. Night air moved cool and strong against my face, and I found a certain strength in the desert wind. I crawled like a wounded animal through the sand to my car.

Moonlight poured a silver path through the darkness and I followed it like it was the road to salvation. The journey took a damn long time.

The light was starting to change when I pulled myself up and onto the seat. Beneath my hands, the steering wheel felt otherworldly.

I have no memory of the drive to Prescott.

Three days later, when I came back into this world, a young doctor with a face drawn by El Greco, told me an old hermit had found me slumped over the wheel in the Wal-Mart parking lot.

The hermit reported that all I said was "Lindsey."

Meet Chris Helvey

Chris Helvey's short stories have been published by numerous reviews and journals, and he is the author of the novels *Yard Man, Dancing on the Rim* and *Violets for Sgt. Schiller (Wings ePress), Snapshot,* and *Whose Name I Did Not Know,* plus the short story collections One More Round and Claw Hammer. He currently serves as Editor in Chief of *Trajectory Journal*.

Other Works From The Pen Of

Chris Helvey

Yard Man - A lonely man simply trying to survive The Great Depression, suddenly stumbles into a job he doesn't want, falls in love with a prostitute who doesn't love him, and incurs the wrath of the most dangerous man in Mississippi.

Dancing on the Rim - The story of one man's journey across a violent wilderness, a journey of revenge, retribution, and a search for redemption.

Violets for Sgt. Schiller - A young German poet is swept up in the maelstrom of World War I.

Letter to Our Readers

Enjoy this book?

You can make a difference

As an independent publisher, Wings ePress, Inc. does not have the financial clout of the large New York Publishers. We can't afford large magazine spreads or subway posters to tell people about our quality books.

But, we do have something much more effective and powerful than ads. We have a large base of loyal readers.

Honest Reviews help bring the attention of new readers to our books.

If you enjoyed this book, we would appreciate it if you would spend a few minutes posting a review on the book's ***Amazon page*** or on its Wings ePress, Inc. webpage ***at*** *www.wingsepress.com*

Thank You very much

Visit Our Website

*For The Full Inventory
Of Quality Books*:

Wings ePress, Inc

*Quality trade paperbacks and downloads
in multiple formats,
in genres ranging from light romantic comedy to general fiction and
horror.
Wings has something for every reader's taste.
Visit the website, then bookmark it.
We add new titles each month!

Wings ePress Inc.
3000 N. Rock Road
Newton, KS 67114